By

John Grit

From the Author

I advise any reader who has not read Apocalypse Law 1 and 2 to do so before reading this third book in the series. Exposition is not a good thing in fiction writing and even worse is the fact those who have read Apocalypse Law 1 and 2 will be bored reading back story that they already know. For this reason, I have not included much explanation of what happened in the first two books and this third installment in the series is not a standalone book. This book starts out in the same scene where Apocalypse Law 2 ends, just before the National Guard team leaves Mel's survivalist retreat and takes two wounded women to a military hospital. In the following prologue, some explanation of the first two books is included, but this in no way substitutes for reading the series in sequence. I have included a list of characters that appear in previous books in the back so readers will know who characters are referring to when they mention a character from a previous book.

I hope you enjoy Apocalypse Law 3.

John Grit

Prologue

Apocalypse Law 1

A plague wipes out ninety-five percent of the world's population, taking Nate Williams' wife and daughter and leaving him with his thirteen-year-old son to survive on their farm. In the bedlam of lawlessness and starvation, hungry, desperate men arrive from the nearest town to take their meager supplies. A benevolent stranger keeps coming in the night to steal food. Sensing the stranger means no harm, Nate leaves food out as charity. But the stranger ignores offers to join them, and then comes to their aid when a gang of prison escapees, led by an old nemesis of Nate's, raids their home. In the end, it is the kindness of a father desperate to save his son that may give two families and the stranger an opportunity to build a new life in a post-apocalypse world.

Apocalypse Law 2

A plague of mysterious origin has swept around the world, killing most of the human population. An ex-Ranger and his thirteen-year-old son are left alone on their farm with no government to rely on. They have taken in refugees, so they may all have a better chance to survive. Together, they farm the land and struggle to feed themselves while guarding against murderous raiders who choose to take from others rather than work for survival. Personal bonds are steeled in a post-apocalyptic world where a friend is defended with your life, a foe fought to the death, and refusing to be a victim demands killing without hesitation.

A son must rely on his father to build a new moral compass in a land of violence. "Dad and I don't quit on each other, and we don't quit on our friends." But despite best efforts, some are lost and others grievously wounded. Their farm is in danger and they face starvation without it.

Chapter 1

Nate Williams could not remember how many men he had killed in the last few weeks. While he, his son, and friends were fighting off one group of raiders in an effort to keep them away from his farm, another group came in from another direction and took all of his food.

"Well," the Colonel asked, "how many?" He stood there in his National Guard uniform looking like he was cool and comfortable in the Florida heat and humidity.

"I wasn't keeping count," Nate said. "And I don't want to guess." Irritation over the question added to the discomfort of the heat.

The Colonel looked at him, his eyes unblinking. "Hmm."

Anger flared in Nate's eyes. "I know how many of my friends died. And that little girl's parents. And Caroline's husband and baby. And probably Carrie's family. But she's not talking. All murdered at the hands of trash taking advantage of the chaos and lack of law enforcement."

The Colonel continued to look at Nate with unblinking eyes. "Maybe you should get with your new sheriff and do something about that."

Nate glared back at him. "I think I have been doing my part."

"The sheriff could use another deputy. He seems to be in over his head in more ways than one."

"And who is going to work my farm? I have people to feed, including myself. I already have a full time job. It's called staying alive."

They were interrupted when Caroline cussed the soldiers as they carried her out of the bunker on a stretcher and past Nate and the Colonel. "I'm not leaving without the M-4." She tried to get off the stretcher, but found she was too weak.

Nate wished she had not said that. The M-4 was government property, taken off a dead man who must have stolen it from a National Guard armory, or perhaps a dead soldier.

The Colonel looked away, pretending he did not hear.

Mel stood by with a smirk on his face, saying nothing. His uniform was not as clean as the Colonel's, and his face was darkened with two day's growth. Still, he stood straight and had an air of professionalism about him. No one ever found his enthusiasm lacking, and he was always fun to be around, no matter how bad things got.

Colonel Joe Greene had thrown the rule book away soon after everything went to hell. The Colonel was a practical man who believed in getting things done as efficiently as possible. When Mel shot a man not long after the plague first hit Florida more than a year ago, the man complained from a stretcher while being treated. Colonel Greene did not bother to look at him when he said, "You pointed a gun at one of my soldiers and you got shot. Stop whining." Colonel Greene walked far enough away the man could not hear and called Mel over. "The next time you shoot one of these bastards, kill him. I can't stand wasting medical supplies and creating more trouble for our overworked combat docs on trash that our country is better off without. If people have to die let it be the scum, so the good people will have a better chance. They have enough problems without having to deal with brigands."

Nate walked alongside the stretcher and looked down at Caroline. "Concentrate on getting well." Nate hesitated. "You may not want to come back here. Who knows? Things may be better where you're going." She reached up, and they shook hands. Nate said, "You have helped us a lot, and you're welcome here anytime. Good luck."

"I will come back if I can," Caroline said. "I don't have anyone else, after they killed my family. Take care."

Mel and Nate left the Colonel to help load Caroline on the helicopter. Deni was already onboard. She was unconscious again from her wounds, so Nate and the others had not been able to say good-bye to her. Mel told the two soldiers who carried Caroline to get on board and ran back to the Colonel. "Ready to lift off, sir."

Nate stayed in the helicopter a few minutes to check on Deni and Caroline once more. He asked the doctor, "What are her chances?"

She knew he was asking about Deni. "I have no way of knowing. I can tell you she is stable at the moment."

Nate swallowed and nodded. He said good-bye to Caroline once more, and then ran back to Mel and the Colonel.

The Colonel reached out and shook Nate's hand. "Good luck to you. We'll take good care of the ladies and have them back here soon." He cleared his throat. Well…the civilian anyway. The soldier will have to report to the Army—what's left of it."

"I'm sure they will understand she was stuck here after everything went to hell," Nate said. "She was on leave and couldn't get back."

The Colonel nodded. "Good luck." He ran for the helicopter.

Nate watched the National Guard helicopter lift off. Backwash from its blades blew debris in his face. He turned and saw his son, Brian, holding his boonie hat on and squinting, as he watched Deni and Caroline being taken away. They needed medical care, but Nate could see that Brian was already missing Deni and Caroline both.

"How long do you think it will be before they come back?" Brian kept looking, as the helicopter grew smaller.

Nate looked at his thirteen-year-old son. "I don't know. Deni is AWOL, and the Army may not let her come back." He noticed the reaction on Brian's face. "She's looking for her fiancé too, remember. So if she can, she might try to find him in South Carolina. Or was it North Carolina?"

Brian did not answer. The helicopter was no longer visible, but he was still looking at the horizon.

"Come on," Nate said, "let's go inside and get our packs and guns. They went inside the bunker and filled their canteens.

Carrie sat in a corner. Her eyes were wide, and she trembled.

Nate walked up to the fifteen-year-old. "They are taking Caroline and Deni to a hospital. The Colonel promised he would get Caroline back here after she has recovered…if she wants to come back." He took a step closer. Carrie cowered in the corner and pushed herself against the concrete wall. Nate sighed. "Now look, you've been with us long enough to know no one is going to hurt you. Caroline not being here changes nothing. She may have been the closest to you, but she was not the reason we never hurt you like those men did. We never hurt you, because we do not want to. You're just as safe now as you were when Caroline was here."

"He's telling you the truth," Martha said. "There is no need to be afraid." The strain of losing her husband, Ben, still showed on her face, but it did not stop her from caring about Carrie's problems. "It's not like you are alone with men now. Cindy and I are still here."

"Yeah," Cindy said. "Mom and I will take care of you."

Nate put his load-bearing harness and pack on. "There will not be any men here for a while. Brian and I are going to try to get some of our stuff back. The raiders left it strung out on the road in pickups."

Martha nodded. "Be careful."

Nate saw the strain on her face. She still had not had time to come to terms with the loss of her husband. "The Guard is going to give us a chopper ride and let us pick out what's ours."

Mel stood by the door, watching. Sweat appeared in rivulets from under his helmet and down his dirty face. "We need to be out of here."

Brian had his pack on in seconds and grabbed an AR-15 off the gun rack. He stuffed four magazines in a load-bearing harness. "I'm ready." He handed his father the M-14.

Nate took it and walked out the door.

"How long are you going to be gone?" Martha asked.

"Not sure," Nate said, yelling over his shoulder. "It's going to be a big job hauling all that stuff back to the farm. I hope we can commandeer a truck if there is one still running. Keep your eyes open while we're gone. There could still be a few of those killers around."

Before Nate got far, little three-year-old Synthia ran out after him and wrapped her arms around his leg.

"Go back inside," Nate said. He picked her up and carried her back into the bunker. "I'll be back soon."

Cindy took her and held her so she could not run back out.

Mel ran to the waiting helicopter and talked to an officer standing next to it.

Nate walked by Brian. "Let's go."

Mel was with a Lieutenant when Nate and Brian walked up, their rifles in hand.

The Lieutenant shook his head and pointed. "No guns. Leave them here."

Mel spoke up. "I've known both of them for years. They know how to handle weapons. I'm sure Colonel Greene understood they would be armed."

The Lieutenant's voice bellowed. "Colonel Greene left me in charge before leaving in the other chopper. I don't need any civilians shooting their guns off in my Huey!"

"Lieutenant," Mel said, "Nate has more combat experience than our entire company. Hell, Brian has more time under fire than any of us did until it hit the fan."

Nate removed his rifle's magazine and deftly ejected the round in the chamber into his waiting hand, pocketing it. He left the bolt locked back, the chamber empty.

Brian copied him. Even though he had little experience with an AR-15, he was nearly as quick and sure as his father.

Nate stared at the Lieutenant.

The Lieutenant nodded and stepped up into the helicopter.

Nate helped Brian get onboard and saw to it he was seated where the flight would not seem so scary. This would be Brian's first helicopter ride. Nate sat next to him, across from the Lieutenant.

Mel sat by a door next to the Lieutenant. There was a smile on his face. He knew Nate was carrying a .45ACP pistol cocked and locked. The Lieutenant never noticed it.

Four more soldiers scrambled onboard and sat down. All the soldiers kept their carbines pointed down at the floor, where a bullet would do the least damage to the aircraft if there happened to be a negligent discharge. The pilot started the engine, got the overhead propeller spinning at high speed, and pulled pitch out of the small meadow. The helicopter almost instantly lifted above the treetops. He must have been in more of a hurry than the Lieutenant for some reason.

Brian swallowed, his eyes rounded. He looked at his smiling father.

Nate winked at him. "The pilot's a hotdog." He yelled above the roar of the engine. "Relax and enjoy the ride. It's good training for a kid that wants to be a jetfighter pilot someday."

The pilot decided to fly down the river valley. He cut hard to the right, following a sharp bend in the river, then the left.

Brian's knuckles were white from grasping the metal bench he sat on.

The Lieutenant held on with both hands. "Shoemaker." He yelled into a microphone. "Stop that bullshit now! This thing has not had full maintenance in months. Treat it like a baby."

The pilot spoke into his microphone, "Yes sir." He pulled out of the river valley, above the tallest trees, and flew level, heading straight to the dirt road.

Mel laughed when he saw the relief on Brian's face. "I guess we won't need a barf bag after all." He winked at Nate.

Nate looked at his son, who was being uncharacteristically quiet. "He looks okay to me."

Brian looked at Mel and all the soldiers in the helicopter. "Of course I'm okay. What makes you think I'm not? Someone should have taught the idiot up front how to fly, though."

The Lieutenant laughed. Everyone in the helicopter was laughing. The pilot heard through his earphones. He looked back and smiled.

When the dirt road came into view, Nate looked out the open door and recognized two trucks he knew were loaded with their stolen property. The trucks were burned-out hulls.

Brian saw disappointment on his father's face, though he could not see out the door from where he sat.

Nate yelled over at the Lieutenant and Mel. "This is it."

The Lieutenant spoke into his microphone. "Find a place to land."

The pilot flew on, following the road. The trees were too close to the narrow road for him to land there, and there was a power line running down the left side of the road.

Nate looked out the door, searching for a truck that looked like it might still be in running condition. They flew over a two-ton flatbed truck that had a flat tire but looked undamaged otherwise. Nate looked it over as best he could.

The pilot flared the craft up to slow down, and then lowered to the road.

Dust billowed up and swirled as soldiers rushed out and ran, forming a defensive perimeter.

Nate jumped out and waited for Brian. "Follow me."

Brian ran a few yards behind his father, keeping bent over out of fear of the overhead prop. His father stopped and looked in the cab of the two-ton truck.

A dead man's body leaned over the steering wheel.

Nate checked for tripwires searching for booby traps. He found none. One hard pull and the body spilled out onto the dirt road. Nate stepped around him and found the key still in the ignition. He looked over the load on the flatbed. "None of this stuff is ours, but we need the truck if it will run."

Brian read a label on the fuel tank's fill cap. "It's a diesel, so it might not run too rough."

Nate searched every inch of the truck for any sign of a booby trap. After checking the hood for tripwires, he lifted it and looked over the engine. He then crawled under the truck and searched underneath. "Get back over where Mel is until I get it cranked."

"What's the point?" Brian stood by the open truck door and looked up at his father.

Nate pointed. "Get over there."

Brian ran over to Mel. "How long does he think I would live without him, anyway? If it blows up we're both dead."

Mel said nothing. He pulled Brian behind the now silent helicopter for cover. "He checked it good. He'll be okay."

Brian glared at Mel. "Yeah. Don't be pulling me around like that."

Mel listened, waiting for the sound of the truck starter.

Nate climbed up into the driver's seat. The battery was nearly dead, but he managed to get it cranked just before it gave out. He kept the engine revved up to charge the battery.

Brian ran over and looked up at his father. "What about the stuff that's not ours?"

Nate opened the door and jumped down. "We'll unload it. But first we need to find *our* stuff."

Yelling from down the road attracted Nate's attention.

The Lieutenant barked orders, his face showing alarm. Soldiers got into firing position, aiming at a line of vehicles racing toward them, snaking around many abandoned trucks in the road.

Leading the caravan was a white four-wheel-drive pickup with red lights on top. The driver brought it to a skidding stop three hundred yards away. When it came to rest it was turned sideways, and a large star could be seen. The word Sherriff was under the star in reflective silver paint. Four more similarly marked pickups raced up behind him. Farther back, civilian pickups loaded with men, rifles, and shotguns, pointed toward Nate, Brian, and the soldiers. There were too many pickups to count, and the line stretched around a curve in the dirt road. The men spilled out of the trucks and lined up, some finding cover, others stupidly standing in the open.

Nate pulled Brian behind the truck. He looked around, searching for the safest route to the woods. Keeping behind other vehicles for cover, he made it to the edge of the road, Brian at his heels. "Follow me."

He ran, jumped across the narrow ditch and disappeared into the woods with Brian two steps behind him. He could not stop in time, so Nate stepped out of the way. Brian crashed into brush. "Shit!" He got up and pulled thorns from his hands. "I hope there is trouble. I feel like shooting somebody."

Nate paid him little attention. He watched the road from behind an oak tree thick enough to stop bullets.

"Aren't we going to help the soldiers if there's shooting?" Brian stood on his toes but could not see anything from where he was.

"We're not part of their team, they and us both are better off out of their way." Nate looked through binoculars. "I doubt there will be a fight. The Colonel said they were working with the sheriff, cleaning out the brigands."

"Then why are we hiding in the woods?"

"Because we have only one life." Nate continued to scan the road with binoculars. He caught motion out of the corner of his right eye and looked at Brian. "Get back behind that tree. There's nothing to see anyway."

Brian hustled behind a large oak tree. Six months earlier he would have argued with his father, or at least said something smart. But the last months had matured him, and he had seen his father proven right so many times he just did what he was told and stood silently, searching the woods behind his father in case someone came up on them. Danger can come from any direction.

"Well, it looks like they have kissed and made up," Nate said. He lowered his binoculars. "We'll get back to work, but keep your eyes open."

They walked out of the woods and searched a nearby truck after Nate checked it for booby traps.

"Nothing here I recognize," Brian said.

They left that truck and came up on another one fifty yards farther. "Stay back until I check this one out." Nate looked into the back of the overloaded pickup. "Bingo. It's full of our canned goods, Mason jars galore."

Brian rushed closer.

"Stay back." Nate watched his son back off a few yards. "Farther. And keep watch."

Nate found no booby traps. He pulled a few boxes of Mason jars out and stacked them on the dirt road.

"Mel and that lieutenant and some man with a shotgun are coming." Brian moved closer to his father.

Nate set a box down and grabbed his rifle. "Careful where you point that AR. They are likely to be as jumpy as us."

"The guy with the shotgun looks mad." Brian shaded his eyes from the sun by pulling the front of his boonie hat down.

"We'll see," Nate said. "Stay behind this truck and overwatch without looking menacing. I will meet them halfway."

"Damn, Dad. Let them come to us and stop worrying about me. The farther away you are from that other bunch the safer for you. Just remember, if there's any trouble it won't be coming from Mel."

Nate smiled and gave Brian a funny look over his shoulders. "Okay, Mr. Brian, but I'm going to walk a ways to them anyway, just so they will be less worried about you back here."

"Yeah, right," Brian said. "You figure I will have more time to stop them if they come for me."

"You're smarter than you look." Nate walked down the road.

Brian held the carbine tighter, keeping his eyes glued to the man with the shotgun. As he came closer, Brian could see he was wearing a uniform.

Before anyone else could say a word, the sheriff threw down on Nate with his shotgun from twenty yards away. "You're under a—"

Mel slapped the shotgun barrel down. "Are you trying to get shot? His son will blow your head off!"

Nate stopped in his tracks and looked the sheriff in the eye. "The next move you make will determine how long you live. Now calm down and tell me what is going on."

The sheriff glared at Mel, then turned his attention back to Nate. "You and that boy are under arrest for looting." Sweat ran down his thin face and down his thin neck onto a frail frame of a chest where he had left his filthy uniform shirt half-unbuttoned.

"Looting hell," Nate said. "We're just recovering what was stolen from us. We'll leave the rest. The Colonel said we could pick out what the raiders took from our farm. When we're finished with that truck, we will bring it back here and whoever claims it can take it and the rest of this stuff. We just want what's ours."

The sheriff stood back on his heels and sneered. "And how the hell are we supposed to know what is really yours?"

The Lieutenant had been quiet until now. "I have orders to let him get his stuff back. Mel says he knows the man and his son. That is good enough for me. But direct orders from a colonel would be more than sufficient anyway, Mel or no Mel."

The sheriff looked at the Lieutenant. "Don't give me any shit. My people need all of that food. They're starving."

"I have orders." The Lieutenant stepped around to face the sheriff.

"And I have you outnumbered today." The sheriff talked through his teeth. "One word on this radio and four hundred rifles will be firing at you and your men."

Nate's voice boomed. "You're a damn fool."

The sheriff's eyes flashed to Nate. He started to speak.

Nate spoke first. "If you were going to play guerrilla army, you should have had your men spread out in the woods, not gather in one wad in the road where a chopper with a mini gun can kill half of them with one pass." He shook his head and looked the man up and down. "This county deserves better than you. Sheriff Fergusson must be dead. I wonder how there was an election in all this chaos. Or were you actually elected?"

The Lieutenant walked away and spoke into his radio. Thirty seconds later, two helicopters flew over low and fast. One fired into a burned-out truck, chopping it to pieces with its automatic cannon. It kept going and flew low over the treetops, turning to the left, until it came back around and hovered, ready to fire again. The other helicopter circled at high altitude.

Mel grinned. "Sheriff, we might not be regular Army, but we are the US military!"

"I thought the sheriff was working with you, Lieutenant," Nate said. "This man is an idiot."

The Lieutenant smiled. "Indigenous personnel are not always of the finest quality, but I have been ordered to work with him and his men."

"Someone needs to tell the Colonel this man is a fool." Nate stared the sheriff down.

Mel smiled. "Yep. A damn fool. Retarded in fact."

"Sheriff," the Lieutenant said, "you need to back off a while and wait until Nate gets his stuff. I'll tell you when he's through."

The sheriff's face turned red and his eyes bulged. "We earned what's in those trucks. If not for us, those thieves and killers would have gotten away." He glared at Nate. "This bum had nothing to do with it."

"You are misinformed," the Lieutenant said. "He and his son and friends had everything to do with the capture and killing of the brigands. They kept the animals penned down at the bridge for days."

The sheriff's eyes narrowed. "Whaat? Bullshit!"

The Lieutenant ignored him. He spoke to Mel. "Escort this man to the ditch," he pointed, "over there. And keep him there until further orders."

Mel smiled. "Yes sir."

The sheriff did not move.

Mel clicked the safety off his M-4. "Come on. We don't have all day. Get that shotgun slung on your shoulder and keep it there, or my trigger finger might get twitchy."

The sheriff walked away to sit on a log on the other side of the ditch. Mel followed him and stood a few yards away.

Nate told Brian, "We better get that truck and get out of here as soon as possible."

Brian followed. "We need our tools back too."

"Yeah. Keep an eye out for them." Nate stepped up his speed. "We may not get more than one truckload."

The truck was still running. There was not much fuel in the tank, but they did not have far to go. Nate and Brian worked fast. Nate took a tire and wheel off a nearby truck and replaced the flat tire on the running flatbed while Brian unloaded it.

When Brian finished, he pointed. "Look. That fourth truck…There's our tools."

Nate climbed behind the wheel and put the truck in gear. He revved the engine before letting the clutch out and heading for the truck Brian pointed at. He stopped next to it and left the engine idling roughly. They worked quickly, loading tools, leaving anything that was not theirs.

Back at the truck parked by the Lieutenant, Nate and Brian spent twenty minutes loading the Mason jars onto the flatbed. The Lieutenant spoke to the sheriff and it looked to Nate like he was giving the sheriff a lecture. Nate and Brian were about to check another truck farther down the road, when the others walked up.

"You're out of time," the Lieutenant said. "I can't stay here anymore. Take what you have and go."

"Shit." Brian looked up at the Lieutenant. "We don't have half our stuff loaded." His ears burned when the sheriff laughed.

"Lieutenant, what do you think is going to happen as soon as you and your soldiers leave?" Nate looked the Lieutenant in the eyes. "I might as well kill that so-called sheriff now." The sheriff stopped laughing.

"I can't stay here and hold your hand, Mr. Williams." The Lieutenant looked at Brian and sighed. "Get in that truck and get back to your farm." The Lieutenant stepped closer to Nate and whispered, "I will try to put the fear of God into the sheriff and make it clear your farm is off limits."

"Get in the truck Brian," Nate said.

"This isn't right." Brian yelled over to Mel, "Can't you do anything?"

Mel looked sick. "I have to follow orders. Sorry."

"Stay safe Mel." Nate stepped up behind the wheel of the truck.

Brian got in on the passenger side. He yelled out the window past his father, leaning forward to see around him. "Come and see us as soon as you can."

"I will," Mel said. "Stay alert and stay armed. You already know this, but it's bloody out there, and the plague is still hot in places. The larger gangs have been just about wiped out, but there are a lot of smaller gangs roving around murdering, raping, and looting. And don't think the government is back on its feet. It's not. They're trying but have a long way to go."

Nate looked out the window at the Lieutenant. "If they come, there's going to be a fight."

"You've got five minutes before we're out of here," the Lieutenant said.

When they were seventy yards down their driveway, Nate stopped the truck. He looked at Brian. "I want you to drive down the east side of the field and get as far into the river valley as you can before you get stuck. Get as close to the river as possible."

"I won't get far," Brian said. "The trees will stop me before the mud does."

"Get as far as you can. Then carry the load down to the river. Start with the tools."

Brian stared back at his father, his eyes slits. "What are you going to be doing?"

"There may be shooting. Just keep hauling the stuff to the river." When the shooting stops, head upstream and wait for me at the first island. Leave everything where it is, just get yourself upriver."

"No way!"

Nate put the truck in gear and continued down the drive. "If I do not show up by three hours after dark, get back to the bunker."

"It's the same old shit. What's the point of you staying? You can't stop them anyway."

"Maybe you can get some of the stuff hid in the swamp, if I slow them down."

Nate drove down their driveway two hundred yards past a curve and then stopped the truck and got out. He grabbed his backpack and put it on.

Brian slid to the driver side. He leaned out of the open door. "Mel won't let this happen."

Both heard the helicopters leaving.

Brian sighed. "Shit."

"He must follow orders." Nate looked down the driveway, and then walked to the cab and looked up at his son. "The way things are, military discipline is likely to be strict. Mel could be shot for disobeying orders. The world is a brutal place right now. Mel would help us if he could."

"He's having fun, though," Brian said. "He's got that smile of his on his face half the time."

"Better get going." Nate checked the driveway again.

Brian slammed the door shut. "What's with that sheriff? I don't think he was elected."

"You think right. I wonder if there are even any real deputies in that mob. That bunch is not a hell of a lot better than what we've been fighting." Nate motioned with his head. "Now stop wasting time and get that thing out of here."

Brian almost killed the engine when he did not give it enough gas before letting the clutch out, but he managed to get the truck moving. He left it in first gear, and the engine whined as he picked up speed. The truck disappeared around a curve in the drive. In less than a minute, Nate could no longer hear its loud muffler.

Chapter 2

Nate waited behind the gnarled oak. It was diseased and past its prime, but its four-foot-thick trunk offered cover capable of stopping any rifle bullet. He could see two hundred yards down the driveway, where it curved to the left and disappeared behind a sun-dappled wall of trees, mostly tall pines. Centuries-old oaks lined the right side of the drive and spread their limbs out, creating shade, and Spanish moss hung straight down from them, as lifeless as the hot, still air.

Thirty minutes went by. Nothing happened. Nate had not slept or even rested for so long, weariness seeped into his bones, and his eyelids grew heavy, but he managed to stay awake, if not one hundred percent alert.

Nate stood silent, dripping sweat, holding his rifle, waiting for trucks loaded with armed men, who would try to kill him. Combat in the Army taught him he did not like this, but here he was, again, waiting to kill human beings. Would he ever survive long enough to get away from it? More important to him, would his son ever survive long enough to live a somewhat normal life again?

The rattle of a vehicle coming down the driveway brought him to full alert. He shouldered his rifle and pushed the safety off with the back of his trigger finger. *Only a fool would come right down the drive knowing a man is waiting with a rifle*. He wondered how many had been sent on foot, walking down each side, back in the woods. Or was the sheriff too stupid to even do that much?

Nate's eyes lit up. He heard a familiar sound, coming in low and fast. Then came the roar of two mini guns, a short burst, and then the helicopter was gone. He had caught only a glimpse of it as it belched flame from both sides, strafing. The pilot's skill and quick reflexes impressed him.

An explosion shook the ground, and a fireball billowed and rose over the treetops, into the clear sky, followed by black smoke. Nate smiled. He could not see around a bend in the drive, but he knew what had happened. *So Mel came through after all.* He heard men running in the woods, back from where they came, back up the drive.

Mel must have more sway than his rank would have you believe. In the end, it had to be the Lieutenant or the Colonel who gave the order. He made his way quietly through the woods until he knew there could be no men close by hunting him, and then ran to help Brian unload the truck.

Nate skirted the clearing around his home and barn, kept back in the trees, and made his way down into the river valley and into the wetlands. He followed deep ruts in the mud left by the truck's tires. He approached the truck with caution. No one was there. Many items had already been unloaded and were piled on a small hill where the ground would be a little drier. He slung his rifle on a shoulder and grabbed a bundle of farming tools. He wanted to take the items to the house, but knew they were not out of danger yet. He sighed. *Things are hard enough on us without being forced to deal with assholes.* Holding the tools as tight as possible so they would not rattle, he started for the river.

It was not easy going. Nate was forced to weave his way through thick brush and closely growing trees while carrying his load. He stopped when he heard boots squelching in mud and heavy breathing. Someone was moving fast, coming upslope out of the swamp straight for him. His hands were full, and dropping the tools would make more than enough noise to alert anyone nearby. He stood behind a bush and waited, hoping it was Brian.

Nate's eyes lit up when he recognized his son. "You're making enough noise to wake the dead."

Brian stopped, froze, and looked around. He held his carbine at the low ready like his father taught him. "You scared the hell out of me."

Nate stepped around the bush so Brian could see him. "The river's not far, is it?"

"No, about thirty yards. Follow my tracks in the mud." Brian eyed him as he walked closer. "I didn't hear any shooting, but there was a big explosion."

Nate did not show any emotion on his face, but his eyes were telling Brian something must have went right. "Remind me to thank Mel."

A smile spread across Brian's face. "I will. Did you see it? I mean, what happened?"

"No. I could not see, but I think they just attacked the first truck in their caravan. Probably killed everyone in it. That was enough for them to get the message: Our farm is off limits. It might not hold them off for long, so we need to get this stuff out of here as fast as possible."

"I'll go on to the truck," Brian said.

Nate passed him and headed for the river. "No, you find a place to sit and rest right here. We'll go together. Stay behind cover and stay alert."

Brian looked around for a place to hide. "You're the one who needs to rest."

Nate was gone.

Brian looked over his shoulder toward the river and shook his head.

Nate found a pile of boxes between a half-rotted cypress log and a palm tree that lay next to it, still living but growing horizontally out of the side of an Indian burial mound that was probably thousands of years old. Brian had been working hard, and the pile was larger than Nate expected. There were a few tools piled nearby, so Nate put his load down on top of them.

Nate looked upstream and saw a good place to launch a raft. The bank was firm there. He looked around the general area for dead standing trees that would float. Finding none, he started back to Brian.

Since his hands were empty, Nate slid his rifle from his shoulder and carried it ready for use. Easing up behind Brian, he was glad to see his son watching their back trail, slowly sweeping the lush green vegetation, trying to see through the brush like looking through a picket fence. Killers could be hunting them.

Brian has learned fast. He needs a rest from the danger and violence, we all do. He's held up well, but how much can a kid his age take?

Nate stopped twenty yards back, behind a cypress tree. He started to speak up, but Brian turned and saw him peering around the tree. Nate smiled and shook his head. *He's learning fast all right. He's already starting to develop the ability to sense when he's being hunted.* The smile vanished from his face. *Too young. Too young. Goddamn it.*

He walked closer to his son, not making a sound.

Brian stood and came out from the thick brush where he hid.

"Anything?" Nate asked.

Brian shook his head. "Nothing." He kept his voice low.

"Stay ten yards behind me." Nate headed upslope toward the truck, his rifle at the low ready position.

After two dozen trips, they had everything carried down to the riverbank.

Nate grabbed the two-man crosscut saw, and they went hunting for standing deadwood that would float. Not wanting to haul the logs any father than necessary, they searched close to the river. Seventy yards uphill, near the edge of the river valley, they found a one-hundred-foot-tall lightning-killed pine that was not too rotted and set to work. They cut the first two logs eighteen feet long; it was about all the weight they could manage in one piece.

"That one is more than two feet in diameter on one end." Brian stopped to catch his breath. "I would never have moved it by myself, even downhill." He pointed. "And that one is about twenty inches across on the big end."

Nate handed Brian a canteen. "Drink. You will be dehydrated if you don't." He sat on the larger log to rest. "Pine's been dead long enough most of the sap has drained out. It would be many times heavier if it had been killed more recently." He mopped sweat off his forehead with his jacket sleeve. "Come on, we're wasting daylight."

They headed back to the dead pine.

Working their way along the downed tree produced smaller-diameter logs, so they cut the next pieces longer. Nate made a harness out of rope, and they took advantage of the downhill route, sliding the logs to the riverbank. "Stay alert and be ready to get out of the way if the log starts to roll or slide on its own," Nate warned.

They went looking for another standing dead tree. They had been keeping their rifles slung across their backs, out of the way, but now kept them ready for use since their hands were not busy. Finding one a quarter-mile upriver, they cut it into twenty-foot lengths and lashed the logs together with vines. Poling the raft downstream gave them a chance to rest from the hard labor of moving the first tree.

Nate jumped ashore and pulled their temporary raft against the other logs. "Get the ax and machete."

In the last half-hour of the dying afternoon, they collected vines, leaving them stretched out near the raft. Nate used his weight to pull them from tall trees, yanking at the stubborn ones. He noticed his son was exhausted, nearly staggering, as he went about the job, uncomplaining. "Sit down and rest while I do the rope work."

Brian sat on a water soaked log, getting his pants wet, but too tired to care. The blue haze of twilight in the western sky gave notice that light to see by was coming to an end, and there was much work yet to do. Purple shadows of the swamp changed to darker hues in the deeper shadows under the most leaf-laden trees. He was bone-weary, but got up to help after only five minutes. Nate lashed the logs together with the vines and one-inch rope he had found in the truck. The rope did not come from their farm, but neither of them felt bad about using it. They had lost a lot, and that rope was small payment.

With skillful use of the ax and machete, Nate cut grooves in the logs for the vines and showed Brian how to use loops as pulleys to double a man's pulling power when stretching them tight before tying them off. "You can't tie these thick vines using normal rope knots. They don't have the flexibility, and can splinter if you bend them too sharp." As he worked, he demonstrated several knots his grandfather had taught him when he was younger than Brian.

"What do you call that one?" Brian asked. He bent over, watching closely in the low light.

"I don't know as there is a name." Nate smiled. "All I know is it works great with vines." He took notice of how his son was deeply interested. *He now understands how this stuff can save a man's life.*

It was completely dark by the time they had the raft finished.

"Start loading the canned goods in the center of the raft," Nate said. "I'll check for trouble and be back here as soon as I can. Then we will head upriver tonight."

"Yeah, okay, but we have to sleep sometime, especially you." Brian looked up at his father, seeing only his silhouette. "Be careful."

"Once we're upriver a ways, we'll stop and get some sleep. Stay alert, keep your rifle handy while you work, and keep quiet. They could be coming up on us as we stand here. Remember, we have to be able to walk down both sides of the raft to pole it upstream, so stack it in the middle." He took a step and stopped. "Also, watch for cottonmouths. They'll be out now that it's dark."

More concerned with Brian's safety than anything else, Nate searched the river swamp in a half-mile semicircle. The far end of the arc brought him back to the river one quarter mile upstream. He used his compass often until he had swung back to the river. The dark forced him to inch along the swamp floor, taking short steps, his rifle held out in front to catch thorny vines before they reached his face. By the time he got back to Brian it was an hour after sunset and pitch-black under the canopy of the swamp.

Nate spoke up to avoid being shot. "It's your father coming in, Brian."

"See anything at the house?" Brian asked, after lowering his rifle. He had heard his father's boots in the mud.

"I never went to the house." Nate could see a dark hulk piled on the middle of the raft. Brian had been busy. "I searched the area so we would know if it's safe to go upriver."

Brian sighed, but he said nothing.

"I've been your father for a long time, and I know that silence means something."

"Everything's loaded. You probably should check it first. I don't always do things the way you like. I didn't have a whole lot to tie everything on with, but I used some smaller vines."

There was no moon out yet and would not be until hours later. They would be cloaked in darkness until then. Nate used his hands more than his eyes to check Brian's work. He spoke as he worked his way around the raft. "I haven't given up on the farm yet, but for now, we will have to stay at the bunker. I'm thinking we're going to have to try to farm there. Staying at the farm is just too dangerous for now."

"Yeah." Brian's voice sounded flat.

"Yeah what?" Nate jumped off the raft onto the bank, felt around next to a cypress, and picked up the two long poles they had previously cut, handing one to Brian.

"I already knew that, that's what. Let's go before those bastards get here," Brian said.

Nate did not move. "I'm sorry."

"Not your fault. Don't be worrying about me so much anyway. It takes a lot more to bother me now and a lot less to make me happy. I just don't want to lose anyone else."

Nate dropped his pole and stepped closer, surprising Brian by wrapping his arms around him. He let him go after one second and picked up the pole. "Let's go. We have a lot of people counting on us."

Brian got on the raft and waited for his father to untie the line and shove off. It was brighter out from under the swamp canopy and in the open starlight. They could see well enough, but soon learned the current pushed strong on the raft, and getting momentum up against it demanded all their strength.

"We need to stay out of the main current by keeping close to this side of the river," Nate said. "Try to be back to the front on your side by the time I am near the back end and hold the raft against the current by jamming your pole into the bottom while I run back to the front on my side."

"Okay. But the raft will turn on us while I'm holding it on this side."

"Yep," Nate said. "I have to move fast, so that will not happen."

It took them some time to get their technique perfected. Then they made progress for more than two hours, until they both grew too tired to overpower the river's current and their progress slowed.

"We need more distance under us." Nate knew Brian was tired, and he hated pushing him. "You have to get back to the front quicker."

Brian said nothing. He picked up his pace.

An hour later, Brian could go no farther. He did not say anything, and he kept working, but Nate could tell he was spent.

Nate held against the current with his pole jammed into the river bottom. "I wish it were more, but I've had enough. We both need rest."

Brian held his side against the current, leaning into his pole. "Don't stop for me."

Nate smiled in the moonlight. "I'm not. We both need rest." He searched upriver, trying to see in the dim light of the rising moon. "That palm tree jutting out from the bank—we'll tie off on that."

When they were close to the palm tree, Nate threw a rope over it. He heard something fall in the water as he tied the rope.

"Watch it, Dad. That moccasin has climbed on the raft."

Nate stomped the snake's head flat and kicked it off into the river. He then used the pole to sweep the palm tree clear of three more water moccasins. They swam for shore.

"Who sleeps first?" Brian asked.

Nate did not answer until he finished rearranging the cargo so Brian would have a place to lie down above the snakes. "You. After three hours, I will wake you."

"Then you sleep until sunup."

"Until false dawn," Nate said.

"Good. That will give you about five hours sleep." Brian yawned and stretched out on top of the cargo. In two minutes, his breathing slowed and he was asleep. His carbine lay cross his chest, his right hand on the grip.

Lying on the five-gallon plastic buckets was uncomfortable, and Brian woke an hour early. He opened his eyes but did not move. The bull frogs were silent on this night, but the mosquitoes were buzzing around his head. Brian saw his father standing still, but he knew his eyes were moving, sweeping the shoreline, penetrating shadows as deeply as possible. He also knew his father's ears were at work, seeking out any unnatural sounds in the woods. He watched as his father turned to a sound upstream, bringing his rifle to his shoulder. A raccoon scampered up on a log, reached into the water, pulled out a crawfish, and bit its soft tail off. Brian could see because the log the raccoon was on stretched out into the river where the sky was clear of any shading canopy of treetops, allowing moonlight to reach it.

Nate slowly turned to look across the river.

Brian sat up.

"Get some sleep, Dad," Brian said, in a low voice, husky with drowsiness. He stood and stretched his aching muscles.

After making his way around the cargo, Nate sat on a plastic five-gallon bucket. "Stay on the front end of the raft, so you will be in shadow, and don't move at all, just your eyes. Keep your ears working fulltime."

"Okay," was all Brian said.

Nate fell asleep in less than a minute.

~~~~

"Dad, someone's out there." Brian shook Nate awake.

Nate opened his eyes and gripped his rifle tighter. Though he had been asleep for only three hours, he sat up fully alert. "Get down behind cover," Nate whispered.

Brian got on his knees and looked over the top of the cargo, his carbine ready.

"Lower." Nate pushed him down.

They heard crashing against palmetto fronds as something took off.

Nate listened ten seconds longer. He sighed and stood up. "Deer," he whispered.

"How can you tell?" Brian whispered back.

Just then, the doe got a whiff of their human scent and blew through her nose, making a sheeew sound, alarming other deer in the area. The sound was familiar to both of them. Bears blow a similar alarm, but much louder. They could tell it was a deer and not a bear. Years in the woods had given them plenty of opportunities to hear both. The dark of night cloaked the doe's retreat, but in their mind's eye, they saw her white tail raised high, as a visual warning to other deer.

Brian stood. "Shit. I woke you for that."

"No problem." Nate pulled a canteen out of his pack and took a drink. He handed it to Brian. "We'll shove off and try to get upstream some more before daylight."

"Aren't we going to eat?"

"We will have to stop when the sun comes up. We'll eat then."

"Okay." Brian grabbed a pole.

"No complains, huh?"

"What's the point? We have to travel at night. It's not your fault."

Nate untied the rope and shoved off. They found the current had slowed some, allowing them to make faster progress. By false dawn, they were close to the island that was not far from the creek that ran by Mel's bunker. Nate tied the raft to a cypress tree growing out of the river bottom. "Now we'll eat," Nate said.

They each sat on a five gallon bucket and ate silently, so they could hear any trouble that approached.

After a few minutes Nate said, "You've been a great help to your old dad. I know this has been hard for you, but you've held up to it well."

"And it's been so easy for you." Brian finished the last of his freeze-dried lasagna. "You're stretching yourself awful thin, Dad. When we get back, you need to rest for a day, at least."

Nate smiled. "We still have to get this stuff to the bunker, boss."

Brian drank from a canteen. "I wasn't bossing you. You're bigger than me, so I wouldn't do that."

"The main thing is I'm your father." Nate stood, grabbed his rifle, and jumped off the raft onto the muddy bank.

Brian followed. "I know that, but you *are* pushing yourself too hard." He checked the safety on his carbine. "I guess we're going to sleep back in the woods, away from the raft."

"Yep. And I'm taking your advice, so I'll sleep first, while you keep watch."

~~~~

There it is again. Now Brian knew someone was in the woods and coming closer. *At least two of them.* Brian kept the carbine shouldered and in the low ready position, like his father taught him. He was well hid in thick brush, and with a three-foot dead cypress log in front and a living cypress eight feet across at his back he had protection from bullets. *Best to stay here and wait. That's what Dad would do.* He looked to his right and was surprised to see his father awake, rifle in hand, and motioning for him to stay where he was. Brian nodded just enough his father could see.

Brian's breathing became labored, and he soaked his dirty clothes with sweat. He saw movement, but could not see anything more than a blur of motion through the brush. Then it was gone. His ears told him more about what was going on in the woods than his eyes. *Just like Dad said.* He became angry. *Why don't they leave us alone? It's bad enough without assholes coming around to kill our friends and steal our food. Who will get hurt this time?* Thinking of Ben and Deni and Caroline made his blood boil. He thumbed the safety off. *No. No more.* He watched the motion behind brush come closer and aimed.

Whaaat? Brian looked over the Aimpoint sight and could not believe what he saw. A teenage girl not much older than him surfaced from the wall of green. She appeared frightened. He took his finger off the trigger. Her attention seemed to be focused to her right, so Brian searched the woods in that area. A man emerged from the shadows and stood still. He held a shotgun, and kept it ready for quick use. The girl was unarmed.

The man eased over to the girl, making little noise. They headed for the river, passing within twenty yards of Nate.

Nate stayed behind cover and kept watch for more danger, keeping them at the edge of his vision, his rifle shouldered, but not aimed at them.

The girl froze. Then she turned, her wide eyes alerting the man, and pointed at the raft. He snapped his fingers and motioned for her to lie on the wet ground. Instantly, she was lying next to a soggy, rotted log.

The man yelled out, "We mean you no harm. We just want to talk."

Nate said nothing. Brian waited for his father to show him what to do next. They were both searching the woods, not worried so much about the two they could see, but those who might be out there they could not see.

After several minutes, the man spoke up again. "We want to talk with you about the sheriff and other things." He searched the woods, but could not see Nate or Brian. "We're looking for Nate Williams."

Nate signaled to Brian to stay put and keep watch for trouble. He aimed at the man. "Drop the shotgun, if you want to talk."

The man put his shotgun down and stepped away from it. He still could not see Nate. "I know you to be a fair man; otherwise I would not have come. My daughter is with me, and I mean you no harm, so don't get nervous."

"I am nervous, been nervous since people first started shooting at me." Nate took one last look around and stood. "But if you're not a danger to me, you're safe enough. Put your hands on your head and turn, so I can see if you have any more weapons on you."

The man did as he was told.

"Now the girl," Nate said.

She stood and slowly turned with her shaking hands over her head. The front of her clothes was wet from lying on the swamp floor.

Nate lowered his rifle, but kept it shouldered. "Come over here and find a place to sit."

There was no log or dry ground to sit on, so the man and girl leaned against a cypress trunk.

Nate walked closer and stood in front of them, but stayed back more than twenty feet. "What is it you want?"

The girl's nervous eyes flashed, and she looked at her father.

"First, we want to apologize about what happened on the road. You can come and get the rest of your stuff now if you want. We won't bother you."

Nate looked the man over. "Well, something has changed. Is the sheriff dead?"

"That chopper killed him and a few of his cohorts," the man said. "There's been kind of a mutiny of sorts. What's left of the sheriff's men are tied up. He was no sheriff anyway. There was no election. Nothing about him being a sheriff was legal. Most of the crowd you saw at the road was not really with him. We came to stop the raiders from hurting anyone else. The sheriff had his own agenda."

Nate's eyes brightened. "How did you and your daughter wind up being with his bunch?"

"We weren't really. I came because the bastards you tangled with at the bridge killed my wife." The man motioned with his head to his daughter. "I had to take her with me because I couldn't leave her alone. Besides, she was rather bullheaded about coming." He looked over at her and she looked down, averting her eyes from him. "Thanks to you, I guess it was you, she got to see the man who killed her mother dead. Found him with the top part of his head missing not far from the bridge."

The girl looked away, her eyes filling.

"It was a terrible thing for a girl to see, him and all the others lying around rotting," the man said. "She's seen too much already, but she insisted."

The girl spoke up. "The bastard's dead, that's all that matters." She wiped her face.

"You two took quite a chance coming out here," Nate said. "Do you know me? I don't recognize you."

"We never met," the man said. "People have told me about you and your family though, one old guy I met a few months ago even knew your father. My name is Austin Stinson. My daughter's name is Renee."

"Who was the old man?" Nate asked.

"Skeeter Thornton." Stinson sighed. "That bunch you've been fighting killed him. "Even though he couldn't run or even walk far, he could still shoot. He took a few with him."

"Those the disease hasn't taken, killers have." Nate swallowed. "I wonder how long it will be before we can get to work rebuilding this country, instead of killing each other. Skeeter was as good as they come. His wife died some years back. They had no kids." There was silence between them for a few seconds. The mosquitoes buzzed.

"What exactly is on your mind, besides telling me I can get the rest of my stuff?" Nate moved closer, reducing the seven yards between them to three.

"There's a big farm. The owners and help all died in the plague evidently. They were what you probably consider to be neighbors in this isolated area, even thought the farm is miles from here, so you probably knew them."

"Yeah, I knew them." Nate took a step closer. "The old man's name was Gary Oak. Everyone called him Red…Red Oak. They called the farm that too."

"Well, it's a big farm, and the owners are dead. We buried them behind the house under a stand of oaks. The looters haven't gotten to it yet, and…well, about two dozen of us were thinking we could start a community farm there." The man seemed to be trying to judge Nate's reaction, but saw nothing on his face. "If any living relatives show up, we wouldn't give them any trouble. Hopefully, we could work out an agreement with them and stay or be allowed to take the crops we grew before we left at least. We're not about stealing. We just want to keep from starving, and that farm is sitting there idle."

"Why are you telling me this?" Nate did not like it when the girl moved to his left. If she kept inching that way, he would not be able to keep both of them in his sight at the same time. He wished he had stayed farther back.

"Back over here, Renee. You got ants in your pants?" Stinson gave her a stern look. "I was one of them chosen to look for you and explain we're not stealing anything, from you or anyone else. We just want to use the Red Oak Farm to raise food on. Another bunch went downriver searching for you." He looked up at Nate. "I guess my girl and me were the ones lucky enough to go in the right direction. You got a lot farther upriver than we figured, but we had an idea you might use the river for travel. Anyway, we were worried you might take us as being like those at the bridge."

"Are you?"

"No sir, we're not. Uh, we also wanted to invite you to join our group. We could sure use a person with real farming experience, not to mention you've proven yourself to be valuable in a fight. Some of us have raised backyard gardens, but none are real farmers. We would ask to join you at your farm, but it's kind of small for the size of our group."

"Yeah, it's too small for that many people." Nate appraised the man. "I won't say no now, but I can't say yes right now either. As far as you moving onto Red Oak Farm, well, it's not mine. If everything is the way you have presented here, I have no problem with it. Red did have children who moved away, and they had children. So don't be surprised if someone does show up in the future."

"We figured that. We don't want to steal anything; we just want to use it to feed our families."

Nate nodded. "I understand."

Mr. Stinson headed for his shotgun. "We'll be going now. If you come with us, I'll get some of the men to help you get your stuff to your farm." He stopped short. "Unless you want us to carry it all the way down to the river, so you can use that raft to take it someplace else."

"I'll have to think on that," Nate said. "In the mean time, I'll be happy to get it all in my barn."

All three walked to Stinson's shotgun. He immediately slung it on his shoulder to not make Nate nervous. "Heading upriver? You have another place somewhere?"

"We were going to hide it," Nate said.

Stinson smiled and kept walking. "Good idea. I heard there might be thieves around."

When they got twenty yards from Brian, Nate spoke up. "See any sign of anyone else, Brian?"

Brian stepped around from behind a hickory tree and shook his head. He looked the man over and then the girl.

"This is my son, Brian," Nate said. "Brian, this is Mr. Stinson and his daughter Renee."

Brian nodded at both of them. "I didn't hear much. What's going on?"

"They're going to help us get the rest of our supplies to the barn" Nate said.

Brian blinked. "Okay. What about the sheriff?"

"Dead. The helicopter," Nate answered. "We owe Mel more than we thought."

Brian smiled.

Renee laughed. "Look Dad, he can smile."

Brian said nothing. He did not even roll his eyes, or turn red. He did not seem to notice that Renee was pretty.

"We have only so much daylight, and we have a lot to do," Nate said. "Let's get back to that flatbed and see if we can get it unstuck."

Stinson checked a compass and led the way with Renee behind him.

Nate checked his own compass while Stinson was not looking. He was not about to rely on a stranger's navigation, anymore than he was completely convinced Stinson had told him the total truth. *We'll see. This might be a turnaround in our fortunes, or it might be a death trap.*

Brian followed behind, as alert as his father.

Chapter 3

"See," Brian said. "There's no way the four of us are getting that thing unstuck."

Nate started walking, leaving the flatbed truck where it sat in the mud. He talked over his shoulder, heading upslope to the farmhouse. "We might get it out, if we had enough manpower pulling on a thick rope."

"We'll bring half a dozen men with us after we have the first load of your stuff in your barn," Stinson said. "It would be a shame to lose that flatbed. It'll haul a big load."

~~~~

Nate stopped just inside the edge of the woods and looked uphill, across his field of now dead tomato plants. He saw the yard was full of trucks and men. He glanced at Stinson, "Stay there for a minute."

Stinson cocked his head. "What is it?"

"Brian, maneuver around real careful and position yourself so you can see me and what goes on, but no one can see you. Keep behind bullet-stopping cover, not just concealment."

Brian nodded, his face serious. "It'll still be dangerous if it's a trap."

"You are going to be my only insurance, so stay alert," Nate said. "Hide in a place where you know the range. If you have to shoot, you need to be accurate."

"I thought we were past that," Stinson interrupted.

"Maybe we are," Nate said. "It all depends on what happens when we get to my house." He kept his eyes on Stinson. "Go on, Brian. You have to be in place before I get up there." He spoke again, before Brian had taken two steps. "Be careful, like I taught you. Don't rush into an ambush. I'll give you fifteen minutes before we move from here."

"Okay." Brian was out of sight in seconds.

"I don't mind you being careful," Stinson said. "All those armed men up there would make anyone nervous. I understand."

"That's about it." Nate noticed unease in the man's eyes. "I'm just being careful."

Stinson did not seem to be reassured. "If something were to happen, you wouldn't hurt my daughter, would you?"

"As long as she stays out of it and stays unarmed, she has nothing to fear from me. There are a lot of guns up there, though. You never know where a stray bullet will wind up." Nate examined Stinson's face, trying to read him. He squared off on Stinson. "Look, if there is something you have not told me, you better speak up before we go out there in the open. There is little chance you will come out of it alive. My son will kill you. He's killed before, and he's getting harder every day. I hate it, but that's the way the world is now."

Stinson's Adam's apple moved up his throat. "It's not a trap. I took a chance coming to you. I brought Renee to prove it's no ruse."

"I thought she insisted on coming."

"I was talking about her coming with me and the group up there. I took her with me to look for you, because you would be less likely to think it's a trap."

"It doesn't really prove anything," Nate said. "Don't worry. If it's not a trap, there will be no trouble. You getting nervous like you are is making me wonder, though."

Stinson looked him in the eye. "It's not a trap. If anyone raises a weapon against you, I'll shoot him myself."

"We'll see," Nate said. "It's time to find out." He motioned with his head. "You and your daughter lead the way."

Stinson pushed through the brush and walked out into Nate's field. His daughter followed.

Nate walked off to the side, keeping them between him and the men in his backyard.

~~~~

Brian rested the carbine on a water oak limb. He gripped the weapon tight, and suddenly felt overheated. Sweat ran down his forehead and into his eyes, but he dare not take his attention away from the crowd. He saw several dozen men turn almost in unison. They watched the trio inch closer, coming from the low end of the field, with Nate seven paces behind.

Brian watched the crowd, his carbine ready.

A man, who was shorter than the rest and on the near edge of the crowd, raised his rifle and aimed at the group.

Brian swung the carbine and held the red dot on the man's chest. His heart rate doubled, and he drenched his shirt. Sweat stung his eyes. The only thing that stopped him from taking up all the slack on the trigger was the fact he knew his father was protected to some degree, because he was behind the man and girl.

A taller man noticed and rushed over. He pushed the rifle down and said something to the short man. Brian did not need to hear. *You better not let that happen again, or someone is going to get shot.*

Brian could tell Stinson was talking as he came up on the crowd. The taller man, who had stopped the short one from pointing his rifle at them, left the crowd and met Stinson, said a few words, and then walked up to Nate and shook his hand.

Brian's pulse slowed, but he kept the sight's red dot on the tall man's upper body. *Careful, Dad.* Using the periphery of his vision, he tried to keep watch on all the others, but watched the tall man the most.

Brian grew more at ease when it appeared Nate was having a casual conversation with the tall man and a few others. A middle-aged woman, thin and small, but carrying herself with confidence, talked with Nate for a few seconds. Nate stepped closer and they hugged each other lightly. Brian's memory started to kick in. *That's Mrs. MacKay.* He thought about the farm her and her husband owned ten miles east of the Williams' farm. Their two outdoors-loving sons moved to Alaska at the age of twenty-one and twenty-two, and had not been seen in the county since. "We want to see a part of the world that has not yet been totally crapped on by people," Stan had told Brian. Clayton, the younger brother, had just smiled and nodded, as was his usual quiet way. That was three years ago. *Where is Mr. MacKay?* He swallowed. *Dead.* Mr. MacKay had been a crop-duster when he was younger, and he continued to fly and owned a small plane. He took Brian on a few rides. He felt bad that he and his father had not checked on them. *We've been too damn busy dodging bullets.* He sighed; bone-deep weariness seeped into him. He was tired of being afraid for his father and his friends and himself. He was tired of killing men.

The crowd began to move, and then formed into separate groups, each group heading for a pickup or heavy-duty truck. Brian thought they must all be diesels. Gas had been unreliable as fuel for vehicles for months and few people had much gas left anyway. He watched as his father headed for a two-ton flatbed. Mrs. MacKay walked beside him, talking. Occasionally, she would put her hand on his shoulder or upper arm, as a sign of friendship, or gesticulate to reinforce her words. Brian knew her as a strong woman who took no lip off anyone, but would give a needy person her last dollar. She often hired legal immigrants to work the farm, but refused to hire a single illegal one. Every farmhand in the county wanted to work for her and her husband. They knew they would be paid well and treated with respect. The MacKays paid all their employees according to their skill and work ethic, not race. Many black and Hispanic employees working for them were paid more than white employees.

He watched as his father helped her into the cab and then climbed onto the flatbed.

What now? Brian's face revealed the strain he felt.

His father signaled for him to stay put when no one was watching.

Brian sighed. *Who's going to watch over you now?*

The pickups and trucks, all loaded down with men and a few women, maneuvered for position, their engines sputtering and running rough, and then snaked their way into the drive and disappeared around a curve.

~~~~

Nate got a good look at the sheriff's burned-out pickup as they went by. It had been pushed out of the way. Its tires were burned, so it gouged a deep scar in the soil when it was pushed by a four-wheel-drive truck into the shallow ditch. The charred bodies in the cab had not been removed. The sheriff had a grotesque permanent smile, the result of his facial flesh being burned away.

At the road, he found more people, mostly men, separating items from the disabled trucks left by the raiders into neat piles, so people could try to pick what they could recognize as theirs and carry it to their own trucks. They were using an honor system and Nate wondered if it would apply to him, or would they not believe him when he pointed something out as his property.

The driver stopped the truck Nate rode in and he jumped off. Mrs. MacKay opened the cab door and Nate helped her down.

She saw nervous tension on Nate's face. "These folks are okay. You won't have any trouble with them. In fact, they feel they owe you, so don't be surprised if they load you down with food that's not yours. We all know you, Brian, and your friends are the only reason the brigands did not get away. Your friend Mel told us."

"We were just trying to protect our farm, so we would not starve. We really had no idea how many people were left alive in this area. We've been busy and have not had time to check. Travel is not exactly safe anyway."

She looked up at him and put her right hand on his shoulder. "You've always been a good neighbor. Your father and mother were as good as they come." The twinkle in her eyes vanished. "I'm so sorry about Susan and little Beth."

Nate's chest rose. He nodded. "Too much death and pain. And some are making it worse." He looked around at others who were standing nearby, listening. "We must do better than we've been. We have to protect the innocent from the predators. If we don't work together, we're all going to die alone."

Several men nodded their heads.

Mrs. MacKay gave Nate a wintry smile. "We're working on that, Nate. We're working on it. This county's got a lot less trash in it today than it had a few days ago."

One of the men standing nearby spoke. "We're setting up roadblocks to keep the killers out of this part of the county." He stepped closer and shook Nate's hand. "Name's Chet Gilmore."

Nate nodded. "You live around here? I don't remember ever meeting you."

"Naw. I used to live in town. Ran a welding shop on Third and Fifth. Lost all of my family to the plague. Wife and three kids." He did not flinch. "They say the Lord never puts more on our shoulders than we can bear. We'll see. We'll see. My shoulders and my back ain't broke yet."

Mrs. MacKay added, "Your spirit is going strong too."

There was silence between them for half a minute.

"What was town like when you left?" Nate asked.

"Well," Mr. Gilmore said, "I left as soon as I buried the last of my kids. My oldest. Chet Junior. There wasn't anything left. Everything edible had been taken long since, and the smell of rotting dead people was enough to run you out of town alone. No, there was not a reason in the world for me to stay there. About eighty percent of the east side was already burned to the ground, and many more homes and buildings were still burning when I left. My old pickup collected a dozen bullet holes on the way out of town. I remember that almost as well as I remember the smell."

"Had the military organized anything in town? I mean had there been any relief or law enforcement?"

Chet shook his head. "Nothing I know of. I doubt there's many left in town now anyway. Those that are, probably are scavenging and looking for trouble."

Nate nodded. "Yeah, just getting there would be dangerous."

A teenage boy ran up to them. "Mr. Williams, we found some of your stuff. At least we found something with your name on it."

"Lead us to it," Chet said.

Nate nodded to Mrs. MacKay and the others and followed Chet and the boy to a truck. They got in, and the boy drove half a mile, the engine sputtering and coughing, and stopped next to several piles of cardboard boxes. The boy got out and pointed. "Those boxes have postage labels with your name and address on them, mostly tomato paste in Mason jars. Some of the other boxes have no labels but contain Mason jars of tomato paste also."

Nate examined three piles of boxes. "Yeah, this is our stuff. We had a good crop of tomatoes and a lot more on the vine, but the raiders got to them." He set a large box of Mason jars aside. "You can have that. We had more tomato sauce than we can use."

Chet and the boy looked at each other, surprise on their face. "Thanks," Chet said.

"We have plenty of tomato paste anyway, thanks to you being honest about things." Nate looked down the road. "We canned a lot of pickles and peppers too."

"There's some of that right over there." The boy pointed to a truck fifty yards away.

"I would like to get our clothes back, especially for a little girl. I don't have much for her, after the raiders took everything." Nate didn't want to push it, but he spoke again. "We're still missing some hand tools for farming too."

"We haven't found much of that kind of stuff yet," the boy said. We're still looking, though, and I'll tell everyone to keep an eye out."

"Thanks." Nate grabbed a box off the clay road. "Can I load it on this truck?"

"Yeah. We'll help you." The boy picked up a box just as Nate slid his against the back of the cab.

Chet grabbed a box. "After we get this stuff in your barn, I would like to talk with you about a mutual defense system. "We need to scrounge up enough two-way radios to communicate long distance. That way when there's trouble, we can call for help."

Nate set another box in the truck bed. "I might have a radio—if the thieves didn't find it. A battery for it too, and a solar panel array to charge it." He headed for the pile of boxes with the other two following. "I haven't had time to check if they found all the stuff we hid in the woods." He grabbed a box and headed for the truck. "I just remembered that we're missing a lot of mechanics' tools also and welding equipment."

"I doubt we'll find everything," Chet said.

"I know. It's just that there are a few projects I have on my mind, and I will need those tools to get them done. If it works, I can build something for Mrs. MacKay's farm too. At least you'll have enough power to charge batteries for a ham radio and a few lights. Maybe you guys can find a steam engine to pump water with for irrigation too. Gas has about run out and is going bad fast, diesel won't last forever either. We've got to start working together and planning ahead to avert a coming famine."

Chet and the boy smiled at each other.

"Sounds like you've been thinking," Chet said. "We just might pull through this if we all work together."

The boy set a box in the truck and turned to the others as they came up behind him, each with a box in their hands. "I just hope we really have cleaned the two-legged animals out of this county for good, so we *can* get to work."

"There will be more," Nate said, "but probably in smaller groups now."

Someone down the road yelled at them. "Hey. I think we found some more of the big farmer's stuff."

Nate felt a need to rush. With so much work to do before dark, and Brian waiting in the woods, not knowing if Nate was safe, he wanted to get back to the farm and Brian as soon as possible. Without a word, Nate took off on a run toward the man down the road. Chet and the boy followed, but could not keep up.

Nate stopped when he reached the man, not showing any affects from the short run.

The boy ran up to Nate, huffing.

Chet slowed to a jog halfway to them. He had to catch his breath before speaking. "You must be…younger…than you look."

Nate looked the items over, not brothering to look up before speaking. "Been working hard on my farm all my life. The last months have either gotten me into better shape, or taken years off my life. I don't know which."

"Yeah, I would guess that's true." Chet looked the items over. "Any of this stuff yours?"

"That gas welder and those tools." Nate pointed. The regulator on the torch had been damaged, but Nate hoped he could repair it. "Those store-bought canned goods aren't mine."

The man who had yelled for them to come over started putting the canned goods in a nearby pickup.

Nate spoke again. "That ammo reloading stuff is mine."

"Okay." Chet hesitated and scratched his whiskered chin. He had not shaved in days. "How are you as far as ammo goes? We're running low."

"Might be able to spare some," Nate answered. "I need to get this stuff to my farm before dark and get back to my son. He's worried, I'm sure."

"Yeah, okay." Chet looked at the boy. "We'll get more men on this."

The boy took off down the road to gather up a larger work crew.

Chet pressed again. "We really could use some ammo."

Nate stopped looking over a box of gun powder and primers and stood. "We need to work out code names for each other so anyone listening in will not know who or where we are when we're on the radio. Maybe call Mrs. MacKay's place "Big Pine" and Red Oak Farm "Big Oak," and my place "Little Hickory."

Chet nodded. "Okay."

"If my radio is still there and working, I'll call you in a few days. We'll work out our plans then. Sometime before, I will see about how much ammo I can spare. We're going to be busy though, so it might be four or five days."

"Sounds good."

The boy drove up in a two-ton flatbed truck with a dozen men riding on the back. They piled off, and everyone went to work loading Nate's property.

Just as they finished, Austin and his daughter drove up in the other truck with Nate's property loaded in the back. "We found some clothes that are probably yours. Some of it was kids' stuff. We threw it on with the rest." He looked out of the right side window past his daughter. "You guys ready to head for the farm?"

Nate climbed on the flatbed truck. He wanted to get back to Brian.

"Let's go." Chet got behind the wheel of the other truck and waited for Austin to get turned around and head for Nate's driveway.

~~~~

Still hiding in the woods and watching the farm, Brian heard the trucks coming. He kept his carbine ready, gripping it with sweaty hands. When he saw his father riding in the back of the rear truck, he started to breathe again.

They stopped in front of Nate's barn and began to unload, carrying boxes inside.

Nate signaled for Brian to come to him, then grabbed a box and carried it in the barn.

Minutes later, Brian walked up to Nate, his face a question mark.

"Everything's okay," Nate told him. "Help us get our stuff in the barn so they can be on their way."

"No trouble at all?" Brian asked, as he slung the carbine on his left shoulder.

Nate grabbed a box of canned tomato sauce out of the pickup and handed it to Brian. "No. We're already starting to form a mutual defense agreement. I think we can trust them."

They both picked up speed and tried to outwork the others, carrying more boxes into the barn than anyone else. With so many hands at work, it did not take long to unload the trucks.

"If we find anything else we think is yours, we'll put it in the barn before we go," Chet promised.

"Thanks." Nate shook his hand. "I'll try to get the radio up five days from now." At least we can see how our communication is going to work out. "The first contact won't be much, as I doubt I'll have any news for you. We'll talk about the ammo situation on the second contact. I won't have much time until then."

"Yeah, you have your work cut out for you." Chet rubbed his sore back. "I take it you'll not be moving back in your farm house then."

"No." Nate looked him in the eye. "And we will not be revealing our retreat's location either. The next time we meet, it will either be here or someplace else, but not our retreat. The whole idea is to keep it secret to anyone outside our group, even to friends."

Chet smiled. "I understand."

Everyone said their goodbyes. Renee made Brian uncomfortable when she offered her hand. He took it, not looking directly at her.

"I'm glad we're going to be friends," she said.

"Uh, yeah. It's better than killing each other." Brian looked down.

She laughed. "Yes, isn't it?"

Chapter 4

Nate woke just after sunrise. He grimaced as he sat up. His sleeping bag gave little comfort between him and the hard concrete floor of the bunker, and he longed for a real bed. The fact Mel had to carry every eighty-pound sack of dry concrete to the site on his back and then mix it with creek water by hand and pour it himself, meant the floor turned out none too smooth. There were rocks poking out of its surface, ready to dig into anyone's back while they slept. Nate felt he would be more comfortable sleeping outside on the much softer dirt. Every muscle ached when he did not move and screamed when he did.

Brian and Nate had come in with the last load four hours after dark, dead tired. Days of carrying heavy packs down to the river and then loading it all on the raft, taking many trips upriver with a load, pushing against the river's powerful flow, and then the return downstream for another load, had worn them out. They still had not gotten it all up the creek and to Mel's bunker. They had at least one more day of hard labor ahead of them. Then they had to pack most of it to Mel's cave, as the bunker was not large enough to hold all of it. That job would not take so long because the cave was not far away.

He saw Brian fast asleep on the floor and hated to wake him. *Maybe I can set up the radio while he sleeps a little more. I'm supposed to contact Mrs. MacKay's group today.*

Cindy stood watch, looking out of a loophole, witnessing the birth of a new day, as the sun turned the woods around them from black to dark grey. The wind had picked up as soon as the sun began to rise. During the height of a gust, wind howled through the loopholes. Because of the wind, there was no possibility of fog, and the sky remained clear. However, Cindy sensed something coming, the wind foretold it. Soon the wind strengthened and the temperature dropped. The treetops swayed and the wind moaned through their branches, sounding as if the forest outside was haunted. She turned and seeing Nate had awakened, she nodded. She spoke low enough not to bother those still asleep. "You two should rest today. Mom and I can haul what's left of the supplies from the river."

Nate put his boots on and stood. He shrugged his shoulders. "I have to set the radio up today. Let's hope the solar panels have charged the battery enough by now."

Brian and he had carried the solar power equipment up from the river two days before and set it up on the bunker's roof. Only the battery was heavy, but the panels were so large, they were difficult to get between the trees and through all of the brush without damaging them, generating considerable cussing from both father and son.

"We're going to get some weather," Cindy said. "No clouds yet, but something's up."

Nate finished tying his boots and walked to a loophole to look outside. "We're in the last part of hurricane season, but that can't be it. The first sign we would see is clouds scudding across the sky. No, this is something different. If it was December, I would say a strong cold front had already passed and it was about to get cold. But it's too early for that." He put on his load-bearing harness. "I'll circle around and look for sign of anyone being in the area, then come back and set up the radio."

"I'll start breakfast when you get back." Cindy lifted the steel bar from the door.

After Nate walked out, his rifle in hand, she put the bar back in place and quickly returned to her position at the loophole to cover Nate while he crossed the small clearing and entered the woods.

Nate had been gone five minutes when Martha woke. She carefully moved away from Synthia, who was sleeping on her right side, Tommy her left. After covering them with a blanket to ward off the growing chill, she stood next to her daughter and looked out of the loophole. "It's almost chilly." She had her arms crossed for warmth. "The humidity has dropped also."

"You should be sleeping," Cindy said. "You just got off security duty two hours ago."

Martha did not respond. She looked out at the thrashing woods and swaying trees and shivered. "Listen to that wind. Makes the woods come alive with motion and sound." She turned her attention to her daughter and touched Cindy's face with the palm of her left hand. "We've been through it lately, haven't we? I miss your father."

Cindy's eyes filled.

"But we'll make it. We've got good friends in Nate and Brian."

Cindy put the rifle down and held her mother. "Nate says it seems like we can trust the others." She sighed wearily. "It's about time. I was starting to think all of the decent people died in the plague."

"I can't say most people are saints, but most are not as bad as the kind we've had to deal with lately. To be honest, I think the worst is over as far as killing is concerned."

A sound from deep in the woods, upwind and carried by a gust, prompted Cindy to let go of her mother and snatch up the carbine. Another gunshot, just recognizable as such, came to their ears, dull and weak, but it was definitely a second gunshot.

They stood, listening in silence.

Cindy looked up at her mother. "Nate is out there."

"It seemed to come from down in the river valley, far away." Martha shivered. "Where did he say he was going?"

"Just to look around and see if anyone had been in the area. He shouldn't be far, and he was not going all the way to the river." Cindy searched the wind-tossed woods. "There might be more of those raiders around though. The soldiers could not have killed them all."

A noise from behind caused them to turn.

Brian had awakened and was stuffing his right foot into a worn-out boot. "I guess you were going to wake me sometime next week." He jumped up from the floor and headed for his rifle. "After you were tired of standing there talking about him being out there alone, that is."

"Your father would want you to stay here," Martha said. "Those gunshots were nowhere near where he is."

Cindy spoke up. "Nate's coming in."

Brian ran to the door and lifted the steel bar off its hooks with one hand; his rifle was in the other.

Nate stepped in and saw the look on everyone's face. "Well, I guess you heard the gunshots."

"Two of them," Martha said.

Nate waited until Brian put the bar back across the door. "I heard three."

Brian looked up at his father. "Someone may have found our cache. They could be loading it back on the raft to take downriver right now."

"I doubt the shooting was in celebration of their find," Nate said.

Brian rolled his eyes. "That's not what I meant. The gunshots tell us someone is down by the river, though."

"Could be a hunter." Nate took his load-bearing harness off. "Could be someone just got murdered. Either way, I'm setting the radio up and contacting Chet…if I can."

"Then what?" Brian still had his rifle in his hands.

"Eat breakfast." Nate looked around the room for a place to set up the radio.

"Well, I think we should get the rest of our stuff up here before it gets stolen again." Brian waited for his father to answer, but Nate was already gathering tools for the job at hand. "I guess you don't care what I think."

Nate moved items from a shelf to make room for the ham radio. He put pliers and screwdrivers on the shelf for later use. "Come on. Help me get the antenna up."

Cindy barred the door once they were outside.

Nate walked as he spoke over his shoulder. "I have cared about what you are thinking and feeling since the day you were born. And lately, you have been thinking more like a man than would be normal for your age, so I always listen to you. I'm in a hurry to get this radio transmitting so we can contact them like I promised. Then we'll eat something and get down to the river as fast as we can."

Nate let Brian throw the rock, as he was a good baseball pitcher. They tied the antenna wire to it for throwing weight, and Brian managed to put the rock between limbs high up in a pine tree. Nate let the rock slide down a few feet and then tied the wire around the tree's trunk, up as high as he could reach to keep it above everyone's head, before stretching it to the nearest bunker loophole fifty feet away.

Brian walked along behind him. "That was easy enough."

"Yep," Nate said. "Let's get inside and hook everything up and see if that old radio still works after being stashed in the woods for so long."

After ten minutes of work, they had the radio ready.

Nate turned the volume up and switched to the frequency he and Chet had agreed on.

"Did you agree to a time of day?" Brian asked.

Nate looked at him and sighed, his eyes bright with self-deprecation. "I was worried about you worrying about me at the time, so I did not think of everything." At the time he suggested he would contact them by radio, he was to some extent just putting them off. He wanted to get the supplies to the barn and get back to Brian.

Brian smiled but said nothing.

"What, no smart aleck remarks?"

Brian shook his head. "Like you said, nobody can think of everything."

"I'll transmit for a few minutes, and you can listen and learn how it's done. Then I'll leave you to it for about thirty minutes while I eat breakfast."

"I can eat while I listen," Brian quipped.

"No, you need to—"

The radio came alive.

"This is Big Pine calling Little Hickory. Come in."

Nate held the microphone close to his mouth and spoke. "This is Little Hickory."

A man's voice came back. "Hey! I've been trying to get you for more than two hours, off and on." Chet sounded relieved. "Nothing to report here. I'm just glad to see our radios are working. How are things there? Come in"

Nate pushed the button on the side of the mike. "Several gunshots this morning just at dawn, long ways off. No trouble though. Come in."

"I'm reading you great. How are you reading me? Come in."

Nate had checked the signal meter when Chet was transmitting. He knew a little about Ham Radio procedures, but his signal communications training was military. Fortunately, Chet instinctively understood how to communicate by radio well enough to make it work, and Nate immediately adapted to his method. "Your signal is 5 x 5. I'm glad we're able to hear each other so well, at least with this frequency. Come in."

"Five by five? Come in."

"Never mind." Nate kicked himself for getting too military. "I mean I read you loud and clear with a strong signal. Come in."

"Great. I've already contacted Big Oak this morning. We had trouble reading each other. I think they don't have their aerial rigged right. I'm going over there tomorrow with a few guys and check it for them. Come in."

"Sounds good. I think we should have our radios on at first light every day, if possible. It's the only way we can be sure someone is listening when we need to communicate. We can't have our radios on twenty-four/seven and manned, but we can run them for thirty minutes every day. Come in."

"I agree," Chet responded. "Come in."

"When you get Big Oak's radio going, try to contact me tomorrow at sundown, or have one of them do it. Come in."

"Will do. Unless you have something else, I'll be signing off now. Come in."

"Nothing else. Little Hickory signing off."

"Big Pine signing off."

Nate switched off the radio.

"Well," Brian said nonchalantly, "can we eat now?"

Martha looked up from the wood stove. "Wild ham and freeze-dried scrambled eggs for everyone. No coffee. We're out."

"We're out of ketchup too," Brian said.

Cindy laughed. "We won't be running out of tomato sauce anytime soon. You can use that."

Brian worked the hand pump so Nate could wash his hands with lye soap. There was no sink, but there was a drain in the floor under the water pump. They used buckets to wash dishes and clothes. "It's not ketchup," he said, "but it will work to make those eggs taste like they're eatable."

"It's not that bad. You've been spoiled by growing up on fresh yard eggs." Nate pumped while Brian washed his hands. "We do need to start a late crop. Only the hardy vegetables will survive though. No more tomatoes."

Brian dried off. "Like Cindy said, we have plenty until next harvest. What I'm thinking is how safe it will be to go back to the farm and work the fields. There are still a few of those killers around."

Martha looked up while taking biscuits from a Dutch oven on the stove, waiting to hear what Nate had to say.

Brian blinked and looked up at his father. "You're planning on farming here, aren't you?"

Nate sat at the small table and filled a glass with water. "It's sandy around here, and not so good for planting. Best land is down by the creek. That's where the water is too. The bugs down there will eat most of our crop, though."

"And the coons and possums and deer and hogs and squirrels," Brian said.

Nate piled scrambled eggs on his plate and grabbed a biscuit. "Won't be fun or very productive, but it'll be safer."

"Damn. It'll be a little patch here and there, wherever we can find sunlight and a clear patch in the bottomlands." Brian's voice revealed his displeasure of even thinking about it.

"Won't be fun, that's for sure," Nate repeated.

Martha pushed eggs onto Brian's plate. "It's crazy is what it is."

Everyone but Carrie, Synthia, and Tommy, who were asleep, looked at Martha.

Martha looked back at Nate. "Why don't we join one of the larger groups? There's safety in numbers, and they still have a tractor or two that runs until the diesel runs out and plenty of land to farm."

Nate's chest deflated and he looked away at nothing. "I don't know if that's a good idea. I never was much for being part of a large organization, not since I left the Army."

"We should at least think about it," Martha said.

Cindy spoke up. "They might not want Tommy, Synthia, and Carrie. They're likely to want only those who can work."

"In that case they can go to hell," Martha said.

"Well, she's right," Nate and Brian said simultaneously.

Brian kept quite while his father finished. "They might not want to take on anyone that can't work."

Martha dropped the lid onto the Dutch oven with a clank. "Then we girls will be staying here. I'm not abandoning either of those girls, anymore than I would Cindy or Tommy."

"I'm not so sure I'm comfortable with the idea of joining them anyway," Nate said. "Once we do, we lose control of our lives, our destinies. Here, no one bosses anyone, but there is probably a pecking order at both of those farms. A group that large must have leaders."

Brian stopped eating. "No one bosses anyone here, Dad?" He had a silly grin on his face.

"I didn't say fathers and mothers aren't fathers and mothers here, smartass." Nate chuckled. He was glad to see Brian still had a little of his old self in him, despite all he had been through.

"I think we should stay here," Cindy said.

"Well, it's still just us thinking and talking about it," Nate said. "We have a lot of work to do around here before we do more than just think about it."

Nate and Brian ate fast and left to haul more supplies from the creek to the bunker.

Brian was impatient and kept pressuring Nate to move faster.

"Rushing could get both of us killed in an ambush," Nate whispered. "Cool it."

Brian said nothing, but he stopped pushing his father to walk faster.

Fifty minutes later, Nate stood in the shade of an oak, listening. With the wind tossing the trees and underbrush violently, he would not be able to hear even if ten men were plowing through the brush at top speed. He scanned the woods, fruitlessly trying to catch movement in a sea of movement. The cache sat only thirty yards away, he knew that, but he could not see it for the brush. And yet, something was wrong—he could sense it. There had been no unnatural sound to alarm him, no fleeting image of a man lurking in the woods, but he knew someone was there.

Nate motioned for Brian to get down behind a cypress stump, his eyes telling Brian something was wrong.

We've got hours before dark. We'll just wait and let him get impatient. Nate took careful, slow steps and made his way to bullet-stopping cover and dark shade for concealment. He squatted down behind a tree and peered around the trunk, trying to penetrate the brush with his eyes, down low where you can often see a man's lower leg when he takes a careful step.

Seeing no sign of a man, Nate searched the treetops, though he knew Brian had already done that.

Nothing.

Time ticked by, and the woods treated them to a natural show of various small creatures at play or on the hunt for food. Three squirrels chased each other in the swaying treetops, despite the wind. That was unusual, since squirrels do not normally come out of their nests on windy days. A raccoon dipped her paw into the creek and pulled out a dead fish, and then a doe came sneaking along their side of the creek from upstream. Like squirrels, deer do not move around much on windy days. The commotion of the windblown woods certainly had this one nervous.

Great. She'll be our alarm. Nate watched as she inched closer to the cache. She stopped in mid step and wrinkled her nose, raising it in the air, sucking in a sent she did not like. She was not smelling Nate or Brian, they were downwind of her. *Maybe the human scent on the cache.* Nate waited.

The doe continued her cautious way down a well used deer trail, stopping to look under brush, just as Nate had done earlier, and listen after every step. A certain scent of danger caused her to hesitate. She inched along, her nose working the air.

Nate and Brian both flinched and dropped to the ground when a rifle boomed from only thirty-five yards away.

Nate tried to find the shooter, but thrashing nearby distracted him for a second. He looked over to see the doe on its side, kicking at nothing and trying to get up. She bled from her chest. Nate checked on Brian, finding him laying flat on the ground, looking back at him, his eyes wide.

The sound of someone bulling through brush alerted Nate. He had his rifle ready, aiming at a form coming closer. An emaciated African American boy not much older than Brian exploded into the small clearing and shouldered his bolt-action rifle. He kept his yes on the thrashing doe as he pulled a sheath knife and bent down to cut the doe's throat. Nate scanned the woods for any sign of more people. He glanced over to Brian and saw that he had his carbine on the boy. *Don't shoot.*

Nate and Brian kept silent while the boy gutted the doe. Nate decided the boy was alone, but did not want to take any chances, so he signaled for Brian to stay where he was and keep his eyes searching the woods for danger. Then Nate stood and slowly crept up behind the boy.

Sensing something, the boy whirled around on his knees and looked up at Nate, terror on his face. He fell back onto the bloody doe and held the knife out, slashing.

"Whoa there. I mean you no harm." Nate tried to sound unthreatening. "Calm down. I just want to talk."

The boy grabbed for his rifle's buttstock to swing it off his shoulder.

"Hold it, damn it!" Nate stepped closer. "I'm not going to hurt you. Just keep that rifle slung where it is."

"This is my deer," the boy swallowed, trying to bolster his courage, "and you ain't taking it."

"No, I'm not. I just want to talk."

The boy looked up defiantly. "I ain't got nothing to say. You might as well leave me alone if you ain't going to steal from me. And if you are, you might as well kill me now, 'cause you ain't gettin' this meat or my rifle without killing me."

"All I want is to talk. You can keep working on the doe if you want."

The boy got into a more comfortable position and sat next to the doe. "There ain't nothing to talk about. You can't have any meat. I need it for myself."

"How about your name? My name's Nate Williams. I own a farm not too far from here."

"I saw that farm awhile back. There ain't nothing there. The stealers got it all." He looked up at Nate with hard eyes and a harder face, his jaw jutting out. "And it wasn't me. It was the stealers."

"I know," Nate said. "The National Guard took care of most of them. "Like I told you, I just want to talk."

"Well, hurry up and talk. I got work to do. Or kill me if you're going to. I don't know as I care much one way or the other. If it wasn't for—" He stopped suddenly and looked up at Nate with hate in his eyes.

Nate understood instantly what he saw looking up at him. "I have people I'm looking out for too. I don't want to hurt you or anyone else. I only kill in self-defense."

"Got any kids?" The boy stood up slowly, obviously mindful to not make Nate nervous. He wiped the knife on a leafy brush and slid it into its sheath.

"Yes. My little girl died in the plague. My son is still alive."

What the boy said next set Nate back on his heels.

"Well, I got a bunch of kids to take care of."

Nate stood there staring through his mask. "How is that?"

"It's a long story."

"I have time."

"I don't. I got to get this meat taken care of. They're hungry. I shot two squirrels earlier, but that wasn't enough for nothin'."

"I guess not. Are there any adults with you?"

The boy almost flinched, but just caught himself. "Three men, all with guns. Should be here soon. I'm sure they heard the shot."

Nate coughed. "Hmm. Well, maybe we should cut that doe in two pieces, and I'll help you carry it. We can meet them on their way here."

The boy's breathing picked up. "Why don't you just leave me alone, if you don't want something from me?"

"Because I have a little food to spare, and I do not want children to go hungry if I can help."

The boy stood there and said nothing.

"How many children are you taking care of? Will you tell me that?" Nate slung his rifle to show he meant no harm.

The boy kept his face hard. "They're comin'." His Adam's apple moved up his throat. "They're goin' to be mad about you messin' with me."

Nate sighed. "Brian, come over here."

Brian stood and walked into the clearing, but stopped ten yards away.

Nate motioned with his head. "This is my son, Brian. My wife and little girl got sick and died."

The boy appeared to be surprised by the fact Brian had been hiding in the woods the whole time. He looked Brian over.

Nate understood that he was looking for signs of abuse. "You can trust us."

The boy's eyes flitted from Brian to Nate.

"Are the children your brothers and sisters?" Nate took a step closer.

The boy shook his head. "I found them in some kind of orphan home when I was lookin' for food. They was alone 'cause the people takin' care of them all died from the sickness. There was more at first." He swallowed, his thin neck rippling with muscles just under his sweat-soaked skin. I lost some. I think they didn't get enough to eat. Two were taken away while I was lookin' for food. I was told when I got back two men took them. Clay was beat up pretty bad from tryin' to stop them from taking his sister. They didn't hurt none of the others though. The ones they took was the oldest girls." He looked away.

"How many are left?" He did not answer. Nate started to speak again but was interrupted by Brian.

"Oh come on. My dad only wants to help. He's not exactly into hurting kids, for God's sake."

"There was eighteen. There's fourteen now." The boy's chest heaved and his face revealed the tress of not knowing if he had just betrayed the children he had been struggling to take care of and protect.

Nate blinked at him for a few seconds. "How old are they?"

"They're just little kids." The boy appeared to be near to tears, his façade of being a hardass melting away. "Some six or seven, some nine, ten years old." He wiped his face. "You really goin' to help? You hurt them, you better kill me now."

Brian broke in. "Jeez. Dad's just bossy, he's not mean. He won't hurt anybody that doesn't try to hurt us."

The boy looked at Brian, his chest heaving, sweat running down his face. As he breathed deep and fast, ribs showed through tears and holes in his filthy brown T-shirt.

Nate slid his pack off. "I have a little rope. We'll hang the doe up and go get the kids."

"What do you want with them?" The boy looked up at Nate, his eyes hard again.

"I don't *want* anything, but it looks like I'm going to have to help you take care of them until we can find some people who can do a better job. Maybe the Guard will take them." Nate looked for a suitable tree. "Help me with your doe."

"Bugs are going to get on it," the boy said.

"It's the best we can do. It'll keep until we get back." Nate threw a loop over a limb ten feet above the swamp floor. "How far is it?"

The boy seemed to be having trouble catching his breath and growing more upset. "I've been huntin' all morning, after I left them those squirrels I cooked. I'm not sure. Maybe a mile. I've been walkin' slow. Still huntin', stalkin'."

"They downriver?" Nate asked.

The boy helped him lift the doe while Brian tied the rope off. When the boy let go, he was gasping. He staggered back. "Yeah. I need to rest for a minute." He sat down right there in the mud.

Nate squatted in front of him. "There are no men with guns, are there?"

The boy shook his head.

"I told you the truth." Nate's voice was soft for such a big man. "I won't hurt those kids. We're with others who will help. You can relax now."

The boy began to shake. He pulled his knees up, buried his face in his arms, and cried.

Nate reached out and put his heavy hand on the boy's bony shoulder. "That's all right. Let it go. It's not all on you anymore. They still need you, but you have people to help now."

Nate waited a minute and then handed him his canteen.

The boy drank eagerly.

"Clean water tastes sweet after drinking river water, doesn't?" Nate waited for the boy to finish drinking. "What is your name?"

"Kendell Taylor," the boy said.

Nate stood and put the canteen in a side pocket in his pack. Okay, Kendell Taylor, let's go help those kids."

Chapter 5

Kendell stopped and turned back to Nate, who was five yards behind. "We're close. Let me go ahead and talk to them before you come in. They'll be scared if I don't."

Nate nodded.

Kendell left.

Brian stood next to his father. "Damn. I hope he's not setting us up for an ambush. There might really be men with guns instead of kids."

"I doubt it. If he's lying, he's a damn good actor." Nate pointed to his left. "But get over there behind cover and wait just in case. I'll get his attention when he comes back. Don't show yourself until I say so."

"Right," Brian said. "We can't be too careful."

Nate's eyes lit up. "You've been learning a lot lately."

When Brian walked away, he smiled.

Kendell came through the brush, not trying to be quiet, crashing over palmettos. He stopped where he left Nate and looked around. "Mr.?"

Nate spoke but did not come out from his hiding place. "Over here."

Kendell hesitated, but seemed to realize that Nate was just being careful. He walked toward the sound of Nate's voice until Nate told him to stop.

"It ain't no trick," Kendell said. "I just want those kids taken care of. Where's your son?"

Nate ignored his question. "Why did you take them out here in this swamp?"

Kendell looked in the direction of Nate's voice. "To get away from people. What do you think those bastards wanted with the two girls they took?" He spit, his face showing hate. "I'd rather they starve. There ain't no food in town anyway. It's all been ate or taken and hoarded. I expect you're out here hidin' too, aren't you?"

"That's about it. People are a source of danger." Nate scanned the woods, buying time while he kept the boy busy. "How long have you been out here?"

"We been in the swamp several months now, but we was a long way south until a couple days ago. There was so much shootin' around there, we headed on up here to get away from the fightin'."

Nate stood, and the boy could see him behind brush. "What have you been eating, besides deer meat?"

"I been feedin' them anything they could keep down their throat." He watched Nate come closer. "You goin' to feed them right off? They're real hungry." He took notice of how Nate kept scanning the woods. "There ain't no one out here except those kids." He pointed. "This way."

"I believe you," Nate said. "But I have only one life, and I'm really serious about not giving it away by being careless."

The boy snickered. "You be different from me then. Except for those kids, I ain't got nothing to lose or be scared of."

"I know what you mean, but you'll think differently once things are better." Nate raised his voice so Brian could hear. "My son is going to stay put while I go in with you. Once I see how safe it is, he'll come on in and we can do what we can for them."

The boy nodded. "Okay."

Kendell led him upslope, out of the wetter areas and into a stand of oaks. Nate stopped and looked at saw palmetto stems that had been pulled out and the white part gnawed off, all the way up the stem to the green part. They had eaten the white part of every palmetto bush in the area. They passed a cabbage palm that had been hacked open and the white eatable material ripped out and consumed.

Oh God. Nate had to catch his breath. He had seen children suffer before, but he could never get used to it. All were skeletons, as close to death as life. Weak from starvation and covered with festering bug bites, scratches, cuts, and bruises, their hair growing long and wild and matted with filth, they watched with terror as Nate came closer. Sick from drinking untreated river water, many were lying down on mats made of palmetto fronds. Evidence of diarrhea was everywhere on the ground. All were looking back at him as if he were a demon come to take them away to hell. But they were already there.

Their fear of this giant washed away when they saw tears running down Nate's face.

One boy, about six, summoned all of his strength to push himself up from the ground and stagger over to Nate. He raised his right hand and scribed an arc in the air. He looked up at Nate. "Hi," he said.

Nate swallowed and said, "Hi there, buddy. We're going to take you to food and give you all plenty to eat. Then we're going to take you home."

"I did the best I could," Kendell said, tears streaming down his face. "I did."

Nate patted him on the back. "Yes you did, and you saved most of them. You did as well as any man and better than most." He looked around the camp and saw lean-tos covered with palm fronds, set like shingles to repel rain. "You did all that with your sheath knife?" he asked.

Kendell nodded. A little girl walked up and wrapped her arms around his leg. "Don't cry Kendell. It'll be okay. We ain't really that hungry today."

"You won't be hungry much longer," Nate said. He looked at Kendell. "We have a cache of food not far from where you killed that doe. We'll cook a meal for them right there. They're so far gone, they probably won't be able to hold it down, though." His jaw set. "Nevertheless, we're going to feed them as soon as we can."

"Some of them can't walk." Kendell picked the little girl up. Her right foot was bandaged from material cut from Kendell's shirt. She had no shoes.

"We'll make a stretcher and carry two at a time on it." Nate took a step, heading for Brian. "Explain to them that we're going to food while I go get my son. That should motivate them to walk faster."

Stunned by what he saw and felt, Brian gave the children what little food he had in his pack, so did Nate. The children drained all their canteens. Kendell refused any food. He plainly cared more for the children than himself.

The condition of the children visibly affected Brian. Tears ran down his face as he carried the little girl who could not walk because of an infected cut on her right foot. She had stepped on something a week before, leaving a festering gash.

Nate and Kendell carried the stretcher Nate had made from poles. Nate came up with the idea to place children sitting on the stretcher with their legs hanging over the edge, making it possible to carry four small children instead of just two. With Brian carrying the little girl with a cut foot, they were able to keep the other children in sight as they traveled through the swamp to the cache.

The children's weak condition forced them to travel no more than a few hundred yards per hour. It took until late afternoon to reach the cache. The wind gained strength throughout the day. The sky did not show any sign of rain, despite the strange wind.

"I don't think they can go any farther," Nate told Brian. "Build a fire and we'll boil water for them to drink after it has cooled."

"What about feeding them?" Kendell asked. "You promised you would feed them."

"We will." Nate pointed to a small clearing that was higher than the surrounding area and at least a little less wet. "Cut palmetto fronds for them to lay on tonight. We've got a big tarp covering the cache. We'll use it for shelter. Cut some poles for a long lean-to. Don't make it any higher than three feet, so it will catch less wind."

"We ain't got much daylight." Kendell pulled his knife and walked toward a stand of palmettos. He went to work with all the vigor his emaciated body could muster.

Nate wondered what would be best to feed starving children. *The main thing now is to get potable water in them so their bodies can start flushing out the bugs they have been drinking.* He pulled a tarp off the cache and searched for something to cook for them, cursing his lack of medical knowledge. *Soup that's mostly broth maybe?*

Brian stretched his T-shirt over the mouth of a two-gallon pot he found among the pile of canned goods and Mason jars at the cache and put it in the creek so the water would strain through his shirt, removing the larger-sized debris. He then put the pot on a fire Nate had started. Nate helped him roll a large log upwind of the fire to protect it from its growing force. The flame still flickered horizontally. Brian searched for more firewood, breaking dead branches off trees. All of the wood lying on the ground was soaked with moisture. It took a lot of heat to boil that much water fast, so he had to spend fifteen minutes searching for more firewood. With a fire blazing, he gathered up every canteen he and his father had. A few minutes after the water started boiling, he used his still-wet T-shirt to grab the pot's wire handle and put the pot aside so it would cool.

Nate called his son over to the cache. "What should we feed them?"

Brian looked up at him confused.

Nate smiled. "Well, you've been reading every survival book we had in the house since the stuff hit the fan. Your dad doesn't have all the answers, you know."

"I don't know…thin soup I guess."

"That's what I was thinking. Did you read that in a book?"

Brian thought for a second. "I don't remember. I know they don't need any deer meat right now. It's hard to chew and hard to digest. Tomorrow we could probably feed them something more solid than soup, though." He glanced over at the children and sighed. "I don't know. They seem really thin and weak and sick."

Nate put his massive hand on his son's shoulder. "I think we can save them. Go help Kendell while the water is cooling."

Feeding all of the children took hours. They had only two cups, stainless steel World War II military surplus—the kind that fit on the bottom of a canteen. The freeze-dried reconstituted soup seemed to satisfy them and relieve their hunger pangs. Each of them got a full cup.

Kendell refused to eat until the last child had been fed. "Look at them," he said. "They ain't hurting as much now. They'll sleep tonight." He wiped his face.

Nate handed him a cup of soup. "It's your turn now."

With Kendell and the children asleep, Brian prepared a meal of spaghetti. There was no soup left, and there was only tomato paste from a Mason jar to go with it. They ate by the fire. By then it was eleven o'clock. The wind continued to build.

"That Kendell is a good guy," Brian said. He ate the last of his spaghetti.

"Yeah." Nate sighed. It was more than weariness.

"How are we going to take care of all of them?" Brian asked. "What if no one will take them?" He looked up at his father as he stoked the fire. "I can see you're worried. And I know you're not going to send them away, even if all of us go hungry. Except me, Synthia, and Tommy. You won't allow that."

"We'll worry about it later. Get some sleep."

"Got to boil more water first, so we'll have some in the morning. They'll want to eat again too, before we head up to the bunker."

"As soon as the water is done, stomp the fire out. It's a beacon for trouble. Then get some sleep. I'll stand first watch."

"You won't hear anything coming in this wind."

"True, but I can still shoot, wind or no wind."

Brian crossed his arms and shivered. His T-shirt was still wet. They had not dressed for the cooler weather that descended on them with darkness. The wind-chill made it worse.

Nate took his off. "Put your shirt somewhere it will dry and put mine on."

Brian stood there. "It'll be too big, and you're going to be cold."

"Go on. I'm your father. Do what I tell you."

Brian took the shirt and walked to the lean-to.

~~~~

The next morning after Kendell and the children were fed, Nate and Brian loaded their packs with food, and they headed for the bunker. It had taken three hours to feed everyone again, but they had gotten up at sunrise, so they still managed to make it to the bunker by afternoon.

Nate and Brian were supposed to have been back the day before. Martha and Cindy had gotten little sleep, worrying about them. Despite their relief to see them back, they wasted no time asking about what happened. They immediately set about taking care of the children.

Brian nearly wore his arms out pumping water so Martha and Cindy could give all the children a bath. The smaller children cried when the lye soap stung their festering sores. Melissa, the little girl with an infected foot, screamed while Cindy held her down as Martha cleaned the gash and put antibiotic cream on.

The children's filthy rags were falling apart, and there were few clothes that would fit them. Most of them wound up with little more than a piece of a sheet wrapped around them as a skirt. Kendell was able to fit into Brian's jeans and T-shirt, owing to his skeletal figure, but the jeans were several inches too short.

For some reason, Carrie came out of her near stupor that had lasted so long, a product of her nightmarish ordeal, and was able to help. The sight of all the sick children seemed to open a door in her mind, and she went to work. For the first time since Nate saved her from the sadists, she showed emotion other than fear.

Though still weak, the children improved rapidly. They sat under a pine tree, clean and wearing clean clothes or at least a swath of clean cloth wrapped around them.

Brian hid in the woods, keeping watch. They had been lax on security while taking care of the children. Now that he was no longer needed at the pump, he resumed their normal security measures.

Nate left for the cave to look for materials to fashion a shelter of some type for the children. There was not enough room in the bunker for all of them.

Kendell took an old tree-saw Nate had given him and set to work cutting poles for the shelter while Martha and Cindy cleaned dishes in the bunker.

"My God, Mom," Cindy said. "How are we going to feed all of them?"

Martha looked at her daughter with worried eyes. "What food we have will not last long now, that's for sure." She forced a wintry smile. "It's not like we have any choice. We're not going to turn them away."

Cindy folded her tired arms across her chest and sighed. "What about the plague? They might be carrying it."

"I thought about that too. More than likely the disease has played itself out by now." Her face contorted in disbelief of her thoughts. "We can't turn children away to die." She shook repulsive thoughts from her head. "No way. We will just have to make do."

Carrie came in and used the pump to fill a pitcher, then went back to the children. She made sure they all got a drink.

"Look at Carrie," Cindy said. "Something good has come out of this already."

"Yes, but we do not have enough food to feed everyone for long." Martha turned to check on Tommy and Synthia. They were sitting side by side on a blanket, sharing the only picture book they had. They looked up and smiled.

With full stomachs and feeling better than they had in months, the smaller children outside grew sleepy, and soon the older children followed suit. Carrie sat nearby, keeping watch over them.

~~~~

Late in the afternoon, the wind gained in strength, and the sky turned gunmetal gray, with clouds scudding across the sky from the west, sinking lower to earth, thickening and growing darker by the hour, but no rain fell.

Nate, Brian, and Kendell fought a flapping tarpaulin, as the wind tried to snatch it out of their hands. They stretched it over a frame of pinewood poles, only to have it blown off before they had time to tie it down.

"Forget it," Nate yelled over the wind. "The kids can't stay out here tonight anyway. A storm is coming, and it's getting colder by the hour. Stretch it over one pole only and make it smaller. It will be less likely to blow down and will still be large enough for us three and maybe Cindy to stay in tonight. The children can sleep in the bunker."

"What about the cave?" Brian asked. "We can leave the door open to let air in."

"I don't want to be that far from the others in case someone comes around," Nate answered.

They struggled against the strengthening wind for another half-hour before they had the tarpaulin secured. Cold rain drops as big as quarters drove down at a forty-five degree angle, pelting them with enough force to sting. The sky continued to grow darker.

Nate looked up and saw a black cloud, its leading edge overhead whirling in a circular motion. He stared at two places where a tight spinning motion formed, becoming more distinct with each moment. Though they had stretched the tarpaulin as tight as possible, it snapped in the wind, sounding like rapid-fire gunshots. A branch from high in a pine tree came down nearly hitting Nate in the face, but he knocked it aside with his right arm. He snatched up a coil of rope. "Get inside now! This is tornado weather."

Kendell and Brian rushed in through the door and into the dim glow of a kerosene lamp. Nate ran in just behind. He leaned against the steel door and shut it. Brian put the bar in place.

Cindy closed a loophole shutter she had been watching from. "I don't think you guys should stay out there tonight."

"We're not," Nate said, "even if everyone but the smaller children has to stand on their feet all night. That's a wall cloud over us."

"What does that mean?" Carrie asked. She held a little boy and Synthia both as she sat on a blanket on the floor.

Carrie had talked little after her ordeal with the sadists, and Nate was surprised to see her talking so much. He did not want to frighten her, so he said, "There will be some rain and wind."

Large hail clattered against the steel shutters and door. The three feet of dirt and sod that covered the bunker's concrete roof blunted the sounds of the wind and hail.

Brian slid a spare bar across the door on hooks two feet above the other bar. "This thing can take any tornado. Don't worry. Mel knew what he was doing when he built this bunker." His white face did not match the confidence in his words.

The wind picked up and began to scream like a thousand demons. All of the shutters on one side of the bunker began to rattle and clatter.

The smaller children cried.

Thunder shook the bunker.

Snapping trees gave them warning.

Nate's ears popped. "Everyone get on the floor and hold on to the smaller kids."

The bunker floor began to vibrate. This time it was not thunder. The children cried louder, until a roar from outside drowned out their cries.

It passed. The roar faded, trailing off into the distance, but the sounds of snapping trees and gusting wind lingered.

Martha, Cindy, and Carrie tried to calm the frightened children.

"Well, I guess the tarp's gone," Brian said. He started to remove one of the bars on the door.

"No one goes outside," Nate said. "There are more storms coming. Hear the distant thunder?"

The wind outside still gusted above hurricane strength as thunder rumbled closer.

Nate opened a shutter and a cold blast of wind chilled everyone. Cold rain hit him in the face. He looked out into the dark. "Bring me that spotlight, Brian."

The light's strong beam cut through the dark and rain, revealing splintered trees cast into piles ten feet high in places. The tarpaulin was gone; the poles Kendell had cut and buried two feet into the ground like fence posts were broken off one foot above ground level.

"Come daylight," Nate said, "you're going to see a different world out there. Most of the trees are gone. We're going to have plenty of firewood lying around, some of it already in small enough pieces to fit into the stove." He turned the light off and closed the shutter.

"Damn, I hope the stuff we left by the creek is still there." Brian exhaled forcefully. "It's not like we can stand losing food, especially now."

Martha turned the kerosene lamp up so she could see the children better. They were still frightened but calmer than a few minutes before. "It's early. We need to keep the children occupied until it's time for them to go to sleep, otherwise, they will be waking up in the middle of the night. "Carrie, will you read to them?"

She shook her head. "No. I couldn't."

Cindy took *The Adventures of Huckleberry Finn,* one of the few novels they had, off a shelf and handed it to Carrie.

Carrie opened it and began to read out loud. She spoke in a low tone at first and read slowly, unsure of herself. One by one, the children sat up and listened. When one on the far side of the room complained she could not hear, Carrie began to speak up and read faster and with more emotion.

After 15 minutes, Cindy remarked, "You're good at that, much better than me."

Kendell came closer so he could talk to Nate without bothering Carrie or the children. "I left that deer hanging. "It ain't no good now. I wish I had never shot it."

"The tornado came from the direction of the river. It might be gone now anyway," Brian said. "It's the cache of food I'm worried about."

"Chances are the tornado did not go that way." Nate laid his hand on Kendell's shoulder. "If a bear does not get it tonight, we can use it for fish bait. We'll make Okeechobee traps tomorrow and set them in the river."

"There's hooks and line in the cave." Brian's eyes lit up a little. "We should set trot lines in the river also."

"Fish are better than nothing, but, pound for pound, they do not offer many calories." While he talked, Nate listened to the sounds of another approaching storm.

"But they'll damn sure fill your belly, and they're fun to catch," Brian said. "If we use traps and trot lines, cleaning and cooking them will be more work than catching them."

Nate turned from the shutter and looked at his son. He started to tell him that fun had nothing to do with it. Instead, he resisted an urge to hold him. He still had his boy after all, and he was grateful for that. "You two try to get some sleep. We have a lot of work to do tomorrow. We've got a mess out there to contend with."

~~~~

Even Nate was shocked by the damage the tornado left in its wake. He guessed it must have been one half mile wide, certainly one of the strongest tornados to ever hit Florida. He doubted even the bunker would have withstood it if not for the berming on all the walls deflecting the tremendous winds and the berm in front protecting the door. It had touched down just one hundred yards from the bunker and then passed over them, continuing on for over a mile before lifting back up into the sky. Later, they learned it came back down less than a mile farther and cut a swath through the forest for five more miles before lifting up again. He worried about the farm house, but had more immediate concerns.

Before the sun had risen above the treetops, Nate, Brian, and Kendell were working in a cold drizzle that streamed down at an angle, clearing downed trees and other debris from around the bunker.

Nate limbed the windfalls with an ax, while Brian and Kendell used a two-man saw to cut the logs into manageable pieces. They labored for three hours clearing debris from around the bunker moving splintered trees away from the door.

Carrie watched the children while Martha and Cindy helped pile logs 50 yards from the bunker. The other debris was scattered out on the ground back in the trees to prevent them from becoming a fire hazard during the dry season.

After all the children were fed and Nate, Brian, and Kendell grabbed a quick breakfast, Cindy went with the boys and Nate to check on the cache. They found the woods to be a mess. Trees were down everywhere. The sky was still overcast, with dark, menacing clouds scudding rapidly at low altitude, and the wind blowing at more than thirty-five miles per hour, sometimes gusting to fifty-five. It was a wet, cold, chaotic world they found themselves in, as they made their way down the now overflowing creek to the cache.

"Can't be any more tornadoes, though, despite the stormy weather," Brian said. "There are no thunderstorms. Right, Dad?"

"Right. No thunderstorms, no tornadoes. This is some of the weirdest weather I've ever seen."

"You mean like the cold winters we've been having lately," Brian said. "Weird is right."

Kendell walked along behind the other three, carrying a military surplus backpack they gave him to carry food to the bunker. He seemed to have little to say. Nate noticed he was still weak, but getting stronger.

"If you need to stop and rest, Kendell, we will not mind. You are not going to be yourself for many weeks."

Kendell shook his head. "I can walk just fine. I'm a lot better now. We have to get that food, if it ain't ruined or gone already."

"We're sure going to need it," Cindy said.

Kendell flinched at her words.

"We'll get by, one way or another," Nate said.

Cindy turned and looked at Kendell, apology on her face. "Yeah, we have enough for now. And we're not going to turn anyone away to starve."

Kendell looked down. "Maybe the government has set up places for kids that ain't got no one."

"They will sooner or later, I don't know about now, though," Cindy said. "For now, they have us, just like they have you. You're not alone anymore."

Kendell blinked and stopped walking. Cindy turned around to see if he was still back there, he ran and caught up with the others. Nate watched for foot prints in the mud. He could not hear anything with the wind slamming the trees against each other, and there was no way he could catch movement in the woods when the woods themselves conducted its wild dance. As they made their way down into the swamp, water became an ever increasing problem, forcing them off course many times to avoid wading in mud. Water moccasins slithered everywhere.

Nate came across a long stick, two-inches think, to use for snakes and picked it up. He did not waste time hitting them with it, just pushed them out of the way, so they could make their escape without getting close enough to be a danger to him or the others.

"There's the cache," Nate said. "Some of it's under water. And it's scattered all over. Look. There's a few cans floating in the creek." The Freeze-dried food was so light, the one-gallon cans were floating. He reached out with the stick to try to get some of them close enough to grab.

Kendell just waded in and started collecting them. "My shoes is worn out anyway," he said. "I ain't got no socks on, so it don't make no difference if I get wet."

Nate looked worried. "The water won't kill you, but there's snakes and gators. Some of that creek bottom is so soft, you can be head-deep and still not hit bottom. I would rather you get out of there now. We have a canoe a little farther downstream to do that with. Come on out of there."

Kendell reluctantly did what he was told and waded to shore.

Nate took the cans and handed them to Brian, then held out his hand and pulled Kendell onto dry land. "While you guys are collecting that stuff, keep an eye out for snakes. You've already seen they are active in this flooded swamp." He went after the canoe.

Kendell watched him leave. "Why did he order me around like that? He acted like he was my father or something."

"He was just worried about you," Brian said. "You haven't seen anything yet. Wait until you see him ordering me around."

"But he ain't my father."

Cindy listened while she worked. She smiled and said nothing.

Brian stuffed a Mason jar in his pack. "He's taken you on as his responsibility, so he's kind of acting like your father too."

Kendell looked confused. As he worked, he seemed to be thinking.

It took them longer to gather up all the jars and other containers of food they could find and set them on dry land than to fill their packs. They lost more than a dozen Mason jars to breakage, but most of the food was retrievable.

"Okay," Nate said, "spread out your hammocks on the ground and put the lighter stuff on them. When you think it is full enough, and remember, don't make them too heavy to carry, pull the ends of the hammock together and tie it off. You will need enough loose hammock material to throw over your shoulder so you can easily carry it."

"My pack's already full of heavy Mason jars," Cindy said.

"I'll carry your hammock," Nate said.

"I wasn't complaining."

"I know that. We need someone with two free hands to keep a rifle handy in case of trouble. Keep an eye on our back trail."

Nate took the lead. They headed upstream and to higher ground.

Kendell pointed. "Look. There's my deer. No bear got it, but the tree it was hanging from blew down." It was floating in the mud.

They stopped long enough to hang the deer in another tree. Nate held the weight while Brian tied it.

"We can still use it for fish bait," Nate said. "The more rotten it is, the more it stinks. Stink makes good catfish bait. We'll cut it up tomorrow, if a bear does not get it tonight."

"I guess we're going to be busy today making traps and trot lines," Brian said.

Nate kept his eyes working, searching the woods for trouble. "We'll make only two traps and one hundred feet of trot lines. I'm not sure all of the children will want fish. We do not want it to go to waste if we catch too many."

Kendell spoke up. "You think we'll get that many?"

"After all this rain, and it looks like it's going to rain more, the catfish will be feeding. I would not be surprised if there were a fish on every hook when we check them the next day."

Brian stepped closer to Kendell. "After a heavy rain, the catfish swim up in the shallows and along the banks and up into the creeks, looking for stuff the rain washed into the water, like worms and grubs and insects."

Kendell nodded. "What about gators? Ain't they okay to eat?"

"Of course," Brian said, "if you make sure to cut all the fat off them. Gator fat is terrible. It'll cure your hunger for gator tail fast. But if you take all the fat off and the gator isn't too old, it's not bad. I like it more than venison."

Nate spoke over his shoulder. "You prefer just about anything over venison."

"Everything but starvation, and even that's a close call," Brian said.

Kendell's face changed. "You ain't been really hungry, then, have you?"

"No, I guess not. Sorry."

"No need for sorrys," Kendell said. "You've been good to the kids and me. I shouldn't have said that."

Chapter 6

Dawn broke clear and cold. The wind had died down to a gentle breeze sometime in the night. Nate struck a match and lit a lamp. The dim, warm, yellowish glow was just enough to see in the small room. He picked his way across the room, careful not to step on anyone. He noticed the children were huddled together under anything Martha and Cindy could throw on top of them to keep them warm. Carrie was in the middle of a knot of the smaller children, her arms encompassing two. What firewood they had in the bunker was used up. The stove sat cold. He saw Martha and Cindy sitting on the bare floor next to each other, their backs against a wall. They both had their arms crossed and shivered through a fitful sleep.

Brian was standing watch, looking out of a loophole. Nate stood beside him. He spoke in a low voice. "We need to go to the cave and bring any winter clothes and sleeping bags we can find to the bunker."

"Have you ever seen it so cold this early in the year?" Brian asked. "It's only late October."

"No. The weather has been off for years now. We've talked about that before."

Brian looked at his father, worry on his face. "If it's going to get cold this early and the winter turns out colder and longer than the last, how the hell are we going to grow any kind of crop until next spring? It's going to be hard growing anything around here as it is."

"Hold on. First, this is probably just a freak early cold snap, a mass of cold air from Canada that came down that will be gone in a few days. Maybe the jet stream has moved south early this year. Normally, the jet stream that crosses the United States prevents cold air from making it this far south until winter. The mixing of cold air and hot is what helped to cause the tornado. Also, I plan to be on the radio this morning, asking if any of the other groups will take the kids in. We can't handle them all by ourselves."

Brian still looked worried. "Aerial's down."

"I will be out there putting another one up as soon as there's a little more light."

"The solar panels blew away."

"Yes, but the battery should still be charged."

Brian turned and looked to see if the others were still asleep or listening. "When it does lose power, it will be the last of the radio. We won't be able to communicate with the others."

"We still have enough gas welding equipment, and I might be able to rig something up using a car alternator. A waterwheel in the creek would turn it fast enough with the proper sized pulleys and fan belt or sprockets and chain. "

"I don't remember seeing any of that lying around here or at the farm."

"The abandoned trucks on the road, and the motorcycles we hid in the woods."

Brian's face lit up. "Oh. The others might not have taken all the batteries also."

"Most of the time and labor will probably go to building a dam in the creek so there's enough of a drop for the water to fall on the wheel and turn it fast enough. An alternator must be spun at least five hundred RPMs to work. I figure we need about two feet of drop when the water spills over the dam."

"You've been thinking about this already."

Nate rubbed his unshaven face. "I was thinking about rigging something up in the river for electricity way back before you got shot."

Brian smiled. "Yeah, you always did think way ahead of everyone else. It sure saved us when that bunch of convicts showed up." His face became melancholy. "I miss Deni and Caroline."

"Caroline promised she would come back if she could. Deni, well, she has the Army to contend with. I doubt she will be in much trouble for not reporting for duty after her leave ran out. She could not exactly just drive or fly back. They're not going to want to let her go, though, even if her time in the Army expires. They're short-handed."

"So she might not ever come back." Brian looked out the loophole, but he was looking inward.

"Oh, I wouldn't say that. She will probably show up someday with her fiancée just to visit and see if we're okay. It might be years from now, though. By then, you will be married and a father."

Brian blew out a lung full of air. "Yeah, right. You're just picking on me now. I know she's too old for me anyway. Or rather, I'm too young for her. I just like her as a friend. Caroline too. They both are hard workers and a lot of help in a fight."

"I agree to all of that."

Brian watched the children sleep. He looked over to the corner where there were a dozen carbines and several shotguns leaned against the wall. "We better get all the guns out of reach of the kids."

Nate blanched. "Damn. You're right. I've been so busy, I didn't think about that." He looked at his son. "I told you many months back I would need your help. No one can think of everything."

"I saw a gun rack in the cave."

"I'll go get it now. We can hang it as high as possible on a wall. It will keep the smaller children from reaching them, anyway." He grabbed his rifle. "First, I will bring in some firewood, if I can find any that's not soaked."

After he left, Brian barred the door.

Nate came back from his second trip with the gun rack, but it could hold only four long guns. "I think I have an idea." He left again, heading for the cave.

Brian heard a metallic sound, like thin sheet metal banging against something. Through a side loophole, he saw his father carrying a metal cabinet, struggling not with its weight but its bulk. It was difficult for him to hold it out away from him so he could walk without banging his legs against it. He put his carbine down, opened the door, and helped Nate get the cabinet inside. The noise they made woke everyone.

Martha threw the coat she was using for a blanket off her and had a shotgun in her hands in a second.

Cindy jumped up and ran to the gun corner, then realized there was no danger.

"Sorry to wake everyone," Nate said. "We're trying to setup something to keep the kids away from the guns. This cabinet will hold them. Adults could break into it easily, but it has a hasp up high enough they can't reach it, so it will do to keep kids out."

Martha carried her shotgun to where most of the other guns were leaning in a corner. "Oh. Good idea." She rubbed sleep from her eyes. "Might as well start breakfast," she said, stretching to get the kinks out of her back.

"Well," Nate said, "it looks like you two are starting to be like combat vets when they first get home. Wives of combat vets often have to use a broom handle to wake their husbands. Otherwise, they might get hit."

"No man is ever going to hit me again," Carrie stood in the middle of the room, surrounded by sleepy-eyed children still lying on the floor, holding a butcher knife in her hand, "even if he doesn't like being woke up."

Everyone but the smaller children had their eyes on Carrie. Kendell stood near her, his eyes fixed on the blade. He carefully backed away. Brian stood next to Nate, his face revealing the tension inside him.

Nate pointed to a small table on the side of the room. "Do me a favor and put that knife over there." He spoke in a calm voice. "It's dangerous to have it that close to the kids."

She took her time, stepping between children, as she made her way to the table. After laying it down, she turned and walked toward the stove, threw several pieces of firewood in, and looked up at Nate. "I laid on it so the kids couldn't get cut." She looked at Kendell. "I kept it close because I don't know him." She motioned with her head toward Kendell.

"Do you think a boy who took care of children, going hungry so they could eat, and placing himself in danger to protect them, would be like those animals who hurt you and Caroline?" Nate asked, his voice still calm. "His chances would have been a lot higher without them."

She threw a handful of tender in the stove and blew on it. The smoldering coals flared up and ignited the thin slivers of sappy pinewood. She closed the stove door and looked up at Nate while still kneeling. "He's probably okay, but I'm not taking any chances." Her voice grew strong with conviction. The scars on her face deepened as her emotion rose to the surface. "No one is ever going to hurt me again."

Nate swallowed. "Not until they kill me and Brian."

"And me," Martha said.

"And me." Cindy took her shotgun and put it in the cabinet. "The kids are up now. We better put these guns away."

~~~~

Chet's voice came in over Nate's radio. "They might be carrying the plague. Did you think about that? Any of them sick?"

Nate keyed the mike. "They were sick from starvation and drinking swamp water, but they're all getting better now. We just cannot take care of that many small kids."

"Sorry, we just can't take on that many kids either. Maybe one or two, but not all of them. We're short on food as it is."

Brian clenched his jaw, but kept quiet.

"I understand you would be taking on a lot, but we are a small group here. Yours is much larger."

"I tell you what: we'll take four of the oldest ones. I promise you they will be treated well, and if they go hungry it will be because we are all going hungry."

Nate was glad they had taken all the children outside before he called the Big Oak group.

Kendell broke in. "Why does he want the oldest ones, for slaves? No way!"

Nate raised a hand to quiet him. "We're not selling the kids out, but the fact is we cannot take care of all of them."

"I took care of 'em all by myself, and I can do it again." Kendell could not stand in one place. He pounded his right fist into his left open hand, while he paced back and forth across the room. His lips moved, but no more words came out.

"Get real," Brian said, "they were starving and so were you."

"Shh." Nate keyed the mike. "We'll get back with you after we decide. Have you made any progress on the security measures we talked about?"

"Some." Chet's voice came in sounding like he had breathed helium but could be understood well enough. "We've had storm damage here, so I called them back to help out."

That bit of information caused Nate to jerk his head and look up at the ceiling. "Security is important, so important it is a twenty-four/seven job, not just when it's convenient."

"I don't see you out there manning the observation posts."

Nate's neck muscles tensed. "This is not something to talk about over the air. I will get back with you on the other problem."

"Okay, fine. I doubt Big Pine will take all of them either. Just because we're larger groups does not mean we're any better off in the food department than you."

Nate signed off and turned the radio switch off to save battery power.

Kendell stepped closer to Nate. "Don't be begging anyone to take those kids. If they don't want 'em and they take 'em anyway, they're likely to not take care of 'em, or worse."

"I understand what you are saying, and I know you are worried about them." Nate looked more exhausted than he did after days of fighting the raiders on the dirt road. "I was hoping to keep them together so you could go with them and make sure they will be taken care of. Not that we are trying to get rid of you. In fact, you would be an asset here."

"But you want to get rid of them 'cause they're too little to work and are just trouble." Kendell's voice rose, bouncing off the bunker's concrete walls.

Brian got in Kendell's face. "He's doing the best he can. You're accusing him of things that aren't true and you better back off." He clenched both fists.

Nate got between them and pushed Brian back. "Calm down, both of you. All of this friction is caused by the fact we all care about those kids and are worried." He looked at Brian and then at Kendell. "And we all know there is not enough food here to last long if they stay."

Kendell seemed to lose all energy and sat down against a wall, staring at something only he saw.

Nate turned to Brian. "Either be quiet, or go outside while I call the other group. "I expect Mrs. MacKay will take them all, but who knows. The way things are now, we cannot count on much of anything."

"I can." Brian stared at Kendell. "I can count on my father doing the right thing." He opened the cabinet, grabbed an AR-15 and stomped out of the room.

Nate switched the radio on. "Calling Big Pine. Come in."

The radio signal from Big Pine was weak and garbled. Their aerial had been blown down by the storm, and they were using a jury-rigged one. Someone at Big Pine was able to listen in on Nate's contact with Chet at Big Oak and had told Mrs. MacKay of Nate's problem.

Mrs. Mackay first asked if any of the children were sick or injured. Her next transmission was, "We will take them all."

Nate looked across the room at Kendell. A light shined in Nate's eyes that was not there before. "Thank you. There is a small chance it will be temporary. I'm going to keep trying to raise the Guard or some other government agency. They have to have set up orphanages by now."

"I wouldn't place my hope on the government," Mrs. MacKay said.

Nate keyed the mike. "I hear you."

They made arrangements for two trucks to be at Nate's farm four days later, sometime in the afternoon. The children were still weak. Nate wanted to give them more time to recover while being fed regularly. Two days for them to rest and recover from bad water and little food, and two days to get them to the farm.

"We're running low on vehicles," she said, "even the diesels are quitting on us one by one. The men are doing their best, but there are no spare parts and the diesel fuel is growing some kind of slime in it."

Nate knew she was referring to what many called dinosaur snot—slime that grows in untreated diesel fuel—but did not want to waste battery power talking about it on the radio. He thanked her again and signed off. "They must have some really old fuel over there." He spoke to himself, thinking out loud.

"Are you going with us to see what's it's like there?" Kendell asked. "I don't want no misunderstanding about how the kids will be taken care of."

"I don't think there are any misunderstandings. Mrs. MacKay is an old family friend."

Kendell appeared to be growing angry again. "If you ain't just dumping them off, you should at least do that."

Nate looked him in the eye and nodded. "Okay. I will go with you. But I hope you understand something yourself."

"What's that?"

"What you are asking, and I'm not so sure it should be called asking, is no small thing. While I'm gone, everyone here will be on their own, and there is still the storm mess to clear out of the way and a field to clear and plow for a winter crop…if we can have a winter crop with the weather acting so strange."

Kendell looked back at Nate, who outweighed him by one hundred pounds, with no fear. "Things is bad for everyone right now."

Nate snickered. "Yeah." He headed for the door. "How about helping us remove storm debris. Brian should be making up trot lines so we can use some of that deer of yours for fish bait. Later, I'll show you how to make fish traps out of vines and sticks. If we hurry, we might be able to set the line and one trap before dark." He looked over his shoulder as he walked. "Then we'll all have fish tomorrow."

~~~~

The next day, Nate, Brian, and Kendell were down at the river. Nate watched Brian pull in the trotline. It quivered and yanked at his hand. The three of them had gotten up before sunrise and rushed down to the river with empty packs to carry more of the cached supplies with them on the way back to the bunker, as well as any fish they may have caught the night before.

"There's quite a few on it," Brian said.

Nate pulled a stringer out of a faded fatigue jacket pocket. He unwound it and handed it to Kendell. "String them on this to carry with."

While Brian and Kendell were busy with the trot line, Nate pulled the trap out of the river. Splashing fish told him they had plenty for a big meal. "We're going to be busy cleaning fish when we get back." There were two bass, about a pound and a half each. The rest were all catfish or bream, mostly blue gills.

They loaded their packs with most of what was left of the cache and headed for the bunker.

It was getting late by the time they cleaned the fish and had a good bed of glowing coals in a fire, ready to shovel into a pit. They found a four-foot square of expanded steel Mel had left for a grill in the cave. After shoveling hot coals into the pit, the grill was put on top and the bream and bass spread out, smothered in barbeque sauce. The children would enjoy the barbeque taste, and they wanted to give them the less boney flesh. The smaller catfish were in a pot of peanut oil, deep-frying over the fire.

"This is the last time we'll be doing this: no more peanut oil," Brian said.

"No more barbeque sauce either," Martha added." We should enjoy this fish fry and barbeque while we can."

Nate lifted a wire fryer half-full of catfish from the boiling pot of peanut oil and set it aside to let it drain and cool.

The sun hung low to the west, just behind the tree line. Nate stopped for a few minutes to take in the colorful show. Back to work again, he checked the fish on the grill. Flakes of flesh pulled away as he used a fork to test how well cooked it was. He pulled a piece off and ate it. "It's ready. Time to start feeding the kids before it gets too dark."

Kendell used a rag to keep from burning his hands on the wire handle and grabbed a large pot of beans. He carried it to a makeshift table, twenty feet long and only two feet wide. "Did all you kids wash your hands?"

They sat on benches made of logs, squirming and impatient. Only three answered, some did not even nod.

"If you haven't washed your hands, go inside and do it now." Kendell nodded at the oldest boy. "Pump water for them and see to it they wash." He ladled beans on plate after plate. "Eat all you can. There's plenty, and we have a long walk ahead of us starting tomorrow." Several of the children scurried off to the bunker, the boy in the lead.

Brian pulled his carbine around from his back where it hung. "I better hide in the woods and stand watch while you eat."

Nate nodded. He slid a pile of cleaned fish off a plate into the hot grease. "I'll relieve you in about thirty, forty minutes."

Brian walked into the woods, his eyes searching for trouble.

Cindy brought a Dutch oven full of hot biscuits out of the bunker and put one each on every plate. She left to bake more on the wood stove.

One by one, the children ate heartily, but they soon filled themselves and pushed away from the table, refusing offers of more. They stretched and yawned, eyes sleepy.

Kendell pulled his jacket closed and buttoned it. "It's gettin' chilly again. At least the bloodsuckers ain't out heavy like usual, but the kids should be inside before they catch a cold."

Martha smiled. "You're a regular mother hen. They're lucky to have you."

Kendell looked uncomfortable. "I wish there was more clothes for 'em. If we leave early in the morn, it's goin' to be cold, and they ain't got hardly a stitch on 'em."

No one said anything. There was nothing to say. They just did not have any more clothes for them.

"We're going to have a hard time getting them to the farm before dark tomorrow even if we leave early," Nate said. "They are a lot stronger now, but most of them are too small to walk fast or far, and we can carry only a few of them."

Kendell threw more wood on the fire for light and warmth, even though they did not need any more coals to cook with. "At least they been gettin' fed lately." The wind picked up, and flames flickered out from the fire, leaning off to leeward in red and orange feathers. "I haveta thank all of you for that. We was havin' a hard time when you helped and changed things."

Martha gave him a quick hug. "You're welcome. We're going to miss you and the kids. I wish we could…we just can't." She stepped back away from the firelight and stood silently in the dark shadows. After a few minutes, she went back to work.

~~~~

The next morning most of the children cried when they were gently shaken awake, knowing they were leaving the only place where they had been comfortable in many months. It was more than an hour before sunrise, but there was much to do before they could leave when it would be light enough to see.

All the children were fed well, shoed and clothed poorly, kept halfway under control, and led into the woods. Martha, Cindy, and Carrie waved their tearful goodbyes. Nate and Kendell carried four of the smallest on a stretcher. They sat with their little legs hanging over the sides, swaying with their carriers' movements. Brian carried the little girl with a cut foot, his carbine hanging out of the way on his back, next to the backpack. Nate was concerned about their lack of real security measures, but there was no way to keep a weapon in their hands while carrying children.

They carried as much food as they could, but if something went wrong and the others did not arrive as planned, they would soon be going hungry. Nate, having learned by painful experience, understood well that plans can go to hell fast. He always preferred to have a backup plan or two, but this time he had none. They carried enough water to get to the farm. After that, there was the hand pump to refill all their canteens. What troubled him was he had no idea if that pump was still in working condition. If vandals had damaged it while they were gone, they would soon be boiling river water again.

~~~~

Nate stood back in the shadows, scanning his field with binoculars, now overgrown with weeds. The barn and house seemed to be untouched. A careful search revealed no danger, no one in the area, and no sign anyone had been there since they left.

Brian kept his carbine ready, looking around behind them, and down toward the river as far as he could see.

Kendell had his rifle in his hands, but his attention was on the children, trying to keep them quiet and still. Most were tired and not too active, several were falling asleep, but the older ones wanted to walk around and play. After spending a cold, uncomfortable night in the woods and walking all of one day and half of a second, none of them were in a good mood.

Nate and Brian could have made the trip in an hour during normal times before it became too dangerous to travel fast in the woods, but the small children could not walk far without resting every thirty minutes. Nate did not hold out much hope they could get the children to the farm before nightfall, anyway and was not surprised they had to stay one night in the woods.

Kendell snapped his fingers. "Git back over here." He kept his voice low, but his tone convinced two wayward boys to obey.

"Here." Nate handed the binoculars to Brian. "Overwatch while I make my way around and circle the farm. I'll be coming back from the river."

"It doesn't look like they've been here," Brian said. "They should have been here waiting, and we aren't late, so they didn't get tired of waiting and leave."

"Yeah. It'll be dark soon. I better get going." Nate left his pack with them and faded into the woods.

The sounds of several vehicles rattling down the long and winding drive alerted Nate. He turned and ran the short distance back to the safety of the woods and waited where he could see as they passed. He was surprised when he saw that the first pickup contained only one person, the driver. The second pickup conveyed only the driver also.

He moved closer to the clearing's edge and waited to see what happened when they drove into the open and up to the house. If anyone waited in ambush, they would reveal themselves soon.

The trucks came to a rattling halt in front of the house. The drivers got out and stretched. Both men left their rifles in the truck cabs, where they would be useless if trouble was waiting. One man walked over to the pump, which looked to Nate to be as he left it, and pumped water onto the concrete slab. The other man walked over and bent down to have a drink while the first man pumped. Then they changed positions so the other could have a drink also.

Nate watched. *Looks like Mrs. MacKay sent us a couple idiots.* He waited, watching to see what they did and giving anyone who might be hiding in the woods a chance to make their move. He wanted any trouble to happen before the children were out in the open.

The men walked back to one of the pickups and one opened the tailgate. They had a wooden box in the back and one pulled items out, handing them to the other who waited beside the pickup. They sat on the tailgate and prepared a cold meal.

While they ate, Nate decided to continue to scout the area.

The men finished eating, had another drink at the pump, and started wandering around the farm, going into the house, coming out empty-handed, and then entering the barn. When they came out, Nate was waiting for them.

Nate stood there stone-faced, his rifle in his hands. "What are you doing here?"

Both men turned white.

The one on the left spoke first. "Uh, MacKay sent use to pick up some kids."

"Yeah," the other one said, "I saw you before. You're Nate Williams."

Nate relaxed. "You two all there is?"

"Naw. There's another truck waiting at the road with four men in it." The shorter man on the left stepped closer. "They're riding shotgun for us."

Nate waved Brian over and then turned his full attention back to the men. "The kids will be here in a minute. You two might as well get back in and be ready to drive. We need to get out of here as soon as possible. We'll be driving in the dark before we get to Mrs. MacKay's farm as it is."

The tall, thin man with rotten teeth gave Nate a cold stare. "You're not too friendly. Are you pissed about us looking around? We didn't take anything."

"Well, it is my home, and you were not invited in, but that's not it."

"What is it then?"

Nate stared back at them in silence for a few seconds and decided not to deride them for their lack of security measures. "I guess all those whining kids have me on edge."

Both men laughed. "Yeah, little brats can run you crazy," the tall one said.

Brian walked up, toting the folded stretcher over his left shoulder, his carbine in his right hand.

Kendell carried the little girl with a cut foot, doing his best to keep the others moving toward the pickups. The smaller children were walking so slow, it took Kendell fifteen minutes to get them across the field.

After all the children had a drink at the pump and Brian had filled all their canteens, they loaded all the children into the vehicles.

The pickup in front would not start. The man impatiently pumped the gas pedal and kept trying until the battery ran down and the starter would just make a clicking sound, not turning the engine over at all. It was the tall, thin man. He got out and slammed the door. His cussing made some of the children laugh. That made him mad and he started cussing at the children.

Kendell jumped down, ready to fight. "Keep your mouth off the kids."

The man bared his rotten teeth with a sneer. "Get back in the truck, you little punk nigger, or I'll leave you here."

Before anyone knew what happened, Nate had the man out cold on the ground.

Several children began to cry.

The shorter man sat behind the wheel of the pickup behind them, its engine sputtering, his hands locked on the steering wheel.

Nate looked up from the prone man with a look that seemed to be asking, "Now what are you going to do about it?"

The man waved out the window. "I didn't see nothing. Somebody steer that thing and I'll push-start it."

Kendell looked up at Nate. "I can drive." He got in and waited.

Brian stood behind the cab of the second pickup, his carbine shouldered, his right thumb on the safety. He watched the man on the ground.

Nate disarmed the unconscious man, finding a knife and a revolver. He noticed the man's jaw was hanging off to the side and knew it was broken. After throwing the weapons onto the truck floor next to Kendell, he dragged the unconscious man to the second pickup. Brian helped him load the man onto the truck and tie him up.

Brian looked closer at the man's face. "Dad. I don't think he's breathing."

Nate put his hand on the man's chest. Looking surprised, he quickly put his hand close to the man's mouth. "Damn." He pushed on his chest, trying to get him to breathe.

The short man got out and walked up.

Brian backed off, his carbine ready.

The man glanced at Brian and then looked down at the dead man. "Don't worry about him. The sonbitch was more trouble than he was worth."

Nate kept trying to revive him.

"I know you didn't mean to kill him," the man said, "but I wouldn't let it bother you. You just hit him. If he dies he dies."

Nate kept pushing on the man's chest.

Blood spit up from the man's mouth and he coughed.

Nate turned him on his side, and more blood poured out. He coughed again, opened his blurry eyes and looked up at Nate. "Waa—what happened?" He blinked and closed his eyes. Soon, his breathing became even and shallow.

"Well, he's went back to sleep," the short man said. "Let's get this show on the road. Time's a wasting." He got back into the pickup.

Nate and Brian turned the man on his stomach so any blood would run out and he could breathe.

With everyone onboard the two vehicles, they drove down the driveway, heading for the dirt road. Kendell had trouble keeping the engine running, but managed.

Chet was waiting with three men. He saw the man Nate hit lying on the tailgate, tied up. "What the hell is going on?"

The short man got out of the pickup. "He had an accident. His jaw conflicted with the farmer's fist. The fist won."

Chet looked at Nate. "Why did you hit him?"

"He deserved it," the short man said.

"I didn't ask you, Eugene." Chet never took his eyes off Nate.

"He was cussing the kids and got racial." Nate sighed. "We don't have much daylight left and these kids are tired and hungry. They haven't eaten since sunrise."

Chet half-smiled at Nate, and then he looked at the unconscious man. "Yeah, let's get out of here."

The trip was uneventful but uncomfortable for the children, who felt every pothole and rut in the road through their bottoms, as they sat on the hard floor of the pickup beds. The unconscious man woke after a few miles and moaned most of the way.

Chapter 7

Two armed Hispanic men guarded the gate in front of Mrs. MacKay's farm. They saw headlights coming, bouncing on the pothole-filled road at twenty miles per hour. They hid in the dark behind massive oaks on each side of the gate, not knowing if it was the party they expected or trouble coming.

Chet stopped at the gate and yelled out the door window. "Hey, amigos! It's Chet and friends. Open up. We're hungry." He killed the headlights so the men would not be lit up as a target for anyone hiding down the road and to preserve their night vision.

Kendell followed his example and so did Eugene, who was in the rear. The two guards opened the gate and the trucks moved down the drive with just their parking lights on, at fifteen miles per hour.

A teenage boy saw them coming and ran into the big house. Mrs. MacKay came out to greet them.

Nate jumped down from the left side of the pickup and started to speak, but Mrs. MacKay spoke first.

"We've got supper waiting for all of you. Come on in." She smiled at the children as they walked by.

Nate scratched at his neck. "We had a little problem at my farm. He's tied up in the back of the truck."

"Oh, Slim again. Did you shoot him?"

"No, just broke his jaw."

Eugene had a rifle slung over his shoulder as he stood by. "What are we going to do with him, Mrs. MacKay? He's hurt pretty bad, almost died. The big guy there brought him back to life."

She tilted her head. "Well, if he was a horse with a broken leg, we would shoot him in the head and haul him to the back pasture. But I guess we can't do that with him."

"Take him to his bunk?" Eugene started for the tailgate and Slim before she answered.

"Yes, take him to his bunk. I'll ask Olga to see what she can do for him."

Eugene spoke loud enough she could hear him from the back of the pickup. "He won't like that."

She sighed. "I expect he will be too weak to protest about being touched with brown hands. Bring a two-by-four with you, just in case. Don't break it, though. No need to waste a perfectly good two-by-four over the bonehead of a mule."

Eugene laughed under his breath. He spoke to the teenage boy who had alerted Mrs. MacKay to the trucks arriving. "Pedro, will you give me a hand with Slim?"

He nodded and grabbed the man's ankles.

"Come in and eat, Nate." Mrs. MacKay smiled at Brian. "Did you see your father hit Slim?"

"Yes Ma'am."

"How many times?"

"Just once."

She chuckled. "That figures. Come on now, let's eat."

Nate and Brian grabbed their packs out of the pickups and followed her inside.

Brian had never been in Mrs. MacKay's home before. He gawked at the signs of wealth that still were evident, despite the great fall she and the entire human race had suffered. Several horses from their farm had produced millions in winnings, and many others were nearly as successful. Their stallions demanded high fees for breeding.

Brian's eyes lingered on a display of trophies, symbolizing hard-won victories at the Kentucky Derby and many other major horse races.

Mrs. MacKay's eyes sparkled. "Days gone by, and never to return in my lifetime, I fear." She shrugged her shoulders. "'Tis a small thing compared to all we have lost."

"I would think horse racing will return someday," Nate said.

They followed her into the dining room. "Yes," she sat at the head of the table, "but long after I am gone." She waved it off. "I still have my horses, more importantly, a few of my dear old friends, and no small number of new friends. Let us eat and enjoy this night."

The dining room was large enough to dwarf Nate's living room. Expensive wood paneling covered the walls four feet up from the floor; above the banister, the walls were intricate white plaster designs. Many paintings of horses in pastures or drinking from a glassy pond in early misty morning were displayed.

Men and women of several different races sat at a thirty-foot-long table, five feet wide and blanketed by a white tablecloth. Brian followed his father's example and put his pack and carbine in a corner. He sat at the big table beside his father and immediately appeared to be uncomfortable, wondering what to do next. He hid his surprise when several women came in from the kitchen and began to put beans, rice, and pork on everyone's plate, starting with Mrs. MacKay's. He had never seen people waited on before, except at restaurants. Not even his late mother waited on him like this, at least not since he was small.

"Uh, where are the kids," Brian asked, "and Kendell?"

Nate gave him a stern look.

"My dear, the children are eating at another table," Mrs. MacKay said. "There simply is not room for them here. Kendell was invited to join us, but insisted on eating with the children."

"Oh." Brian noticed no one had picked up a fork or spoon, or even a glass of water. He took that as a cue and waited. Mrs. MacKay waited until many at the table spoke prayers under their breath and crossed their chests, then said, "Let's eat."

Everyone started in. Brian looked around before starting and watched how they put small amounts of food on a spoon or fork and slowly brought it to their mouths, looking like they were trying to savor the taste. He ate some rice. It tasted Mexican, spicy. He saw no bread on the table. The Mexican-style mixture of rice and pork and two kinds of beans seemed to be the complete meal.

As they ate, Mrs. MacKay asked Nate, "Have you managed to get a winter crop in the ground?"

"No." Nate drank some water to clear his throat. "With one thing after another, we haven't had time. When Brian and I get back, we will finish clearing an area for planting."

"Yes," she smiled, "you've had your hands full with the children. Did you have much trouble with that freakish storm?"

Most everyone at the table seemed to be interested in the storm. They stopped eating and listened.

"We had a tornado pass over. Our shelter withstood it, but there's still a mess to clean up. We have to clear downed trees before we can plow."

A woman in her thirties mumbled something in Spanish and crossed her chest.

Mrs. MacKay glanced at her, a worried look in her eyes. "We were fortunate enough not to have tornados to deal with, but one man was killed when struck by lightning while repairing wind damage to one of our barns." She looked down, not saying more.

"I'm sorry," Brian said.

Nate glanced at him. "Yes, we both offer our condolences."

"He was a good worker, and honest," Mrs. MacKay said. "In a way, it's fortunate that he was not married and had no family. He left behind enough of a vacuum as it is. Like I said, he was a good man. We all miss him."

One of the Hispanic men spoke up. "Have there been any recent signs of the sickness?" He spoke with little accent and in prefect English.

Before Nate could answer, Mrs. MacKay spoke. "This is Ramiro, my foreman and best friend."

Nate nodded. "No. We have not seen any sign of the plague lately."

"Have hungry people been coming?"

"No one but Kendell and the children," Nate said. "We haven't had any beggars, just takers."

"Ah." Ramiro smiled under his thick mustache. "But you fought them off. I am told you are hard to kill."

"I'm sure you've had your troubles too." Nate took a drink of water.

"Yes, but we have many guns, you have few."

"I have Brian. That makes a lot of difference."

Brian turned red.

"Ah. Another Nate Williams."

Brian looked at his plate.

"He has carried his own weight many times over." Nate finished his meal. He was still hungry, and he knew Brian was too. He also knew there would be no second serving.

"Well, we're getting by," Mrs. MacKay said. "I expect you and yours are too."

Nate drank more water to clear his throat and to fill his stomach. "Yes, for now. The future is questionable, though. We must get at least two good crops in and harvested and stored."

Everyone at the table nodded.

Ramiro sat back in his chair. "The bandits make things worse. Too much time is wasted fighting and fearing attack. All of these wasteful security measures are draining our resources, keeping people busy and away from producing food."

Nate looked down the table at Ramiro. "We just have to deal with it all. Doing one thing perfect while neglecting to do another that is just as important, is not going to keep us alive. We must do all things well to survive. It does no good to avoid starvation if we are killed while working our fields."

Ramiro shrugged. "Yes, complaining changes nothing. I do wish God would deal with the bandits, so we can work more productively."

Brian's voice raced down the table. "God didn't help my mother and little sister. I don't expect he will help us with the bandits…or anything else."

A woman in her forties scolded him. "You must not lose faith. God is always listening."

"He wasn't listening when millions of people were dying." Brian got out of his chair.

Nate stood. "Calm down."

"I didn't mean to be rude." Brian picked up his pack and carbine. "Thank you for the dinner."

Mrs. MacKay got out of her chair. "Pain is a dirge that hangs over all of us, Brian. I will have someone show you where to sleep tonight."

Nate grabbed his rifle and pack. "Good night to you all."

"He is angry with God," Ramiro said. "That is not good."

Brian looked as if he wanted to say something, but he just looked away. Then he walked out the door. Nate led him outside.

Brian set his pack down on the red brick walkway that crossed the front of the house. "I wonder where Kendell and the kids are."

Nate stepped closer. "Brian—" He put a hand on his son's shoulder. "If you want to talk, we have plenty of time. There is nothing else to do tonight."

Brian looked away into the dark. "Nothing to talk about. You can't change anything. It's just the way it is."

"I'm not so sure there is a God, put hating is not healthy."

"I shouldn't have said anything, but it's too late now."

"Religion means a lot to some people, and it's best not to get between them and their beliefs. They have a right to believe what they want, as do you."

"I guess they're Catholic."

"Probably. They're good people, or Mrs. MacKay would not have them around."

Brian's face changed, and he looked up at his father. "What about the guy you hit?"

"Sometimes groups like this get stuck with undesirables and can't get rid of them. Every time you take someone into your group, you're taking a chance. We have certainly taken chances."

"Maybe we should have let him die. It would have been doing Mrs. MacKay and her people a favor. I doubt that he's anything but trouble for them."

"There is a time to be hard about killing because it's a matter of your life or his, but I do not like killing someone because of his mouth. People say things sometimes they really don't mean. In his case, I think he meant it, but human life is not so valueless that I will kill a man for a surly mouth. Knocking him down was enough. It was more about Kendell than him. Kendell is a good person, and he does not deserve to be treated like that."

Brian smiled and looked away. "You would have killed me a long time ago, if you killed people for talking back to you."

"Ah, yes. Your grandfather was a lot harder on me than I have been with you. Maybe I'm weaker than he was. It's just that I remember what it was like to be beat on by someone who is supposed to love you. When I was your age, I would never have had a conversation like this with my father. He did not believe in communicating much. Still, he had his way of showing me he loved me. I turned out okay."

Brian's voice sounded mature and confident. "You're not weak. Maybe you're stronger than your father was."

"I'm just doing the best I can. And I know that's what my father did. He was just different."

"Maybe someday I can take care of you when you're old and repay you."

Nate's eyes lit up, but Brian could not see in the dark. "Hah! You will be busy with your own children. The sentiment is appreciated, though."

"Well, I'm sorry about all the times I made another hair on your head turn gray."

Ramiro stepped out of the house, obviously looking for someone. He saw Nate and Brian and started over to them.

Nate saw him coming. "If you want to apologize for your comments on God, now's your chance."

"Mr. Williams, would you like for me to escort you to your sleeping area?" Ramiro asked.

"Are you taking us to Kendell and the children?" Nate picked up his pack.

Ramiro rubbed his chin. "They are sleeping, but I suppose you can look in on them."

"That would be fine," Nate said. "We just want to check on them."

"Uh, Mr. Ramiro," Brian said, "I want to apologize for saying what I said about God."

"That is no problem." Ramiro shrugged. "We are concerned with what's in your heart, not your words. It is not good for a boy to hate God."

"I...I don't know what I feel about God."

"And that is probably what is troubling you as much as all the rest." Ramiro held his left arm out, welcoming them to the door. "We do not have time to discuss why God allows terrible things to happen tonight. Your apology is accepted. For now, let us rest. Mrs. MacKay has much to ask of you in the morning."

"Oh?" Nate stood in the stream of light escaping the open door, looking at Ramiro. "We are not planning on staying long. The others are not able to maintain security long without us."

"She will speak to you tomorrow about many matters." Ramiro led them to a room upstairs.

The children were lying on thin mattresses on the floor. Kendell slept on the floor with no pad, just a blanket, where he could keep an eye on them and anyone coming into the room would have to go past him to get to the children. His rifle lay beside him.

They left the room quietly and went down the hall to a room nearly full of snoring men lying on blankets or thin pads on the floor. It was obvious to Nate that they did not have enough beds to go around. Nate and Brian were both so tired they fell asleep within minutes, despite the snoring and hard floor.

~~~~

For some reason, perhaps because he had not slept for more than a few hours at a time in so long his body's inner clock was not used to sleeping for seven hours straight, Nate woke up. He opened his eyes and looked around the room. Brian slept quietly beside him. He could make out most of the room in what little light came in through the one window in the eastern side. The sun still hid behind the earth's horizon, but false dawn gave faint illumination, enough he felt he might as well wake Brian and start the day early. He had no idea what Mrs. MacKay had in mind, but he had his own plans too.

Nate shook him, and Brian woke instantly, looking at his father with questioning eyes, wondering if something was wrong. They grabbed their packs and rifles and headed down the hall, stopping to check in on Kendell and the children.

Already awake, Kendell said nothing, but joined them in the hallway. They continued on, down the stairs, and into the living room, careful not to disturb anyone's sleep.

Mrs. MacKay sat in a chair. She looked up from her Bible. "Oh. I am glad you are up so early. I am certain you are hungry. Let's have breakfast and plan the day ahead of us."

For the first time, Nate noticed the aroma of frying bacon and eggs. He could not smell any coffee—that would be too much to expect. His stomach growled, and he remembered the meager supper the night before. The look on Brian's face told him he was hungry too.

They washed their hands with water poured over them into the sink, taking turns with the pitcher, careful not to waste the water. It was a long haul from the solar-powered pump in the nearest pasture. The well and pump were originally installed for watering livestock and the well was shallow, not intended for human consumption. To be safe, they boiled all water before drinking, but considered it safe enough for washing hands and bathing in.

An elderly man put two eggs on each plate. Water would be their drink, nothing else. He offered red peppers, but Nate, Brian, and Kendell turned him down. There was no bread of any kind.

Mrs. MacKay looked around the table at the others. "I am sorry this is all we have to offer. We have enough eggs for everyone, but we're not exactly over-blessed with them. More chicks are being raised, and soon we will be making a meal out of the older hens, but for now this is breakfast."

Kendell held his fork in mid air. "Thanks for sharin' what you have. It's easy to share when you have a lot. It ain't so easy when you have little yourself. I and the kids have come across too many takers lately." He nodded to Nate and Brian. "They are givers, and so are you. You give even to your own hurt. There ain't no reason for you to apologize."

Her eyes lit up. "You're welcome, Kendell. We share what we can here, and we all do our best to give back." She chuckled to herself. "It's not that this is a commune, and we don't follow the Communist Manifesto, I am as much a capitalist as always. It's all about survival. If I did not think we could handle the children, we would not have taken them in. It's a risk, but one well worth it to my mind. Still, if we were starving there would be no point in taking them in and watching them starve along with the rest of us. There is only so much we can do in the way of charity, but I think we can do this. The children will be the last to go hungry here."

Brian finished his eggs. "We lost all of our chickens and our milk cow to the raiders. Kendell is right about the takers. There's plenty of them, too many."

She took a sip of water. "Supporting yourself today is hard work. It's not as easy as it was before the plague. Some get it in their head stealing is easier." Her eyes twinkled. "You and your father taught more than a few that stealing is not so easy after all."

"Mrs. MacKay," Nate said, "I would like to use your radio in a few hours to contact our group and let them know we're okay."

"Certainly." She sat back in her chair. "There is a favor I would like to ask of you before you leave. I wish you would look over the place and help us improve our security measures."

"We have a little time before I am supposed to radio home, so I'll get to that right now. Mind you, I'm no expert, but I will tell you what I would do if this were my place."

She smiled. "Wonderful. We have a few military veterans among us, but none as experienced as you, and no former law enforcement. Any advice you can give would be a great help." She got out of her chair and stood.

Nate stood and so did Brian and Kendell.

"I was never in law enforcement." Nate rubbed the stubble on his chin.

"Of late, you have been this county's de facto sheriff." She gave him a half-smile. "And a good one at that."

"It was all in self-defense." Nate grabbed his rifle and pack. "There was no playing cop, just surviving."

Brian followed his father's cue and grabbed his carbine and pack.

"Where do you want to start?" Mrs. MacKay asked.

"Your outer perimeter. I need to see your first defense measures."

Everyone but Kendell headed out the door. He stayed behind to help in the kitchen and make sure the children got breakfast.

Mrs. MacKay talked over her shoulder while walking to a pickup. "Let's hope at least one vehicle wants to run this morning. Transportation is becoming more iffy as time passes."

"How are your liquid petroleum supplies?" Nate asked. "You might be able to refit a couple trucks to run on LP."

She stopped at the door of a pickup. "We have a half-full one-thousand-gallon tank of LP behind the heavy equipment shed. Some of the men were able to convert a couple generators and a small utility vehicle. It's called a Gator. None of our gas is any good for motor fuel, and the diesel is nearly useless also. It will not be long before LP is all we have for fuel."

Nate slipped his pack on. "Might be worth the risk to go looking for more LP. Maybe you can trade something for it. Some places, empty farms and the like, there might be some that have not been looted yet. If the whole family is dead, there's no reason not to take it before someone else does."

Mr. Ramiro drove down the drive on a Gator. He stopped and walked over to them. "Good morning."

Everyone but Brian answered, "Good morning."

"I'm glad you're here," Mrs. MacKay said. "Nate is going to look over our security measures. Would you show him around? I have much to do in the house. You can use the utility vehicle."

"Of course." Ramiro turned toward the Gator.

Nate and Brian followed.

Ramiro slid behind the Gator's steering wheel. "There is no need for the boy to come, is there?"

Nate threw his pack in the back and sat on the front seat beside him, the butt of his rifle on his right leg. "Why not? He has been to hell and back with me, there's no reason why he can't be with me now. He might learn something."

Ramiro shrugged. He waited for Brian to get seated in the back and then headed down the drive. "We might as well go to the gate first, so you can see it in the daylight. You could not have seen much last night."

Nate nodded.

When they stopped just short of the gate, Nate got out and looked the area over, then he used his binoculars to scan a wooded area to their right. "I hope those men hiding in brush under that stand of water oaks are yours."

Ramiro jerked his head around and then his body, to face Nate. He smiled. "You found them?"

"One has a bolt-action, the other, what looks like an HK-91. They need to utilize concealment better, and more importantly, bullet-stopping cover."

Ramiro's smile grew wider, and he cocked his head, but said nothing more.

Brian still sat in the back of the Gator his carbine in his hands, pointed skyward. "Dad, they might have someone across the road."

"They *should* have someone across the road. If he's there, I haven't found him yet." Nate walked closer to the gate but did not go directly; he walked off the drive and into some brush, and then worked his way to the fence. He scanned down the road with his binoculars in both directions, concentrating on the brush growing up to the edge of the clay road.

Nate emerged from the brush and examined the gate and looked down the fence line.

Ramiro watched with interest. "Do you see anyone else?"

Nate came back to him before speaking. "There's a woman on the left side of the road, about a quarter mile. She saw me watching her. Whoever it is, is alert. She needs to stay farther back in the brush and in shadow, though. If she and I were enemies, I would not have let her see me. She would be dead now."

Ramiro's face turned hard. "She is my wife."

"Well," Nate said, "she needs to cover her pretty face with something green. Even black would be better than nothing. A hat would help also."

Ramiro nodded.

"The gate is not strong enough to withstand ramming with a car or truck and the fence will not stop anything either."

"Yes, but what can be done? We have little materials."

"Do you have a gas welder and gas?"

"In the shop."

"Then you can make a stronger one with a few scrap water pipes. How about a tractor with a front-end loader?"

"It still runs, but there is little usable fuel," Ramiro said. "We hope to use it for pumping water for the crops with its power take-off. The drought season comes soon."

"Well, if you have enough fuel, make the ditch along the road deeper and wider. Push the dirt up against the fence. Make it as high and steep as possible, so a truck or car can't get over it. You can drag big logs up too—anything to stop vehicles or at least slow them down to give you a chance to shoot them. Those cypress trees over there would be great for that."

"Men can make the berm with shovels," Ramiro said.

"It probably would be more accurate to call it a rampart. Yes, men with shovels can do it, if you have the manpower and the time."

"We can use horses to haul logs."

Nate mentally measured the property's frontage. "I think you really need the tractor. You've got hundreds of yards to deal with. The creek on the north side is a natural barrier, but the other side is open all the way to those trees."

Ramiro looked to the south. "The trees grow close there. No car or truck could get through. It is wet and muddy in the rainy season. Their tires would spin and get stuck."

Nate motioned with his head. "Let's go over and look that creek over. I have an idea."

They rode the Gator over to the creek as close as they could before it got too wet, passing within seventy yards of the men hiding in brush. Nate waved as they went by. This time Brian got out with them. They walked into the wet area, through a stand of cypress trees as large as any likely to be found still surviving in Florida. Nate turned upstream looking the topography over. Nearing the house, they came to a place where the creek ran through a ten-foot-deep ditch cut out of a hill. Generations past, the ditch had been dug to drain an area and turn lowland into pastureland, some fifty acres, off to their right, farther north of them. The area around the house and the five hundred acres behind it was much higher ground, but the land north of that dropped off into what was the previously wet fifty acres, with the creek draining it and cutting through the hill.

Nate looked all that he could see over. "Do you really need that pasture over there?" He swept the fifty acres with his left arm. "What I'm thinking of suggesting you do will cause some of that pasture to be flooded."

Ramiro tilted his head and looked at Nate with narrowed eyes. "How will this help security?"

Nate noticed that Brian was looking more perplexed than Ramiro. "Well, I suppose it would make it a little more difficult for anyone to get through there if it's under a foot of water, but I'm thinking of a way to produce electricity for you. At least a small amount anyway."

Ramiro's eyes narrowed further. "Electricity?"

"Yes. To recharge batteries for your radio and a little light so you can stop using up kerosene at night. Perhaps set up some car headlights to blind attackers at night. It depends on how much work you want to put into making a bigger system. I've been planning on doing something similar, but much smaller, for our place but have not had the time."

Nate glanced at Brian. "What time is it?"

Brian checked his wristwatch. "Fifteen to nine."

Nate directed his attention back to Ramiro. "I have to use your radio to contact home." He headed for the house. It would take him less time to walk than to go all the way back for the Gator.

Brian followed.

It took ten nerve-racking minutes to contact Martha on the radio. With each passing minute, Nate and Brian's apprehension grew. They both released a heavy lung full of air when Martha's voice finally came through the speaker.

"All is well here," she said. Synthia is crying for both of you, though. She thinks you're gone for good, like Kendell and the children."

Nate talked to Synthia for a few seconds to assure her he and Brian were coming back. Nate informed Martha of his plan to stay one more day and start for home at sunrise. He would radio them at 9 AM the next day if there were any more changes in plans. He finished the call and switched the radio off.

"Well, I am happy you were able to check in on your friends and that they are doing well," Mrs. MacKay said. "Ramiro tells me you have many helpful suggestions for us. Let us go into the study and discuss what you have in mind."

Nate discovered the study was as large as most people's living room and had walls of books in fine wood cabinets. There was a computer sitting idle and a large oak desk with a few papers stacked on it.

"I will need paper and pencil to make a list," Nate said.

"Of course." Mrs. MacKay went to her desk and got out a few sheets of paper. "You're welcome to sit here while you write."

Nate sat in the chair. "Do you have any topographic maps of this area?"

"Why…yes. My late husband had some around here somewhere."

"I think you can use the creek to generate power, but I would like to get a better idea of the topography of your land and the surrounding area first."

"Ramiro," Mrs. Macy said, "would you search for those maps? I am certain he kept them in this room somewhere."

Ramiro nodded. He opened a cabinet door, starting his search at the far end of the room.

Mrs. MacKay turned back to Nate. "Are you thinking of a waterwheel?"

"Yes." Nate kept writing as he talked. "It will turn two alternators to produce twelve volt direct current electricity. That power can be used to charge batteries taken from all those wrecked pickups and trucks on the road by my place and at the bridge. You need to grab every car battery you can get your hands on and plenty of alternators. Get the highest capacity ones only. Some of those larger trucks should have high-output alternators."

Mrs. Mackay looked at him in amazement. "You have gone beyond the call of duty here."

Nate continued. "I'll draw up plans for it, and your maintenance people can fabricate it in your shop. More than likely, someone here will improve my design anyway. It's just an idea I've had kicking around in my head for months, but

I've never had the time to actually act on it. The creek near our place is nowhere near as suitable for the purpose as yours, but a smaller rig could be set up there too. The real work will be building the dam. You will need as much drop at the dam flue as possible, the farther the water falls, the larger diameter the wheel can be and the better it will work. The trade off is that fifty acre pasture on the low end of your property will be flooded by the backup of water."

She pulled on her right ear, thinking, then said, "We don't have half the livestock we normally have, so I think that will not be a problem. But we can't buy feed for them anymore either and must harvest hay."

"I doubt much of it will flood except during the wet season." Nate kept writing as he talked. It's during the dry season you will need the extra pasture, and most of those fifty acres will be usable during a drought. There might even be times when there is not enough water in the creek to power the wheel. I don't live here, so I do not know the history of the creek."

Ramiro spoke up. "I believe I have found the maps you need." He handed them to Mrs. MacKay.

She put them on the desk next to Nate.

Ramiro cleared his throat. "What he is speaking of will be much work. We need to get the rest of our crop in the ground before we start on his project." His eyes flickered with fire. "And the security measures are more important than electricity."

"Yes," she said. "I agree. But I think you should get those batteries and other things from the wrecked trucks when you take Nate and his son back home. That will not take too much time, and we will have the parts needed when we have the time to complete the project."

Ramiro nodded. "We will take extra men and plenty of tools to remove the alternators, batteries, and any other items we may need. That is a good idea. The trip will have more value to us that way too."

Nate finished his list and turned the swivel chair around to face them. "Keep in mind I have included things here you probably will find too arduous to do, so they are just suggestions. I included all I could think of, whether I thought you would be likely to go through the trouble of carrying out the suggestion or not. Some of them presuppose access to that electricity a waterwheel would provide you."

Mrs. MacKay brought a chair closer to Nate. "Please go over the items on the list so Ramiro and I can discuss them with you."

Ramiro brought a chair closer and motioned for Brian to sit, then brought another chair and sat down by Mrs. MacKay.

Nate looked at his list. "Item number one: Everyone old enough to be trusted with a firearm should carry a rifle or at least a handgun at all times. If doing work that makes it difficult to carry a long gun even slung on the back, then at least have a handgun on the hip in a holster. There are few jobs you can't do while a handgun is holstered at your side."

Mrs. MacKay chuckled. "I used to be a pretty good shot, but that was many years ago. Perhaps I should exempt myself from that rule."

"That's up to you." Nate rubbed the back of his neck. "I would certainly include Kendell as someone who can be trusted with firearms, if I were you."

Ramiro smiled. "Yes. It would be difficult to get his rifle from him anyway."

"More like dangerous," Brian added. "I feel sorry for anyone who tries to hurt those kids."

Ramiro looked up at the ceiling and scratched his neck, a half-smile on his face. "I would agree. Many of us here have seen that already."

"Next item." Nate continued. "Develop some system of alarm that can be triggered and a code to signify what type of emergency it is. Car horns, maybe. Eighteen wheeler horns, if you can find some. If you could scrounge up a few of those battery-powered megaphones that come with a siren button that would be great for guards to use. Anything you use, except for the megaphones, would run on twelve volt auto batteries that will have to be recharged someway."

Ramiro seemed to be thinking. "We will look at your plans for the waterwheel as soon as possible."

Nate checked his list. "Have SOPs—Standard Operating Procedures—for when the alarm is sounded. Everyone should have a battle station to go to with their weapons and equipment. At least one person should be assigned to gather the children and put them in a safe room and guard them, and perhaps another to keep them quiet and comfort them, make sure they have water, etc."

He went to the next item. "The alarm can be used to tell a little about what is happening: One two-second blast could mean an attack from the front, two from the back, etc. You can add more, but don't make it so complicated people can't remember it while scared."

Ramiro and Mrs. MacKay looked at each other but said nothing.

"The next two items are to be done only if you have the manpower for it. Set up camouflaged OPs—observation posts—and man them twenty-four/seven. You already have that to a degree, but you need to refine the concept and make it more worthwhile. I'm saying you can make it safer and more efficient."

He looked up from his list. "This one will take a lot of manpower, manpower you may not have to spare. Implement roving patrols, each patrol consisting of at least three people. The idea here is to keep informed of what's going on in your area and to form an outer ring of protection. You want at least three rings of protection that will be retreated from if the threat is too much to handle. Each ring will be smaller and closer to the center: this house. And each ring of protection will be defended with ever more vigor. The house will be defended to the death."

Mrs. MacKay did not flinch, but Ramiro blanched.

"What about an escape plan?" Ramiro asked.

Nate sat back in his chair and looked Ramiro in the eye. "If it gets that bad, the only way you would get out of here alive would be through a tunnel that gets you into the trees back behind your pastureland. I'm talking about a very long tunnel. I don't think you have the time or manpower to dig it."

Brian spoke. The sarcasm of his days before he left most of his boyhood behind returned for a moment. "It would fill full of water anyway, and I doubt you could hold your breath that long."

Nate gave him a hard look.

Ramiro looked away, nodding. "To the death."

"Yes," Nate said flatly. "Even if you make it out of here and retreat to my farm, there is nothing to eat there, and my little group does not have enough to last long, feeding your large group. We could not even handle Kendell and his kids."

"You are not saying anything I did not know," Mrs. MacKay said. "I have never given the idea of abandoning my home to brigands a second's thought. This is our Alamo."

Ramiro laughed.

Smiling, she said, "Sorry."

"Not quite like the Alamo." Ramiro smiled back. "I believe the largest raiding gangs have been cleaned out of the county now. We can handle the smaller wolf packs."

"I hope you're right," Nate said. "You need this farm. You cannot survive without it."

Ramiro's jaw set. "So it is to the death. We will protect the women and children to the last man."

"And you better let the women and children who want to fight defend themselves too." Nate added.

There was silence in the room for a few seconds.

"Is there more on your list?" Mrs. Mackay asked.

"Yes." Nate looked at the paper in his hand. "Use some kind of visual identifier so everyone will know anyone walking around in the pastures or gardens is part of the group. A hat or jacket, something that can be seen from a distance, but not too bright, or it will destroy any camouflage qualities of his clothing."

"I suppose we can come up with something," Mrs. MacKay said.

Nate continued to the next item on his list. "Get with neighbors for mutual defense. I do not know anything about your neighbors or if any are still alive, but if you have any you can trust, you should contact them and try to cooperate."

"We have already looked into that," Ramiro said. The nearest neighbor is many miles from here."

"Well, even if they are twenty miles away, you probably should see about an alliance with them." Nate put the paper down. "This one is just an idea. Use creeks to flood the road. I'm thinking of any creek that crosses the road between you and any source of trouble. It depends on the topography as to whether it will work or not. A dam in the right place that backs water up can make it difficult to get to you. This is just a suggestion to keep in back of your mind. It probably will never be called for now that we have removed the two big raider groups from the county and the Guard has taken what's left of them away."

"That would only work during the rainy season," Ramiro said. "And it would be something to do way ahead of the threat arriving. It would take some time for the creek to back up enough to flood the road enough to stop four-wheel-drive trucks."

Nate nodded, not wanting to elaborate on his suggestion any more. "Since your potable water source is the livestock well in the pasture, store plenty of water in the house. Same goes for food, firewood, anything you must have to live should be kept here so you do not have to expose yourself to gunfire while under siege. You should boil the water a little to sterilize it before putting it in the containers, and whatever you use to store it in should be put in boiling hot water first too, unless it's plastic and will not take the heat. If the water and the container that holds it is sterile when you put it away, there should be no problem with drinking it after it's been stored a long time. Keep it in a dark, cool place if possible."

"We have many large glass jugs that would work," Mrs. MacKay said. "Usually there is a couple days' worth of water in the house, but we will increase that to a couple weeks' worth. It will take up a lot of room, and we are already crowded with so many people, but we can make it work."

"As for protecting your water source," Nate picked up one of the topographic maps and unrolled it, "that solar panel for your pump is vulnerable to gunfire and so is the PVC piping. You should put up protection around the well. A wall of logs just high enough to protect it but not so high as to shade the solar panel and bermed with dirt on the outside will work. You will have to move the water tank over a little so it will be outside the wall and livestock can get to it of course."

"That will not be difficult," Ramiro said.

Nate looked up from the map. "Back to the three rings of protection. You will not be able to protect the cattle, horses, and other livestock if it gets bad while under attack from a large raiding party. The outer buildings, including the barns, will also probably be lost. Your farm is too large to protect it all. Some of your crops in the field will be looted. If you try to protect everything, you will probably lose it all."

"I would die for my horses." Mrs. MacKay clenched her jaw. "If they're hungry, they can have a cow, but not my horses."

"If it's a large raiding party, they will take everything, including the women here." Nate was not trying to frighten her, just help her put things in perspective. Her love for her horses could get people killed.

Ramiro looked at the two of them and cleared his throat. "I still do not believe there are any large raiding parties left in the area. Certainly, the Guard has been at work all over the county. I doubt the two groups on the road are the only ones they have hunted down."

"We will just have to deal with whatever comes," Mrs. MacKay said.

Nate picked the list up, checked the last line, and put it back on the desk behind him. "Okay. The last item may require more manpower than you want to spare, but could make a lot of difference during a raid and will help you keep an eye on the outer reaches of your property, including your livestock." He cleared his throat. "Set up sniper nests in the top floor, and put up bullet stopping barriers so they can shoot from the window. Choose the windows carefully, so the sniper can cover the most area, one window on each side of the house. Put up sandbags or steel plates to stop bullets. Build a shooting bench for each sniper hide and make it as comfortable as possible. They will be spending a lot of time there. Make sure the sniper is set back from the window to make it more difficult for them to discover which window is being used. You do not want to have their rifle barrels sticking out the window."

Ramiro rubbed his chin in thought. "We have discussed armed lookouts on the top floor before, but have not acted on it yet." He sighed. "There is so much to do. Oh how easy we had it before the curse of the shadow of death. We had no idea. God is teaching us." He turned to look at Brian.

"I guess so," Brian said. "It sure is a painful lesson, though. And a lot of good people have paid with their lives."

Ramiro nodded. "I understand what you are saying. The loss of a loved one is difficult to bear."

Nate looked over the topographic map again. "Looking at the contour lines here tells me nature has given you a pretty good setup for waterwheel-powered hydropower. You will lose some of your lower pastureland, but not as much as I was thinking. You lucked out on another thing, too. It looks like the best place to put the waterwheel is directly across from the house."

"Even so, Ramiro said, "we do not have the wire to reach all the way from the house to the creek."

Nate shook his head. "No. That's not what I was talking about. You will be dealing with direct current. DC current cannot be transmitted far without losing voltage. The big advantage to the waterwheel being closer to the house is you will not have to carry the heavy batteries so far. In other words, you are going to have to carry the batteries to the wheel to recharge them. You can use maybe twenty feet of cable, but you certainly will not be able to wire the power all the way to the house."

Ramiro gave Mrs. MacKay a wintry half-smile. "Of course. Why should anything be so easy? This is now, not before the shadow of death cloaked our world."

"Well," Nate said, "the amount of power the waterwheel can produce is substantial. You will have enough to power a couple fans so the kids can sleep better on hot nights and will have light to keep from stumbling around the house in the dark. Also, you will be able to continue work after sundown, processing food during the harvest, for example. Canning is time consuming, and you will be in a hurry to get the harvest taken care of before it spoils. Using car headlights to see attackers will make a big difference too."

Mrs. MacKay stood. "There is still some time before lunch, and I have many things to do. Will you make a list of items we will need to make the waterwheel generator work?"

"Of course. There are many things that you should take off the abandoned trucks besides the headlights, alternators, and batteries. All of the twelve volt light bulbs should be taken, and the fuses."

"What will the bulbs be for?" Ramiro asked.

"They will provide just enough light to see in the house at night without attracting unwanted attention from a distance. You can even read with them. It isn't much light, but it's enough, and they do not run the batteries down so much as a more powerful light will."

Ramiro's face lit up. "We must get to those trucks before others do."

"Make sure you take the sockets the bulbs fit into also," Nate said. "I will draw a design for the waterwheel, but it will just be loose plans. It all depends on how well the creek dam works out. The more the water falls the better."

Nate spent the rest of the day and part of the night drawing plans for the waterwheel generator and explaining to those who would build it what was needed.

Just before sunrise the next morning, they managed to get four of the larger trucks cranked and running and Ramiro felt they might make it to the abandoned trucks and back.

Nate and Brian said their good-byes to Kendell and the children the night before. They were glad to be heading home.

Chapter 8

They were many miles from Nate's farm when Ramiro stopped next to the first truck they came to. It was a large flatbed, heavily damaged, but it appeared to Nate the engine compartment was still intact.

"If you're going to stop here," Nate said, "we're going to have a long walk ahead of us. I'm anxious to check on my people. We've been gone too long already."

"Do not worry," Ramiro said. "You are a good friend. I will take you all the way to your farm. Let us just check this truck for usable parts. It will take only a few minutes."

Everyone piled out of the trucks and milled about in the road, stretching their backs and legs. They left the engines running because they might not start again.

Nate said, "Follow me," and headed for the woods.

Something on Nate's face prompted Brian to ask his father a question. "What's wrong?"

They stopped just inside the woods line.

Nate shrugged. "They could put a little more common sense into this operation."

Ramiro heard. He stopped looking under the hood of the abandoned truck and joined them, jumping across a three-foot-wide ditch. "What foolish thing have we done?"

"You are assuming because we are a fairly large force, no one will take a shot at us." Nate swept the road with his left hand. "Everyone is out in the open and no defense perimeter has been setup. There has been no scouting of the surrounding woods for trouble." His face hardened. "Luck is a bitch. If you rely on her, sooner or later, she will let you down."

Ramiro scratched the back of his neck, a strange smile on his face. He looked at Brian, his eyes lighting up as he spoke. "There is a reason you still live: You have a guardian."

"Like my dad says, you have only one life, act like you value it. I used to think he didn't know anything. That was before the world went to hell."

Ramiro's smile broadened. "Ah yes, every son starts out worshiping his father, then goes through a stage when he thinks he has the worst father in the world." He cleared his throat. "Then he grows up." He jumped back across the ditch and into the road. Heading for the still running truck, he spoke over his shoulder. "We will go to the farm first. You two need to be with your people, protecting them."

Nate climbed onto the back of a flatbed. He made sure Brian sat down just behind the cab, where he would be best protected from bullets.

The convoy rattled along at fifteen to twenty miles per hour for many miles, coming to a sharp curve in the road where a creek crossed under a decrepit bridge. Nate was standing, watching the woods on both sides of the road, looking over the top of the cab. He pounded on the roof. "Stop!"

Ramiro hit the brakes. He yelled out the side window. "What is wrong?"

Nate jumped from the truck onto the dirt road. "This is a bad place."

"A bad place?"

"I mean it's a perfect place for an ambush. Wait until I have scouted the area before you approach the bridge."

Ramiro had his head half out of the window, looking back at Nate. "We went through here the other night with no problem. *Any* place along the road could be an ambush. We will never get there if we keep stopping."

Brian jumped down and walked into the road, away from the truck. He stood there, looking around.

Nate took several quick steps, reached out and grabbed Brian by the shoulder, pulling him back to the truck. "Stay down, beside the wheel."

Brian's eyes rounded, he held the carbine tight. "Did you see something?"

Nate reached over, grabbed Brian's pack, and handed it to him. While putting his own pack on, he said, "Buzzards. On the blind side of the curve. I smell trouble."

Brian looked up for the first time and saw the buzzards. "There are bodies around from the fighting before."

"No. It's a fresh kill," Nate said.

Ramiro started to open the truck door, its squeaking sounding loud in the silent tension. Just as he put his left foot down onto the dirt road, a bullet struck the windshield. He slid out of the seat, hit the dirt on his side, and rolled under the truck.

Everyone on the flatbed jumped down and sought cover. Several in the other trucks raced into the woods. Bullets screamed by, impacting in the dry clay down the road. One man grunted, stumbled, and fell. "Son of a bitch!" He held his side. Blood flowed between his fingers. He tried to crawl to the ditch, but collapsed after moving only three feet.

"One rifle so far," Nate yelled out. "He's not a very good shot, but is close enough to get lucky. Don't expose yourself if you want to live."

Brian pressed his body against the truck's back wheel. "It's going to be hours before dark."

Nate turned his head to check on Brian. "Relax. We're going to be here a while."

Brian blew out a lung full of air. "Yeah."

Ramiro was forced to yell over the chatter of the other men. "What does this killer want?"

"Good question, but who knows?" Nate answered. "It's hard to believe a lone gun would take on a force this large. There must be more than one." He got up on his haunches.

"I'm afraid the shooter is keeping us pinned down so a killer squad can come up on us through the woods." He prepared to jump up and run. "On the count of three, have your men lay down cover fire. I'm going to try for the woods." Nate looked at Brian and saw him coiled and ready. He pointed, his voice rising. "You stay where you are!"

Brian was not ready to give in. "I can help."

Too afraid to chance Brian not obeying him, Nate got his binoculars out and scanned the trees. He had a feeling the sniper was shooting from up high. He could not be that far away. The road curved to the left, limiting the distance to the farthest trees.

He swept his binoculars slow and smooth, scanning the trees up high, finding nothing. He scanned lower, just six feet above the ground. He stopped short, dropped the binoculars, and brought his rifle up to his shoulder. Two seconds later, he fired.

Ramiro yelled, "You got him! I saw him fall out of the tree on the far side of the curve." He started crawling out from under the truck.

"Stay where you are," Nate said. "I still need you and your men to provide cover fire while I run for the woods. We don't know for sure he was alone."

"Say when." Ramiro got ready to shoot.

"Tell your men to get ready." Nate set himself to jump up and run. He pointed at Brian. "You stay there. Don't move an inch!"

Brian nodded.

Ramiro spoke in Spanish and then English, telling his men to be ready to provide cover fire for Nate at his command.

Nate yelled, "Now!"

Everyone but Brian shot. He could not see from where he sat behind the rear wheel of the truck.

Nate ran across the road and disappeared into the woods. To Brian's relief, no one shot at his father or the others.

Twenty minutes went by. Brian grew more impatient with each passing moment. He kept checking his watch. Nearly an hour spent in silence but for the heavy breathing of several men who had taken refuge behind the truck eroded Brian's resolve to obey his father. He scooted around and got on his stomach, trying to see by looking under the truck. He was just in time to see his father stagger out of the woods where the bend in the road started and fall to his knees.

"Dad!" Brian exploded from around the truck and ran all-out toward his father.

Ramiro started to yell for him to get back behind the truck, but stopped short. Brian was already halfway there. Instead, he shot into the woods a few times in case someone was out there aiming at the two. Most of the other men followed his example.

Brian stopped a few feet from his father, expecting to find blood, but there was none. Instead, he saw bewilderment and pain on his face.

Nate's eyes were distant. "It was Carrie. I killed her."

Brian could not comprehend what his father was telling him. He stood there frozen, staring.

Nate dropped his rifle and opened his arms.

Brian rushed to his father. "It wasn't your fault. How could you know?" He blinked, and then his eyes rounded. "She was shooting at us."

Nate held his son. "I'm tired, Brian. I'm tired." He held his son to him for several minutes, seemed to catch his breath, and released him. He stood. "Tell them there are no other shooters and that they can drive on up here."

"What happened?" Brian looked up at him, still not understanding.

Nate touched his son's face with his callused open hand, as if he were a small child again. "She broke. I guess she couldn't live with it any longer. For some reason…I fear what we will find at the bunker."

Brian backed away, shaking his head. "No! She wouldn't." His eyes looked inward. "They would never let her get her hands on a gun."

"We don't know what happened yet. All we know is she is out here alone, she shot at us, and I killed her."

Brian looked up into the sky to his left. "The buzzards."

"We'll find out." Nate walked up to him and put his left arm over his shoulder. "I'm sorry about being weak a minute ago." He shook his head and sighed. "All I did was make it worse for you. It didn't change anything. It's just that killing her…I thought she was getting better, and now this."

The rattle of trucks approaching alerted them. They turned and watched Ramiro drive the lead truck, heading toward them. All the men had left the woods and climbed on. They surmised the danger was over.

Ramiro opened the squeaky door and got out. "You two look like you have seen the devil himself."

Nate swallowed and cleared his throat. "I just killed one of our own people. A teenage girl who had been through hell. She wasn't right in the head. I don't know why she shot at us, why she was out here, or what has happened at our place." He looked at Brian. "I fear the worst."

Ramiro made the sign of the cross. "I am sorry."

"So am I," Nate said. "Will you bury her while I scout around the curve?" He pointed. "She's just back in the trees over there."

"Yes." Ramiro nodded. "We will do that, and pray over her."

"Thank you." Nate motioned for Brian to follow. "We will be back in an hour or so."

The two of them disappeared into the woods.

Nate walked fifty yards and stopped.

Brian caught up with him.

"I'm not expecting trouble," Nate said, keeping his voice low. "There probably are no more people out here. It's the buzzards that have me worried. We can never be too careful, so stay back thirty yards except where the woods are too thick for you to see me. Even then, stay back as much as possible."

Brian nodded. "You think she might have killed someone out here?"

"All I know is there is something or someone dead over there."

They made their way through the woods, Nate stopping often to look and listen, never moving fast, and always with fluid motion.

Brian followed behind, watching his father and learning more about hunting the most dangerous prey. He kept his thumb on the carbine's safety switch.

Nate kept back from the woods' edge, swinging close enough to see from the woods every thirty minutes and checking the road. When they were on the back side of the curve, he could see half a mile down the dirt road. Nothing moved but the buzzards above.

After they got closer to the area the buzzards circled, Nate was able to see there were not one but four items of interest for the buzzards on the ground. He could not see what had died, but knew their approximant location in the weeds beside the road because of the mass of buzzards moiling around and over them, hiding whatever was dead from sight.

They made their careful way, moving closer.

Nate stopped and used his binoculars to scan the area, not dwelling on the dead. The dead cannot kill you. Besides, he could not see that close to the ground because of the weeds and the mass of buzzards feeding and fighting each other for scraps.

There were more buzzards perched in trees. "Nothing moving out there but buzzards as near as I can tell." He let the binoculars hang from his neck.

Brian stood behind a three-foot-thick pine tree. He had the carbine shouldered and at the low ready position.

"Use that pine for cover and overwatch while I see what has died." Nate took one step and stopped. I will come back to you. There is no need for you to move from this spot."

Brian nodded as Nate walked straight across the road and stopped when he was close enough to see what was lying rotting in the sun. The flapping of the buzzards' wings as they reluctantly took off alerted other buzzards perched in nearby trees, and they too took off to rise above and circle in a thermal draft. He turned and headed down the road to see what was under the next mass of buzzards.

Again, Nate took a quick look, keeping his distance, and went down the road to the next buzzard gathering.

The next and last gathering of buzzards was behind a burned-out pickup. He took a quick look after scaring the buzzards away and headed back to Brian.

When he got within twenty yards of Brian, he shook his head. "Just dogs." He kept walking, into the woods, toward Brian. "They probably attacked her. I noticed she had a rag tied around one hand. The country is probably full of starving dogs roaming the countryside in packs."

Brian took his hat off and mopped his forehead with his jacket sleeve. "We still don't know why she shot at us and what she was doing out here."

"But we have an idea." Nate put a heavy hand on Brian's shoulder. "It will be tomorrow before we know. Until then, don't let it eat you up. There's no point in going through it but once."

"What if they're alive but hurt? We should get there fast."

"We would kill ourselves just to save a little time that will make no difference." Nate motioned with his head for Brian to follow. "We will ask them to take us to the farm and then we will go straight down to the river and use the canoe. It's the fastest way."

~~~~

Nate and Brian found no sign anyone had been at the farm. All doors and windows were still secure from weather if not thieves and vandals.

They spent only a few minutes there before saying their good-byes to Ramiro and the others and going on to the river, moving quickly and quietly through the woods. They found the canoe where they left it hidden in brush during one of their many trips between the farm and Mel's bunker.

Nate handed Brian a paddle. "I don't like traveling by canoe in broad daylight."

"I know, but we need to get there as fast as possible." Brian sat in the rear.

Nate sensed Brian was afraid he would wait until dark before traveling farther, but he had no intention of waiting. He shoved off and leaned into his first stroke with the paddle. "Keep your eyes and ears working and stay quiet. We will keep to the right side of the river until the sun is low and producing a shadow on the west side, then we'll cross and hug the western shore."

Brian said nothing but put all his strength into paddling. They found the river current to be weaker than usual and made good progress, reaching the creek in record time. Nate thought they would be there before sundown. Impatient, Brian kept the canoe going too fast for safety. It had gotten to the point Brian was doing all the paddling. Nate just tried to steer clear of snags.

Nate finally spoke up to warn him. "You're pushing it too hard. There are too many submerged logs. We're going to be in the water if you keep it up. Slow down."

"It'll be dark soon."

"We will be there before dark. I want to know too, Brian, but it either is or it isn't. Getting there ten minutes sooner will not change a thing. Turn this canoe over, and we will get there later, not sooner."

He listened to his father's words, and they made it farther up the creek than ever before until they reached a point where the creek became so choked with logs and other debris they could go no farther. Nate turned the canoe toward shore that was only four feet away, and where the creek was narrow.

Nate got out and pulled the canoe halfway onto dry land with Brian still in it. "We'll have to walk the rest of the way."

They traveled at three miles per hour. Still, Nate refrained from bulling his way through thick brush and making enough noise to alert anyone in the area.

Sunlight streamed in at a steep angle, struggling to penetrate the treetop canopy. Wide areas of the forest were cloaked in dark shade, other, much smaller spots, were bathed in warm yellow sunlight, casting freckles on the forest floor. Nate avoided the light. Shade is life when being hunted in the woods. He did not know if danger lurked near or not, but he did know they were getting close to the bunker. The closer they got, the slower he walked. Brian followed impatiently behind.

Stopping in mid-step, Nate lifted his nose and took in the smell of food cooking, along with the smell of hickory smoke. *They're alive!* Maybe. He motioned for Brian to come closer. Whispering in Brian's ear, he said, "You overwatch for me. I'll make my way around to the front of the bunker and yell out while staying behind cover in the woods."

Brian nodded. "Someone is cooking. I smell it. They must be okay."

Nate shook his head in disagreement. "We still do not know who is in there. I don't hear the kids playing." After placing Brian where he wanted him, Nate started his stalk.

Slowly easing his way through the woods, Nate turned to his right, heading for the front of the bunker. Something on the ground caught his attention.

Blood.

On closer examination of the forest floor, he found drag marks and more blood. Then he found another blood trail and more drag marks. His heart jumped up into his throat. Following the trails led him to a depression that seemed to be filled with loose debris. The branches had been cut from nearby brush. He pulled the covering aside and saw a little hand. Frantically, he pulled more of the covering debris away and found what he was afraid he would find. He staggered back, his chest heaving. All of them, Martha, Cindy, Tommy, and Synthia, lay dead in front of him. There was a man too. He appeared to have been nearly disemboweled. Nate had an idea what happened to him and what had caused Carrie to go off the deep end. His grief already overcome by rage, he headed back to Brian, dreading what he was going to have to tell him.

Brian knew as soon as he saw his father's face. "No!"

Nate put a hand over his son's mouth. "Quiet. Carrie got one of them, but we don't know how many more there are." He could see hate washing over Brian. "That's my job." He motioned for Brian to follow. "We will back off until we learn what we are up against."

"They're dead," Brian hissed.

Nate turned to him. "Sshh."

They moved back into the darkening woods as the day died and faded into night.

When Nate found a big root they could sit on and stay off the wet ground, he stopped, took his pack off, and told Brian to do the same. They held each other in silent grief. The night did not compare to the darkness in their hearts.

Nate thought out loud. "If there's only one left, he's got to sleep sometime."

Brian wiped his face. "But the bastard's in the bunker."

"If we catch him sleeping, we can get to him. We could shoot him through a loophole. The trouble is there's no way to open the door if he has it barred. We can't kill him while he's inside, or we'll never get back in that bunker again."

"Might be able to put something through a loophole and lift the bar out of the hooks. It would sure be a lot safer to shoot the bastard through a loophole while he sleeps."

"I'm thinking there is more than one. We could shoot two just as easily, but I fear we would never be able to lift that heavy bar off the hooks by sticking something through a hole. It would have to be a long rod, and the leverage would be wrong. I doubt there's a rod in the cave or at the farm. There's some rebar in the barn, but it's not long enough. No. We will just have to wait for them to open the door for us."

"We'll have to take turns watching them."

Nate sighed. "Yes. One will sleep while the other watches."

Brian stood. "Let's go. We can't see anything from here."

~~~~

Rain drops the size of quarters hitting Nate's face woke him. He opened his eyes, only to be forced to close them again. He sat up and put his boonie hat on to shed rain. He saw Brian who looked back at him and put a finger to his lips. Nate grabbed his rifle and got to his feet. He saw that the woods were just turning from black to gray and the sun was about to rise over the horizon.

"They just woke up," Brian whispered. "They've been talking, so there's more than one. I heard two voices so far. Both men."

Nate put a hand on his son's shoulder. "Good work. You were supposed to wake me several hours ago." He kept his voice low.

"I was okay, and you needed the rest."

Nate appraised the scene. "Well, get your poncho out and go to sleep. You wake up to shooting, it will be them dying."

Brian did as he was told, curling up with his carbine under a magnolia tree not ten feet away.

Heat and mosquitos woke him. He opened his eyes and saw his father standing in the exact spot he had been when Brian went to sleep. Judging by the position of the sun, it was midday. He sat up, stretched, yawned, and then got to his feet, keeping bent over. After shedding his poncho, he grabbed his canteen and took a drink then grabbed his carbine and joined his father.

"They have not come out," Nate said.

Brian's eyes scanned the scene. "Yeah, I figured that. They're not dead yet."

"They'll come out. We have all day and all week."

"And all year," Brian added.

The day dragged on. Both father and son were hungry, but did not want to bother with preparing something. At any moment, they may have to kill. The thought encouraged them to ignore their growling stomachs.

As Nate prepared to remind Brian again how he should be watching the woods behind them and let him watch the bunker, the murmuring of low voices inside the bunker grew loud and drew his attention.

"Get your lazy ass out there and get some more firewood," someone yelled.

The bunker door opened and a man in his late twenties appeared.

Nate had his rifle ready. "Do *not* shoot. We need them both outside."

"I know." Brian clicked the carbine's safety off. His eyes became slits. Hate hardened his face.

A man's voice from inside the bunker yelled out. "Did you check to make sure no one was around before opening the door?"

The man at the door kept walking. "Of course. There's no one out here."

When Nate's friend built the bunker, he included many security measures, one of which was a five-foot-tall wall across the front of the entrance, making it necessary to turn at a right angle when entering or exiting. The man walked around the bermed wall and turned to the firewood pile under a tarp. Halfway there, he stopped and headed back. He yelled at the open door to the bunker. "I forgot the ax. Hand it to me over the wall, so I don't have to go all the way back around."

"Just grab some small pieces," the man inside yelled back.

"We used all of the smaller pieces that will fit in the stove cooking breakfast."

A man materialized from out of the shadow of the bunker's interior. He was a few years older than the first man and a lot larger. He reached over the wall with an ax.

It was an easy shot at fifty yards. Nate's rifle boomed, and the man dropped out of sight, along with the ax. Nate fired again before the younger man could react, and he too fell. He lay on the ground, breathing but not trying to get up.

Someone fired out of a loophole. Nate saw the rifle muzzle poking out and fired into the bunker through the loophole. A high-pitched voice screamed. The shooting stopped.

"Time to relocate," Nate whispered. "We will let them bleed out."

More shooting erupted while they were repositioning. They kept low, crawling along the ground, staying behind cover.

After settling in a good hiding spot, they watched, listened, and waited. The man on the ground made a wet sucking sound as he tried to breath. Nate glanced at his son's face and saw that it bothered him, despite his hatred of the killers. He sighed and put a hand on Brian's shoulder. "He's out of it, anyway."

Brian's eyes flared. "I hope he's hurting."

"Well…keep your head on straight. It's not over."

Brian nodded and kept his eyes sweeping the woods on his side.

They heard no sound from the bunker. All they could do was wait.

Someone in the bunker started crying. It sounded like a woman. She yelled out, "Shaun! You hurt bad?"

"Shaun!"

She got no answer.

Another volley of rifle shots rang out.

It was the same loophole she shot from before. Nate took careful aim and shot into the bunker through the loophole.

Brian fired two shots into the open doorway, but his shots went high. Lying on the ground, and being forced to shoot over the wall, he could do no more than waste ammunition. In frustration, he yelled, "You murdered our friends. Now it's time to pay. Did you thi—"

Nate's callused hand covered Brian's mouth. "Not another word!" Nate whispered in his ear. "We have to move again, thanks to you." He took his hand away. Follow me. Stay low. That means crawl."

Brian's face told Nate he was angry, but he did as he was told. They moved more to the left front of the bunker and waited.

Sunlight reached farther into the doorway as the day grew older and the sun inched across the sky. Nate waited patiently for a shot.

The bunker door swung closed by four inches, then stopped. Nate knew she was trying to get the door closed, but the dead man on the floor was in the way. He readied himself for a snapshot. A flicker of movement, a flash vision of her head as she bent down to grab the dead man to move him out of the way. Nate squeezed the trigger. He thought he saw her head explode, but it was just a ghost of an image in his mind. He could not be certain.

After more than an hour, Nate decided to move in. "Cover me. This isn't going to be fun. I doubt there are any more, but it's only our life at stake."

Mel had designed his retreat well, leaving no blind spots for anyone to sneak up on the bunker. Death could explode from anyone of those loopholes, and Nate knew it. He looked at his son. *I'm not leaving him alone in this world.* "We'll wait."

Brian looked back at him from where he lay and nodded.

The sun dropped behind them and below the tree line. Day faded into twilight. Nate backed off into the trees, took his pack off, and got out a pair of dirty socks. A search of the surrounding area netted him a rock of the proper size. He put it in the sock. He always kept a small can of lighter fluid in his pack for starting fires. The can and a cigarette lighter were put in a jacket pocket along with the sock, so he could reach it quickly.

"Brian." Nate motioned for him to come closer. "Leave your pack here and listen carefully."

Brian slipped his pack's shoulder straps off and let it swing off him and land near his father's. "You still mad at me?"

Nate's face softened. "No. Keep your mind on staying alive." He put a hand on his son's shoulder. "We're going to finish this in a few minutes. When I throw a burning sock into the bunker, I want you to shoot into the doorway twice. You understand? Just two times, then stop and lay flat on the ground."

Brian nodded in the dark of the woods.

"If you shoot more than twice, you will kill me, because I will jump up and roll over the wall and run into the bunker after that second shot."

"Two shots," Brian said.

"Also, keep your eyes and ears working. There might be more than the woman in the bunker. I'm saying there could be more out here in the woods, so do not assume the threat is only in the bunker."

Brian nodded again.

"Let's go. Stay alert."

They moved through the woods, slow and quiet, keeping in the shadows.

Since there was no way he could sneak up on any alert person in the bunker, it wasn't dark enough yet, Nate kept behind cover as long as possible, sprinted forty yards, then dropped and rolled until he was up against the bermed wall in front of the open door. *No gunfire. That's encouraging.*

While on his knees to keep low, he got the sock and lighter fluid out, soaked the sock, and lit it. He then swung it over the wall and through the open door. It hit something inside, sounding to Nate as if it knocked a can or metal cup off the table. Brian fired two quick shots. Nate jumped up, his rifle shouldered, aiming through the doorway. The fire lit up the bunker's interior. He could not see anyone inside but the dead man, who must have managed to crawl a few feet before passing out, his feet still in the doorway. He did see crimson brain matter on the floor that he was sure had to be the woman's, the only one he might have shot in the head.

There could be someone standing behind the door, so he rolled over the wall, landing on his feet, and dove through the doorway, landing on his back with his rifle aimed at the front wall. He swung his rifle to the other side of the door, his eyes looking over the sights. He found only the woman. She lay on the floor. The door hid her head from view, so he kicked it, but it was already against the man's body and would not move. A shot into her chest made sure. He slid on the floor until he could see her ruptured head. It was then he noticed for the first time she was pregnant. *If you had asked for help, you would be alive now.*

Nate swallowed, got up, and put the burning sock out. "It's over."

He went to the door and motioned for Brian to come on. "It's over."

Chapter 9

Brian kept watch while Nate dragged the bodies out of the bunker. They locked the door and spent the night in the woods. The smell of blood was too strong for them until they had a chance to clean up the mess, and that would have to wait. Many graves had to be dug. He insisted Brian not look while he carried all of their friends to their graves. He did not want him to see the condition of their bodies. Though Brian had seen plenty of dead people, these were friends. Only after Nate had them buried under a few inches of dirt, did he allow Brian to help. Nate felt that they were more than friends. They were family, and he knew Brian felt the same. He drew a diagram on paper, showing who was in each grave. They planned to make markers later.

After the job was done, Brian, who had cried the whole time without a word, looked up at his father and said, "I'm tired of losing people. If it wasn't for you, I wouldn't see any point in living like this."

Nate's face was as wet as Brian's. "I know. I'm tired too. But we do have each other." He dropped the shovel and held his son. "It will get better someday, I promise."

"Even if it does, it's too late for them." Brian picked up the shovels and walked away, heading for the bunker. He had his carbine slung on his back. When would they ever feel safe enough to leave their guns in the bunker while they worked? When would they ever feel safe enough to go home to their farm?

There was no way to understand what happened, but Nate surmised the three somehow surprised the women during some incident that caused them to let their guard down. He thought of many scenarios that might have provided an opening for the men to take advantage of and move in for the kill. Carrie had killed one of them with a knife and escaped with his rifle. He believed he knew why he let her get that close. More than likely, he was forcing himself on her. The attack was enough to send her over the edge. Everyone knew she had been put through hell and was on the edge of sanity. This last horror was the final blow. Nate knew he and Brian both would spend the rest of their lives regretting staying away for so long. Thinking it best for both of them to stay busy, he had Brian help him clean the bunker. It was a mess, and it gave them a chance to talk about what they should do next.

Brian pumped water to clean the bloody floor. "I guess we have plenty of food now, with just us to feed."

"We're back to two people providing security twenty-four/seven. That's going to get old fast. We have to sleep, and we have to work, not just stand guard."

"Yeah," Brian looked out the door, "a lot of things got old a long time ago. I guess we can't raise a garden now, not unless we want to take a chance on winding up like them."

"We will talk more about that later. Let's get this blood up and leave the rest. I want to drag those killers farther away so we don't have to smell them."

Thirty minutes later, Nate grabbed a rope and they locked the door behind them. "Look for a pole we can use. We'll tie the rope to one of them and the other end to a pole, so we can both pull."

"We're not going to bury them." Brian's face was distorted with hate. "They don't deserve to be buried. Let the bears and hogs and buzzards have them."

Nate found a suitable pole left over from tornado debris. "We don't have time to bury them. I just want them far enough away we don't have to smell them."

He saw something in Brian's eyes when he looked up from tying the rope on the woman. "Turn away. There's no need for you so see her. I'm the one who killed her."

"It doesn't bother me," Brian said.

"Just the same, keep watch for trouble. Ignore her. She's no danger."

They spent two hours dragging the bodies into the woods. All of them were emaciated, and that made their work easier, but the job was still laborious.

With the last one in tow, Brian was losing his patience. "These bastards are still causing trouble for us, even after they're dead." He stopped pulling on his end of the pole because a tree was in his way. He took the opportunity to mop sweat off his forehead.

Nate yanked on the rope and pulled the man around the tree.

When the man's body went by, Brian kicked at it. "You son of a bitch."

"Hey. Get up here and help me." Nate tried to read his son's face. "He was a murdering bastard. He was a son of a bitch. But now he's dead. He's paid up here on this earth. The rest is between him and God."

Brian almost snarled his words. "So we should respect their bodies? They're just dead meat."

The father looked at his son with sadness on his face.

The son saw it and looked away. "I'm all right. Just mad." He took his end of the pole in his hands. "Let's get this over with. The hogs and bears are hungry."

Twenty minutes later, Nate said, "This is far enough." He coiled the rope and stuffed it in a pocket. "We will not be coming back to this area anymore, unless we just have to for some reason."

The mass of cold air had reversed course and headed north, and it was a warm day. It was nowhere near as hot as it had been only a few weeks before, but they were both soaked with sweat from their labors. Brian pulled his T-shirt up to mop his forehead with, exposing his thin waist. Nate saw how thin he was. He had seen it before, but at this moment it cut into him. *Overworked and underfed.* He turned his strained face away and looked inward. *But full of pain and hate.*

Brian stared at his father. "I'm glad that's over. I don't want to see them ever again. It's our friends I want to remember, not them."

They went back to the bunker to get their packs.

"First we'll check the cave. It's not likely they knew about that, though. I would feel better if we scout the area and make sure there's no one else around," Nate said. "There's plenty enough time before dark."

Brian nodded while drinking from a canteen. He put it in his pack. "Okay."

Nate looked at him. "You haven't eaten all day."

"Neither have you. I'm not hungry." Brian checked his carbine. "Let's go."

They found no sign of any others in the area, but did find a jon boat dragged up on the bank of the creek, not far upstream from the river. There was no outboard, just two paddles and one long pole. They hid it in thick brush and left it turned over to shed rain.

No more than three or four adults could have fit into the boat, so it was a clue there probably were no more of the killers.

"So," Nate said, "these bastards came from up or down river and decided to go up the creek and then, what? They stumbled onto the bunker? There is more to it than that."

Brian did not have an answer. In fact, he did not seem to care. He looked off into the woods, his mind focused on something.

Nate nudged his shoulder. "Brian, this is important. More killers could show up."

Brian jerked his head and looked up at his father. "Of course. There are probably millions of them. This will never end. One day it will be you or me."

"Hey…" For several seconds, Nate had no words. "We've been through this before when we lost your mother and sister. There's no point in giving up."

The look on Brian's face worried Nate.

"When you rushed the bunker…" Brian's Adam's apple moved up his throat. He turned away. "I was thinking if you got killed, I would…"

"You would what?"

"You took a big chance. You don't normally do something like that."

"I…was almost certain that there was no one left alive in the bunker. You're right, though. I got impatient. Should've waited overnight. Was worried if there was anyone left alive in there, he would get the door closed in the dark before I had a chance to shoot."

There was silence between them all the way back to the bunker. Nate's concern for his son rose to new heights.

~~~~

The next morning, they finished cleaning up the bunker.

Brian seemed to be better, but had little so say. He just threw himself into the work.

"It's almost noon." Nate appraised the bunker. "This is good enough. Let's eat."

"One of us should stand guard while the other eats." Brian went to the corner where his carbine leaned against the wall.

Sighing, Nate said, "No. We will have a meal together and discuss what we should do next."

"Well, I don't see any point in starting a garden here." Brian slung his carbine on his back. "The weather's so screwy nowadays it will probably be a waste of time, anyway."

Nate noticed Brian seemed to be reluctant to be even a few feet from a weapon and knew he was feeling insecure after what happened to their friends. "We won't have time for that." He put plates on the table. "With just the two of us, security will be more than enough to keep us busy." He put wood in the stove and piled tender on dying coals.

"What are we going to have for lunch?" Brian sat at the table, using a stool so he would not have the back of a chair banging against the carbine hanging on his back.

"You put a bullet hole in a can of freeze-dried spaghetti. We might as well eat that before it spoils."

Brian almost smiled. "Finally, a break from wild hog. How do you know it was my bullet?"

"I can tell the difference between a hole made by a .223 and a .308. Besides, it was on the top shelf and I never shot that high." Nate filled a pot with water from the hand pump. "What do you think we should do, stay here, or join Mrs. MacKay's group?"

"What?" Brian looked sick. "Stay here. Why would we want to have to put up with strangers? You never know when they will turn on us."

"Lost faith in your fellow man, huh?"

"Haven't you? What if that guy you hit dies? They might hang you for killing one of their people. You broke his jaw. How's he going to eat? There's high chance he will die."

"They didn't seem too upset about it at the time. He didn't seem to be too popular around there."

Brian looked down at his plate. "I'm just saying you never know with people."

"Actually, you have a point. There is no way to predict how people will react to things. I doubt they will hang me if that idiot dies, though. Joining them would have benefits and added dangers both, no doubt about it. I would not even think of joining any large group, but Mrs. MacKay is as good as they come, I've known her all of my life. And the others there seemed okay to me. Mr. Ramiro impressed me with his common sense and seemed to respect Mrs. MacKay. In fact, everyone there did."

"What about the fact you won't be the boss around there? It will be you taking orders, not giving them." Brian looked serious. "They will probably tell me to do things you don't want me to do."

Now Nate's face lost all humor. "A father's right to raise his son will never die, not as long as people love their children. Any sign they don't defer to my rights as your father, we're out of there."

The pot of water on the wood stove was not hot yet, so Nate sat across the table from his son. "You're right, though. It will be different there, in many ways. It didn't seem to me they had a dictatorship set up, but a democracy can be just as bad. They may put justice up to a vote. I mean, they may let the people decide on the punishment if someone steals or doesn't pull their own weight. A democracy can be nothing more than a lynch mob. We will be safer from external threats there, but the internal threats would increase."

"Yeah, they might shoot you for falling asleep on guard duty." Brian was not smiling.

"We could have asked a few questions about how their little commune worked, but I was busy with one thing and another, including designing that waterwheel generator for them."

"It was obvious who was boss: Mrs. MacKay."

"Which is a good thing," Nate said. He rested his hand on his pistol. "Still, our reluctance to trust people is based on experience. If people were angels, there would be little need for government, and certainly no need for law enforcement."

"What's the point in even thinking about joining them, then? We did okay alone before. What if Caroline and Deni show up and we're not here?"

"The point is, we're in here talking and neither of us is watching to be sure no one is out there sneaking up on a loophole to shoot us as we talk."

A sudden realization came over Brian. "Yeah. It was easier when there were more people to keep watch."

Nate's face softened. "I didn't want to tell you, but more than likely Caroline lost her leg. She may not have survived. I doubt she'll be coming back if she did survive. And Deni, well, she was hurt inside. Who knows if she lived or not? And if she did come out of it healthy and able-bodied, the Army is not going to let her go when they need all the manpower they can get. If they did, she's most likely to go looking for her fiancé."

Brian's chest deflated. "I guess. But one of them might comeback."

"Maybe." Nate noticed the water was nearly boiling. He got up and put some spaghetti in the pot, guessing on how much to use. It was still thin, so he dumped more into the pot and stirred it with a fork. The smell of cooking food made both of them suddenly realize how hungry they were.

"I guess you made up your mind before you asked," Brian said. "All you're doing now is pretending I have a choice in the matter."

Nate grabbed a rag and put the steaming pot on the table. "You're getting to be quite a thinker lately." He used a large spoon to load their plates. "Growing up fast. Perceiving things only a man would. But this is a conversation between us that is exactly what it seems to be." At that moment, he made a decision. "We will stay here. At least for now."

Brian's eyes locked with his father's. "A week?"

"Longer than that. Unless something happens to change things, we might as well stay here all winter. Come planting time, we will need to decide if we're farming here or joining them to help with their planting."

Brian's eyes lit up. "So I guess you do listen to me sometimes."

Nate drank water from a glass. "I always listen. Sometimes a father has to override his son's vote. There's a reason kids have parents. We're older and more experienced, and kids need guidance."

"People have kids just so they'll have someone to boss." Brian smiled.

"It's not as fun as you seem to think. The thing is, once a man becomes a father he can't take it back. He can't say he changed his mind and just shirk his responsibilities. He can't say, never mind, I don't like this. I quit. Fatherhood is forever." He watched Brian fork spaghetti into his mouth and hoped it would put some pounds on him. "Being a parent does force a man to put his priorities in place and keep them there."

~~~~

Brian watched his father work. "We're going to use up all the fishing line on this."

"It's worth it." Nate stretched the line in a large square that ran just inside the woods line that surrounded the small clearing around the bunker. Each side of the square was a separate line that led back to the bunker and through a loophole on the nearest side. "We'll use traps to catch fish, if we have to." He kept the line three to four feet above the ground, so anyone approaching the bunker would walk into it.

Brian kept his eyes busy, scanning the woods for danger, his carbine in his hands. "Well, it's going to be interesting to see how you make your contraption work. Seems to me the wind will be setting it off all the time."

"You'll see. The main problem will be deer walking into it. It's high enough hogs won't, but deer are a different matter." Once Nate had the trip line stretched and ran through the nearest loophole, he began work on the alarm system inside the bunker. "Put your sleeping pad in that back corner under the shelf." He pointed. "I'll sleep in the front corner over here."

"What are we going to use to make noise with, empty cans?" Brian talked as he carried his sleeping pad and sleeping bag to the corner. He grabbed a spare pad that had been used by one of the women to make his pad thicker.

"No. It will be a silent alarm. I'm going to fill a small can with water. When someone walks into the trip line, the can will be pulled off the edge of that self and spill water on your face, waking you."

Brian threw an extra blanket in his corner. "Nice. Are you going to set it up so you take a bath too?"

"Of course. It's the best way to wake someone from deep sleep. We have four independent trip lines, so we can tell which direction they are coming in from by which can is pulled off the shelf. We will paint them with the letters, E, W, N, and S. I'm leaving plenty of slack on this end so wind blowing trees and brush around and pulling on the lines will not make the cans fall, but someone walking into the line and pulling it a couple feet will."

Brian considered his father's words. "You probably already thought of this, but we should tie a cord around the bottom of the cans so they will fall only a foot and not hit us in the face along with the water."

Nate smiled. "That's right. I already thought of it, and it is a good idea. Get the cord."

When they finished, Nate grabbed his rifle. "I'll go outside and trip the west side line. You watch and see how well it works."

"Okay," Brian said, "but we should put something in the cans so they'll be about the same weight they'll be when full of water."

"Why not water? We'll put a five-gallon bucket under the can." Nate put the bucket on a chair and made sure it would catch the water when it fell.

Brian pumped water into a pot and filled the cans. "I've been thinking about those bastards finding this place by chance. I mean the odds are slim that they just happened onto the bunker."

"I brought that up earlier, if you will remember. And, yes it's been bothering me. Still, just because the odds of them happening onto this place are slim, does not mean it's impossible. I've seen a lot of things happen that were harder to believe than that."

"Like what."

Nate smiled. "Well, I saw a man get struck by lightning once. The thing was…he was not hurt. I thought he was dead, but he just got up and checked himself over and he said he was okay."

Brian's jaw dropped. "Wow. Was he a soldier?"

"No. He was a farmer working in the fields. I was a kid then. Your Grandpa hired me out to him. That old man nearly worked me to death. Thunder storms were coming closer, and I had asked him if we could go to his barn for safety, but he said no, there was too much to do before sundown. Fortunately, he got hit and not me. Anyway, the next day his wife told me he was too sore to work, so he paid for it, despite being able to walk away. He also had to see a doctor and could not work for the rest of the week. I wound up having to work even harder because of it."

"You didn't work in thunder storms, though, did you?"

"No. I told your Grandpa about it, and he made it clear that I was not to be out in the fields when there is thunder within hearing distance."

"I wonder what Grandpa would've done if you had been hit after you asked that farmer to go inside."

"Let's put it this way: Old Man Harrison was lucky he was the one that was hit by lightning and not me."

Brian looked out the open door. "Your dad was a rough old cob, but he seemed to go easy on Beth and me."

"Grandparents are that way sometimes, doting on their grandkids after being tough on their own. Besides, you and your sister were not his children, not his responsibility."

"I miss him. I miss everyone." Brian turned his back on his father.

Nate sat at the table. "Let's sit and rest for a few minutes."

Brian turned around. "We probably should get this done as soon as possible, before more killers show up."

"Are you sure you don't want to talk?" Nate's chest rose and held as he looked at his son. "You've been through a hell of a lot. Sometimes, it's almost been too much for me, and I would not hold it against you to need a shoulder to lean on. I will always be there for anything you need."

Brian shook his head, his face stoic. "I'm okay. Let's get this done."

Nate stood. "Okay." He walked out the door, rifle in hand. They tested all four trip lines, and were satisfied with the results. When Nate walked into the lines, he stopped short of breaking them, as that was not necessary for the test, even though a stranger walking into them would keep walking and break the fishing line.

"What now?" Brian refilled the cans from a pot of water.

Nate bolted the door and sat at the table. "We rework our security measures and settle in for a long stay here." He motioned toward a chair. "Sit down and rest. We need to talk about a few things."

"What? Are we going to dig a moat around the bunker now?" Brian sat down and drank from a canteen.

"No." Nate appeared to be deep in thought. "We do need to strengthen our defenses, though."

"Well, I guess you'll think of something. More like ten somethings. What about bombs on tripwires?"

Nate ignored the question. "Those bastards showing up here out of the blue still bothers me."

Brian leaned back in his chair and stared at his father across the table. "I thought you said—"

"I know. I'm thinking maybe one of those raiders running from the Guard and posse found the bunker and told others about it."

"But even so, they wouldn't want to tell everyone about the bunker. They would want to keep the food to themselves. We probably got them all."

Nate unloaded his pistol to clean it. "You're right. And that's damn good thinking." He reached over and slapped Brian on his right shoulder. "You've really been adjusting to this survival stuff, learning fast."

Brian flinched, but said nothing.

Nate noticed the look on his face. "It will get better, I promise. They're already rebuilding somewhere. We don't know what all is going on with the government, but I would bet they are moving now, with growing speed. In the meantime, we have to hang on."

Brian bit his lower lip. "But you're still worried more killers might come."

"Well, we have to be ready for anything."

Brian got up from his chair and looked out a loophole. "I guess that's one thing we have learned: Anything can happen."

Chapter 10

Brian woke up before sunup the next morning to the sound of his father's voice.

"Time for breakfast." Nate heated canned wild pork in a pan. The meat sizzled and fried in its own grease; just enough to make it taste like it had been fried and not canned. A pot of water steamed on the stove, ready for four cups of freeze-dried scrambled eggs to be dropped in. He worked by the light of a kerosene lantern, turned down so much he could barely see. Light shining through the loopholes could attract trouble, and he wanted to preserve as much night vision as possible.

Brian sat up on his sleeping pad, stretched and yawned. "Why so early? It's still dark."

"We need to patrol the area, see if anyone's been around. Then we'll go down to the river and come back up the creek on the way back. I want to be back here in time to contact Mrs. MacKay or Ramiro and check on Kendell and the kids."

Brian stood and grabbed his carbine. "That means we have to be back by nine o'clock. We'll have to move fast, and moving fast is not the thing to do when men are hunting you in the woods."

"No. We'll do it right." Nate put two plates of steaming scrambled eggs on the table. "We're just going to patrol a mile-wide perimeter and then go straight down to the river. There's plenty of time for that."

Brian pumped water into two cups and set them on the table. "I guess we should leave as soon as it's light enough to see." They ate quickly. In fifteen minutes, they had their packs on and were in the woods.

Nate spent a lot of time looking for boot prints, broken brush, or any other sign people had been in the area. He found none.

After circling the bunker, they went down to the river. They worked their way upstream, eyes and ears on full alert. A deer distracted Nate for a few seconds, until he saw the white tail bouncing away.

Brian stood at a muddy area on river's edge. He waited for his father to look his way and motioned toward the ground. Nate moved over and saw it. A boat, probably a flat bottom jon boat, had been eased up on the bank. Both of them ratcheted up their alertness.

"Damn," Nate whispered, "it's getting crowded around here." They moved farther upstream, Nate in the lead, where they found no more evidence men had been in the area. Still, they went back to the bunker worried they could be attacked at any moment.

Brian had the only watch between them. "What time is it?" Nate asked.

Brian checked his wristwatch. "We have fifteen minutes."

Nate turned the radio on and checked several of the most used frequencies. There was no voice traffic, so he switched to the frequency they used to contact Big Pine, Mrs. MacKay's farm. He took his load-bearing harness off and sat down to rest. "Pump us some fresh water, will you?"

Brian did as asked. He handed his father a cup and sat down across the table. "I wonder why there are so many people on the river now."

"Like you, I've been thinking about that." Nate took a drink from his cup. "It's only a guess, but I think maybe it's because a few people have been staying in fishing and hunting camps upriver. They've been raiding those camps and living on what little supplies they found there. Probably, they've been working their way downriver, from camp to camp. If they found someone at the camp, they killed them. Well, it's been just long enough that they have worked their way down to us. They should drift on downriver. There's nothing to tip them off that we're up here so far from the river valley. They will check out our farm, though. They can see the barn from the river."

"And maybe burn it and the house to the ground, just to be assholes," Brian added.

"That's possible. I still have no idea why those who killed the women and children went up the creek and stumbled onto this place, but the river traffic might be caused by what I just explained." He looked across the table at his son. "Who knows? I'm using logic, but it's still just a guess."

Brian put his cup down. "Sounds reasonable, though."

"Still, it could be something else entirely." Nate stood and walked over to a loophole, looking out.

Brian grabbed his carbine. "See something?"

Nate turned to the radio. "No. It was nothing. Time to radio our friends at Big Pine."

"It's past nine o'clock now, they should have called us," Brian said.

The radio came to life, sounding like a man with a lung full of helium. Nate fine-tuned the frequency and the voice became clearer. Ramiro used a rather unpolished technique, but it worked well enough. "We'll finish our conversation after we're done with this," Nate told Brian.

In five minutes, Nate and Brian learned that nothing of consequence had happened at the MacKay farm since they last talked. There had been security changes, based on Nate's recommendations, and they were still hard at work on them. Kendell was allowed to talk with Nate for several minutes. He seemed fine, and said the children were all okay, also.

Ramiro got back on the radio. "We have a surprise for you and will deliver it three days from now. So be waiting for us at your old location."

Nate's eyes narrowed and he glanced at Brian, who stared back, listening. "A surprise?"

Ramiro said, "That waterwheel plan of yours has been completed, and it works great. We wanted to repay you, so we made up a smaller one for you."

"I was not expecting that," Nate said. "Thank you, and tell everyone involved thanks, especially Mrs. MacKay."

"We will," Ramiro said.

Nate hesitated. "I have a tragedy to report. When we got back, we found all of the women and children murdered."

Silence on the radio lasted for several seconds. Ramiro keyed the mike to speak. Kendell could be heard crying in the background, until Ramiro spoke. "You have my condolences." He kept his voice controlled, but emotion came through anyway. "Is there anything we can do to help?"

Nate keyed the mike. "No. The killers are dead, and we are not injured."

Mrs. MacKay's voice came over the radio. "Oh dear God, I'm sorry! When will the needless violence stop?"

Nate answered, "When the worst of what's left of the human race is gone." He swung his head to look for Brian and found him facing away, his head down. Nate and Ramiro made plans to meet at the Williams farm in three days, and Nate signed off.

Brian turned to his father. "What do we do between now and when we meet them at the farm?"

"For now, we'll sit down, rest our legs, and finish our conversation about river traffic," Nate said.

Brian put his carbine on the table and sat down. "I think I should clean all of my guns."

"Yes. Do that, while we talk." Nate laid his rifle on the table, also. "When you're finished, I'll clean my M-14. I cleaned the .45 already."

"What about the increase in river traffic?" Brian continued to dismantle the carbine.

Nate finished the water in his cup. It was warm. He got up and pumped more water, getting both he and Brian cool refills. "I'm thinking there are two kinds of people left alive by now. Small groups like us, the big groups like at Big Pine and Big Oak, and the most vicious kind of killers and takers. Just about everyone who was not prepared to survive is dead by now. That leaves people capable of taking care of themselves, and those who have survived by killing and taking from people like us. Anyone traveling is likely to be the latter. They're hunting for more victims."

"The bastards." Brian pushed a cleaning patch down the carbine's barrel with a steel cleaning rod. "We better get more ammo out of the cave."

"This stage, too, will pass. First, we have to get through it." He looked at his son, his face hard. "The killing is likely to increase over the next few months."

Brian's eyes narrowed. "I guess the Guard is busy."

"Yes. They have their hands full."

"And the Army and Marines."

Nate's jaw set. "Whatever is or isn't happening in Washington, I guarantee you that the great majority of surviving military personnel are doing all they can to help innocents."

Brian put an old toothbrush he used to scrub gun parts with on the table. "I know."

Nate continued. "The killers and takers are probably running out of food to scrounge or steal. They are more desperate than ever, so they're moving on, hunting for more victims. We must be ready."

"That's why so many in boats, drifting downriver?"

Nate nodded. "Gas has run out. What's left is bad and useless for car or truck fuel. Diesel is running out and the older stuff going bad by now, too. You saw how much trouble Mrs. MacKay's bunch is having with their vehicles." Nate drank from his cup. "Most people are on foot by now. Some are traveling by boat."

"The river is both a good thing for us and a curse," Brian said.

"Yes, the same as the road." Nate reached for the carbine. "Let me show you how to clean the receiver without scratching the aluminum up. AR's are different from the steel guns you're used to."

"I noticed you were watching me close," Brian said. "You've been waiting for me to mess up, so you could set me right."

"You've done well, considering the AR is new to you. Let me explain about AR gas rings."

They spent the next hour cleaning all of the guns they used and carried regularly, including the shotguns. They reloaded all of them afterwards and replenished the ammunition pouches on their load-bearing equipment.

Brian loaded both of their packs with freeze-dried food while Nate patched his worn boots for the third time in as many months. Nate wished they had bought extra foot gear before the plague hit. There were so many things they could have bought so easily in town before the world went to hell, but now all those things were not available at any price. One item they could not have stocked up on any better than their friend Mel had, was medicine. They had almost no medical supplies left that were not so out-of-date as to be dangerous to use. The cave still contained plenty of non-perishable medical items, but the medicines were too old, except for some antibiotic cream, and that was out-of-date. Nate feared for Brian. Death could come to him by illness or accidental injury as quickly as by violence. He still remembered the terror of the day Brian was shot in the leg by men who came upriver from town. It was during the early days of violence, when Mel's cache of meds was still fresh. Thank God for Mel and his survivalist ways. Those antibiotics saved Brian. What would he do if Brian were injured now?

"Dad?" Brian stared at his father from across the room. "Are you all right?"

Nate nodded. "Yes." He tried to smile. "Just missing everyone we have lost."

Brian froze for a second. "Well...those old boots are on their last mile. Are you sure none of those boots Mel has in the cave will fit?"

"Way too small. The boots those men we killed were wearing were too small too."

Brian tried to bring comic relief to the conversation. "That's what you get for having such big feet."

Nate raised an eyebrow and shrugged. "It's what I get for not keeping several extras for everyone. Mel had it right. He may be a survivalist nut, but he was right. I should have listened to him."

"I made fun of him all the time about it. You shouldn't be blaming yourself for not knowing the whole world was going to get sick and die." Brian looked inward. "You're thinking of all the stuff we could have done to prepare. Hell, we're doing a lot better than most. And I would have been dead a long time ago if not for you."

"We need each other. I told you that from the beginning, if you remember."

"I remember, Dad. I notice more than I used to, and I don't forget, not anymore."

"Yeah." Nate nodded, his eyes locked on his son. "Yeah. You're not the same person you were back then. I was proud of you then, and I'm proud of you now." He jacked a round into his rifle and clicked the safety on. "And I promise it will get better."

Brian swallowed. "It's not your fault." He hung his backpack from a peg on the wall. "I didn't believe you back then, but I do now. It will get better. Maybe in a year or so."

Nate took gun-cleaning items from the table and put them in a military surplus ammunition can. "It may be sooner than that. Even so, in a year, you'll still have your entire life ahead of you, and all we've been through will have been worth it."

~~~~

Two hours before sunrise, Nate woke to the sound of distant gunfire. He lay in the dark, his eyes open. Another shot echoed from more than a mile away. He did not get up, but he reached for his rifle next to him. He saw Brian's shadow when he moved from a loophole. "That shot was a long way off," Nate whispered.

"Yeah." Brian moved closer. "Most people are dead, and we're out here in the sticks, but we still can't have any peace."

Nate laughed under his breath. "Get some sleep. I'll stand watch until sunrise." He sat up and stretched, his rifle lay across his lap.

Brian did not wake until after nine. He sat up and saw his father looking out of a loophole. "What are we going to do today?"

Nate turned and looked across the room at him. "We need to clean this place up some more and be ready to head for the farm tomorrow."

"We're not going to check the area after those gunshots last night?"

"No. We are not going to be working a field, so our perimeter is smaller now."

"Let trouble come to us, I guess." Brian folded his arms. "It's cold. I'll get the stove hot."

"No," Nate said, not bothering to turn to his son as he spoke. He looked out of another loophole. "No smoke."

"Oh. Okay." Brian stood and grabbed his jacket off a hook on the wall next to him. "Winter's sure early this year…again."

"Yep." Nate stopped looking out loopholes and turned to his son. "We'll use a couple of Mel's chemical MRE heaters to warm our breakfast."

Brian rummaged in a cardboard box under the table they used for eating. He held a can in his hand and slid the box back under the table, out of the way. In his other hand, he held up a small paper packet. "Look what I found."

Nate set his rifle down against the wall and turned to look. "Coffee?"

Brian smiled and nodded.

"You drink it."

"No, Dad. I have some orange juice powder. You haven't had coffee in months."

Nate rubbed his whiskered face. "Okay. The juice has vitamin C in it. It's better for you anyway." He looked out a loophole again. "It's going to be lukewarm at best."

"Unless you let me start a fire and get the stove hot." Brian's voice sounded hopeful.

"No. Not that I'm expecting trouble."

"Hmm." Brian coughed. "Why do you have that look on your face, then?"

"What look?" Nate spun around and faced him.

"That look you always have when you think you're going to have to kill someone soon."

"I hope not." Nate sighed and looked out of another loophole. "Wash your hands. Then make breakfast."

"Okay."

Brian finished warming their breakfast. "Time to eat. The alarms we set up should warn us if anyone comes around. You might as well set at the table and eat."

Nate left his rifle in a corner. He washed his hands while Brian pumped water.

"You think we should be traveling while there are people in the area?" Brian asked.

"No." Nate dried his hands on a towel. "But it's too late to contact them now, unless they are keeping their radio on longer now that they have power. I'll try to raise them after we eat. If we can't, we'll have to meet them at the farm anyway. I don't want them waiting around there for us, wondering what happened."

"Yeah. That wouldn't be right." Brian sat down to eat.

They ate fast, before the lukewarm food got cold. Nate got up and went straight to the radio.

"I'll wash the dishes after you're through," Brian said. He wolfed down the last of his meal and went to a loophole to stand watch.

Nate tried for ten minutes, but could not raise either Mrs. MacKay's group at Big Pine, or Gary at Red Oak. "Battery's getting low," Nate said. He reached up to switch the radio off. His hand stopped just before reaching the knob when Gary's voice emanated from the radio.

Gary informed them that many at Big Pine were busy, but he would not speak of it over the air. "You will have to wait until they're finished," Gary said. "If you need to get in touch before the next appointed time for radio contact, try after dark. They and our bunch both like to listen in when the traffic is heaviest. "We have a little solar power here to keep our batteries up, so we can listen as much as we want. You would be surprised at the traffic at night nowadays. Things are starting to cook out there. We've managed to contact other groups. It makes you feel not so alone."

Nate keyed the mike. "That's great to hear. Unfortunately, we have no way to recharge our battery and must conserve power, limiting our radio time. Our battery's running low, so I'll sign off now." He switched the radio off after Gary wished them luck and signed off.

Brian commented wryly, "He's getting long-winded, isn't he?"

"Yeah." Nate thought out loud. "We can sure use that generator Ramiro was talking about. I'm worried about the noise it will make, though. It could attract unwanted attention."

Brian looked over his shoulder. "Can't be that loud, can it?"

"Well, the waterwheel has to turn fast to produce enough RPMs for the alternator to kick in, and there will be water spray and the water will have to fall at least two feet. All of that together will produce enough noise to be heard fifty, maybe even one hundred yards away. Anyone walking along the creek will happen on to it even without the noise. The main problem is we will have to carry batteries to the generator every day, exposing us to ambush. The last thing we want to do is present a routine for anyone to pick up on. Also, we do not want to wear a trail through the woods going to and from the creek for anyone to find."

"Every little thing's more complicated now," Brian said.

"Yes. And even good things can cause more problems to solve and more dangers to overcome."

"What fun," Brian said.

Nate's mind turned to how to set up the generator. He looked across the room at his son.

Brian smiled to show he was not complaining then looked out a loophole. "What Gary was saying sounds encouraging, doesn't it? I mean, you've been promising the world will rebuild someday. Maybe it's starting to happen."

"Maybe. If so, it's just the beginning. We need law and justice—something to restrain people. We also need to organize better and produce more food. Hungry people are not kind people."

"It seems like Mrs. MacKay's group is trying."

"Yes," Nate said, "but the effort needs to be more widespread to have any real force behind it. I mean, there should be survival groups like that everywhere."

Brian became serious. "If you think they are doing so well, maybe we should join them. I know what I said before, but it might be the best thing, at least for a while. I don't really want to join them, but it might be safer."

Nate sat at the table and leaned back in his chair, stretching his legs out. "So now you're looking at it from my side. That's good. We need to reason this out, consider the pros and cons. For example, your reluctance to join them is well-founded...for several reasons."

"Why? They have a lot of fighters for protection and plenty of land to farm."

"There are many advantages," Nate said, "but there are a few disadvantages and even safety risks."

"Risks?" Nate now had Brian's full attention. "Shouldn't we be safer with so many armed people to fight off attackers?"

"Well, first, there's the sickness. With that many people living so close together, if the plague started up again, it would spread fast. If it was weaponized, and I think it was, it would have been designed to spread from person to person. In fact, it had to have been, to spread so fast and kill so many. Usually, a disease that kills its carrier fast does not have time to spread to many other victims, but this one was able to both kill in a weak or two *and* spread around the world in a short time. It was highly contagious and deadly, with a mortality rate of near one hundred percent. I doubt nature produced anything like that. It's been almost a year since we've seen the last death from the sickness, and the danger may have passed, but who knows?" He saw worry in Brian's eyes. "It's also possible that most of us survivors have already been exposed to the disease and have a resistance to it, so the plague can't restart."

Brian had nothing to say. He appeared to be deep in thought.

Nate continued. "Another problem is we will lose a lot of our autonomy."

"What?" Brian asked.

"Freedom. We will pretty much have to accept their decisions. We are just two votes, and they may not count yours, since you're only thirteen."

"Almost fourteen now," Brian said.

"Anyway, we will be outvoted whenever they do not agree with us. I'm not sure we could just pack up and leave so easily either. Once you join a group like that, it's not easy to part ways. They will expect us to contribute all we have. Mel's supplies included."

"Jeez, you *have* been thinking about it, haven't you?"

Nate sighed. "I try to think before I act. It comes with being a father."

Brian flinched. "Well, worry about yourself some too, not just me." He sat in a chair across the table from his father. "There wasn't any chance of getting the others to join any group, especially Carrie. They're gone now, so it's up to us." He was silent for a few seconds. "Or do I have a choice?"

Nate rubbed his whiskered chin. "Okay, I'll ask you flat out. What do you think?"

Brian's eyes rounded. "Uh, I don't know. I need to think about it a few days."

Nate chuckled. "Some help you are."

"Well." Brian threw his hands in the air. "You've had longer to think about it than me. You just brought it up."

Nate laughed. "Making decisions isn't so easy, is it? And this isn't the first time we talked about it"

Brian rolled his eyes. "I didn't say it was. Besides, we need to know more about how things work in their group and ask a lot of questions before we decide. They may not want us anyway."

"We certainly need to learn how difficult it will be to leave when the time comes. I doubt such a relationship will be forever. Someday, we will want to come back to our farm." Nate's eyes lit up. "You're thinking more like a man every day. Yes, we need more information before we can decide. The list of things to be worried about is long. Now you see what I meant by considering the pros and cons. This is a big decision."

"We need to spend more time with them to get to know what they're like under stress, that's for sure." Brian looked down at the table.

Nate looked at his son. *God, he's growing up fast*. "I know I can count on you when it hits the fan. You have proven that to me many times."

Brian raised his eyes. He turned red, but he smiled.

"I'm not sure exactly what kind of system of government they have there. It seems to be a commune, but with Mrs. MacKay as kind of a leader. Many of the people there are former employees, so she's the boss."

"They call her *Mrs.* MacKay, even when she's not around; that's a good sign," Brian said.

"Yes it is. They respect the fact the farm is hers and accept her as their leader for that reason. She's also a good farm foreman, and they know that. The thing is, she was a horse person, not a farmer of crops. She needs someone to help her. I would bet many of her former employees know a little about farming from working as migrant workers on vegetable farms, but they do need help if they're going to produce enough food to feed them all."

"That means we will be bringing something to the table even without Mel's supplies." Brian thought for a second. "I don't feel right about giving away his stuff."

"I agree."

"So when we go to get the waterwheel generator we might as well go with them to Mrs. MacKay's farm and stay long enough to see if we might want to join them?"

"Yes. We'll leave the generator at our farm until we get back." Nate stood and looked out a loophole to judge the time by the sun's position in the sky. "Mel's supplies are not really ours to give. He said we could take what we need, not hand it out to people he does not even know." He turned back to Brian. "Grab your rifle. We're going to the cave. We can give them some of our ammo and leave Mel's stuff alone."

~~~~

Nate waited for his eyes to adjust to the dark cave's interior. What little light there was came in through the open doorway. "Grab an empty pack and put some ammo in it to give to Gary. He's been asking for some. Just take our ammo, not Mel's."

Brian found a well-worn ALICE pack and slapped dust off of it.

"Put in twenty rounds of buckshot," Nate told him. "We don't have much, and that's about all we can spare. There's plenty of 7.62 and 5.56, so put in two hundred rounds of each."

"Okay." Brian opened a second military surplus ammunition can. "It's going to add a lot of weight. Our packs and load-bearing harnesses are already heavy with our usual ammo load and more food than we usually take on a trip."

"We're going to be carrying more than you think." Nate searched through tools leaning against the cave wall. "Cold weather's here early, and it looks like it's here to stay for a while. We better take our sleeping bags and a heavy coat this time."

Brian nodded and raised an eyebrow. "Yeah, we better." He shoved two more boxes of rifle ammunition into the old pack. "My socks are all holey, and I don't mean Godly. I wish I had some thicker ones for cold weather."

"There are some wool socks in the back end of the cave, where Mel put all of his extra clothing." Nate found the tools he had been looking for. He carried a shovel and an ax out of the cave, left them leaning against a pine tree, and came back in to help Brian. "Let's go back there and see what we can find."

"Okay. I've got the ammo packed."

Besides two pairs of wool socks and three more of thin nylon for both of them, they found nothing else that would fit. Everything was too large for Brian and too small for Nate.

Outside the cave, Nate closed the heavy steel door and pushed the hidden bolts home. Brian put the padlocks in place.

Nate pointed to a limestone rock. "Put the pack over there out of the way." He waited for Brian to return. "Here." He handed Brian the shovel. "Follow me. We have to plant some brush in front of the door and try to hide it."

"Are we going to try to hide the bunker too?" Brian asked.

"Maybe we'll put in a little camo," Nate said."

Nate dug around several large bushes, saving as much of the roots as possible. Brian gathered leaves to cover the holes, so as not to leave them for anyone to find. Brian helped him carry them to the cave entrance. There, they dug holes and planted the bushes to hide the cave door.

"Let's get to the bunker." Nate slung his rifle on his left shoulder and carried the tools. "Grab the pack, but keep your carbine in your hands and your eyes working."

They filled two five-gallon buckets with water from the hand pump in the bunker and carried them back to the cave and watered the bushes in an attempt to help them survive their transplant.

"Chances are they will die, but that's all we can do," Nate said. "It would be better if they live, because when they turn brown it will be a dead giveaway to anyone looking for sign of artificial camouflage."

Brian did not say anything, but he had that look he often had whenever he learned something from his father.

Nate noticed Brian's interest. "When you cut green brush to camouflage, say a sniper hide, you have to replenish it with fresh brush every few days, or the dry, browning camo will give your position away faster than if you had not bothered to camouflage it at all. Here, I'm trying to transplant brush so they will live and stay green while we're gone."

Brian nodded.

Nate picked up a bucket. "Let's get back to the bunker. We need to hit the sack early tonight."

They woke the next morning and dressed without benefit of any light. Nate wanted to protect their night vision. They sat in the dark and ate a cold breakfast of canned wild pork and biscuits. Just as the dark woods began to grey into false dawn, they locked the bunker door and headed for the farm, heavily loaded with supplies and extra ammunition.

Chapter 11

Nate stood just inside the woods line and glassed his farm with binoculars. "Looks like we got here before they did."

Brian swept the woods behind them, searching for signs of danger. "How does the place look, anyone tear the place up?"

"It doesn't look like anyone's been there since we left." Nate lowered his binoculars. "Let's ease around to the north and wait for them by the driveway."

Thirty minutes later, they found shade to make it more difficult for anyone to see them while they waited. "Take your pack off and sit down." Nate pointed to a log. "You might as well relax." He took his own pack off and repositioned where he could keep watch over the drive and his home.

Brian sat down and arched his tired back. "You still thinking about joining them?"

"We won't be making that decision any time soon." He glanced at his son and then continued to sweep the area with his eyes. "You be thinking about it. Over the next few days, we will get to know them a little better and see how they do things. I figure we can stay with them a while a few times and learn more about their ways before deciding."

"Before you decide you're going to talk with me first, aren't you?"

Nate turned to his son. "Of course. This is a big decision, and we need to consider all the angles first. There's no hurry. Judging from our conversations about it, I don't think either one of us has decided yet. That's why I want you to keep it on your mind between now and then. If you do not want to join them, we won't."

Brian's eyes looked inward. "Okay."

Nate became more alert. "We have pickups coming."

Brian jumped to his feet, carbine in hand. "Is it them?"

Nate nodded. "Ramiro is in the lead pickup."

Brian put his carbine down long enough to slip into his pack's shoulder straps. Nate did the same as soon as Brian had his carbine in his hands again.

Nate watched four pickups loaded with armed men stop between the house and barn. He scanned the far woods line with his binoculars, looking for anyone who might be waiting in ambush.

Brian continued to scan the woods behind them. "You're waiting to see if they are attacked before we show ourselves. That's almost like using them for bait."

Nate's eyes darted to his son. "Are you judging me? If they are attacked, we can help them from here a lot better than if we are in the kill zone with them. It's not my fault they didn't send scouts out on both sides of the farm before driving up like it's normal times and there's no danger." He resumed scanning the woods. "Besides all of that, I will always value your life over any other, even our friends."

"Sorry. I wasn't judging you, Dad. I was just observing."

Nate let the binoculars hang from his neck and turned back to his son. "Keep doing that; it's how you learn. What you said is basically correct, but I did not set them up as bait. They made mistakes, and I adjusted to that. We've been through this exact same thing before, and we were standing in about the same place, but you didn't say anything then. You probably didn't notice what was really going on. This time you did. It shows you're learning. Remember what I said about you having only one life. Never forget that."

Two men carried something out of the back of the pickup closest to the barn and set it down in front of the barn door. Nate took one last look at the far woods line. "Let's go. It appears safe. You stay back twenty feet and don't come out of the woods until they have seen and recognized me."

"Right." Brian held his carbine so the muzzle pointed skyward.

Nate stepped out into the open, holding his rifle above his head with both hands. A man pointed toward Nate and yelled something. Several other men unslung their rifles and prepared for trouble, some got behind pickups for cover. Nate kept walking. Ramiro met him halfway and shook his hand. Brian stepped out of the woods and walked up to them, taking quick steps.

Ramiro welcomed Brian. "I am happy to see you again also, my friend." He shook Brian's hand.

"Yes sir." Brian stepped back to let the men talk.

Ramiro became serious. "We are all so saddened by the needless tragedy you have suffered. The news hit Kendell hard. He must have thought much of those lost."

"The boy didn't know us long," Nate said, "but he seems to care about people more than the average person. He went through hell for those children he's been taking care of."

Ramiro nodded. "Kendell has already proven to be a great asset to the group."

"Well, let's not stand here any longer," Nate said. "There has been shooting along the river lately, and we are perfect targets out here in the open."

They joined the others in front of the barn. "Throw your packs in a truck," Ramiro said, "then show us where you want the generator."

Nate and Brian looked the waterwheel generator over. Brian turned the wheel, moving a paddle a few inches. "You're right, Dad. It will take a pretty big waterfall to spin this fast enough."

"They did a good job on it. Someone at the horse farm knows how to weld," Nate said. "Brian and I are going to have to scrounge up a few car batteries and some heavy wire, also, some thin wire for lights."

Ramiro smiled. "We brought four batteries with us. We had only twenty feet of large gauge wire, though."

"It's going to be fun carrying all this heavy stuff down to the river," Brian mused. He glanced up at his father. "But I'm not looking a gift horse in the mouth."

Nate smiled. "No, of course not." He turned to Ramiro. "We might as well put this back in the truck with the batteries, so we can drive as close to the river as possible and leave it all hid in the woods. It will be as safe there as in the barn, and rain will not hurt it."

A man helped Nate lift the generator into the back of a pickup. Nate and Brian rode in the back while the man drove down to the lower end of Nate's field. They unloaded everything, hid it in brush, and rejoined the others.

Ramiro was sitting on an open tailgate. He motioned for Nate to sit beside him. Brian sat on the ground under a nearby tree, his carbine across his lap. "We were hoping you would join us on a trip north of here." Ramiro's feet did not reach the ground. He swung them back and forth in the air as he spoke. "The town fifteen miles north of Mrs. MacKay's farm may still offer scavenging possibilities. We need fuel, especially LP and diesel. We also need wire and more twelve volt light bulbs, so we can wire the house. There are many other items, too many to name."

"I guess you have scavenged all the light bulbs, batteries, and other items you can from the abandoned vehicles around here," Nate said.

"Yes," Ramiro said, "we took anything of use." He shifted his sitting position to face Nate more squarely. "Before the plague, there were several distribution centers just outside of town, warehouses full of food and merchandize."

Nate cleared his throat. "I thought of that too. But I'm sure those warehouses were emptied within weeks. Any that have not been picked clean are probably being held by armed men, waiting to kill anyone who shows up."

"I want to be clear: we do not want to go on a raiding party. The idea is to collect what has been left by the dead, not to take from the living. The warehouses may be empty, they may be held by others, but one of them may be sitting full of needful things with no one to protest us taking what will go to waste anyway. On the way, we can stop at homes and offer help to the living and collect what has been left to waste by the dead."

"All right." Nate rubbed his whiskered chin in thought. "You know, the Guard may have taken over those warehouses and distributed the merchandise."

"I think we would have heard about such things, if that were the case. We have been listening to the short wave radio since the power grid went down and have heard nothing about the military handing out food anywhere in this county."

"The government fell flat on its face at all levels. You can't blame them though; they lost people so fast they were short-handed in no time." Nate's eyes focused on Brian, who was close enough to hear. "If we go, my son stays by my side, and I have total authority over him and his safety."

Ramiro nodded. "Of course. You are his father."

Nate continued. "And, if at any time, I do not agree with what's happening or I think things are getting too dangerous for Brian, I reserve the right to depart your group. If we have to walk all the way home, so be it."

"Agreed." Ramiro revealed white teeth under his thick mustache. "But I am certain you will find us to be a careful people. We do not want to put your son in danger either, not to mention our own lives."

Nate nodded. "I am not a bad judge of character, and I think you are not the kind to go animal, and that goes for the others in your group, but in case I have miscalculated, let it be known right here and now, I have no interest in harming innocent people and will not tolerate it in my presence."

Ramiro slid off the tailgate and stood. He held his right hand out. "Good. Then we are in agreement on several matters." Nate stood and shook his hand. "If there is nothing else," Ramiro said, "let us go back to Mrs. MacKay's farm and prepare for the long trip. We will be taking every running truck we have, including two flatbeds."

"Oh?" Nate motioned for Brian to come closer. "I hope we are successful, and manage to overload those trucks."

Ramiro raised his eyebrows, his smile stretched across his face. "We are all hungry and losing weight, and I see you are in need of a new pair of boots. Yes, hope for success, but prayer is more powerful than hope."

Nate got in the back of the truck and pulled Brian up with one hand. The heavy load they carried made getting up on the tailgate a chore for someone like Brian with short legs. "We will see," Nate said, and sat down next to Brian.

Two minutes later, the caravan of pickups headed up Nate's drive. They turned north when they reached the dirt road.

They stopped at several homes along the road, finding them looted and ransacked. It appeared the owners had all died in the plague or from starvation or violence not long after. They found no bodies fresh enough to have been victims of the bands of brigands that Nate, Brian, and their friends had fought many weeks before. The looters had left nothing of value to them. Nate did find an old garden tiller in a shed behind one home, but they had no usable gas for it. Brian looked it over. "I guess those lazy thieves had no use for farming equipment." He looked up at his father. "We should remember this tiller, in case we find a kit in town to switch the engine over to LP."

"Small chance of that," Nate said, "but we will keep our eyes open for small engine repair shops. Places like that might have such carburetor kits. We could also use them for gas-powered tractors and pickups. If we are able to scrounge up propane gas, converting gasoline engines would be a great help."

"Should be some LP not taken yet, the carburetor kits, probably not so easy to find." Brian said.

They went back to the trucks and waited for the others to finish searching. In a few minutes, they were on the move again, heading for Mrs. MacKay's farm. They passed a few more homes, but Ramiro did not stop. It was getting late, and all the homes along the dirt road were likely to have been looted by the gang of raiders before the National Guard killed or captured them.

When they rolled up to the gate, the engine of every truck running rough, they learned those on security had recognized them from a distance, using binoculars. They had the gate open and were waiting for them. Ramiro and others waved as they drove through.

Brian and Nate both noticed the tall berm along the front of the property and the barbwire fence on top. "Looks like they followed your advice," Brian said.

Nate saw where they had put up scavenged auto headlights in strategic places to illuminate the perimeter in case of night attack. "They've been busy all right."

A young Hispanic man riding in the truck with them spoke up. "We're not finished yet. We ran out of wire."

Nate nodded. "I think electrical wire was one of the last things people had on their mind when they were looting in the early days of the plague. There's a good chance we will find plenty in hardware stores."

The trucks were parked in front of a building where most of the men slept. Ramiro let everyone but Nate and Brian off, and then drove up to the big two-story house. They were greeted by Ramiro's wife, Rita. The two held each other for a second. Rita's eyes revealed relief that her husband had returned safely. She directed her attention to Nate and Brian. "Please prepare for dinner. There is water for you to clean up." She motioned to the bathroom down the hall, where water had been carried in by hand. "Mrs. MacKay is waiting in the dining room."

After Ramiro introduced his wife to Nate and Brian, she left, and Nate and Brian took their packs off. They took turns watching their rifles and packs while the other cleaned up in the bathroom.

~~~~

At the dinner table, Mrs. MacKay used the opportunity to bring up a few issues while they ate. "We are running very low on usable diesel. Your trip tomorrow will be the last, unless you can find usable diesel fuel."

"We are hoping to find some liquid propane, too." Ramiro drank water from a glass. "The mechanics among us say it's possible to convert gasoline engines to run on LP."

"I have heard of that, but didn't think it was an easy job." Mrs. MacKay saw something on Brian's face. "Do you have something to say, Brian?"

Brian's eyes flashed to his father and back to her. "Yes, Ma'am. They used to make kits to switch engines from gas to LP. LP does not have as much energy as gas, so the engine will not be as powerful, but it will work okay on LP." He motioned toward Nate. "My Dad did it before."

"If you're going to convert gas pickups," Nate said, "you will need LP tanks of around one hundred pounds and gas line tubing. You will also need tools for fitting the tubing end pieces."

"Our diesel fuel went bad because it was already so old," Ramiro said. "Newer diesel should still be good." He raised a fork loaded with rice and stopped. "We should have treated it with biocides and stabilizers." He shrugged. "We should have bought more before the plague, but who knew the world was going to suffer like this?" He put his fork down and lowered his chin.

Nate cleared his throat. "Diesel can last ten years if stored properly and water is kept out of the tank, so I'm sure there will be some in town. Your trucks may be running rough because of lack of maintenance as much as old fuel. You need fuel filters; yours might be partially clogged. I would suggest you make a list of things to look for, so we will have it when we leave in the morning. Brian and I have our own list."

Mrs. MacKay grew serious. "Perhaps you should leave Brian here. The trip could be dangerous."

Nate did not hesitate. "He stays with me. He may save my life. We're both safer together."

Brian's chest swelled. "Yeah, we're safer together."

"Have you asked yourself if the trip is worth the risk?" Mrs. MacKay asked. Personally, I'm still not certain it is. Ramiro and others have told me there are many things we must have, but I fear for the safety of everyone who goes on this trip."

Ramiro shrugged. "Risk is everywhere."

Nate put a glass down. "Of course, Brian and I have talked it over. We are thinking of asking you to let us join your group. Going on this trip will demonstrate our trustworthiness. Also, Chet, at Big Oak, informed us by radio that pockets of the country are starting to organize and rebuild local government. I think it's time we take a look at the nearer towns and see what's going on."

Mrs. MacKay seemed to be deep in thought. "Are you asking to join our group tonight?"

Nate answered, "No, not yet. We want to see how things are done around here first."

"Oh," Mrs. MacKay said. "Ramiro and others have told me that they wished you two would join us. I felt that you are free spirits, not in the habit of having others make decisions for you."

"That may be true," Nate admitted. "Certainly, we must learn your ways before we decide. Other than the fact you are in charge and Ramiro is your foreman, we are not certain exactly what kind of a system you have. We're thinking maybe it's a commune."

Mrs. MacKay and Ramiro both laughed. She held a hand to her chest and caught her breath. "No, we did try something similar in the early days. We learned, to our regret, that some will not work if everyone eats from the same pot. 'From each according to his means; to each according to his needs' did not work for us. We would have all starved by now. Our rule is not a hard and fast rule of, if you don't work you don't eat, but it's close to that. We expect even the children to do their part, though; we do not make slaves of them. The smaller ones take naps during the midday and all of them receive some instructions on reading, writing, math, farming, etc."

"Well, that sounds good. We will have to spend some time with you before Brian and I can decide. You will also have a chance to get to know us better before you decide if you want to let us join."

"But," Brian broke in, "I don't need any schooling. Dad is teaching me how to survive. Maybe they will start new schools someday, but for now, Dad is my teacher." He looked at his father. "I guess I can forget about being an Air Force fighter pilot. It looks like I'm going to be a farmer."

Mrs. MacKay gave him a wintry smile. "None of us know what our future holds. You may be a pilot someday."

Ramiro's wife walked in and announced to her husband and Mrs. MacKay both, "The children are all asleep." She grabbed a plate.

Nate stood and motioned for Brian to do the same.

Mrs. Ramiro stood frozen for a second, a look of surprise on her face. "Oh. Please sit down. I apologize for being late. Some the children were not cooperative and did not want to go to sleep."

Ramiro moved rice closer to his wife. "You work too hard, Rita. Someone else could have put the children to sleep. We do not often get to have dinner together, and tonight we have quests."

Nate and Brian sat down and finished their meals. The five of them added to their lists of items to look for during the trip and discussed how the waterwheel generator and security plans Nate had given them on the last visit had worked out.

"Brian and I need our sleep. We must be ready to rise before sunup, so we should excuse ourselves now. Thank you for the meal and hospitality." Nate stood, and Brian followed his example.

Ramiro stood also. "Let me show you where you are to sleep tonight."

Nate and Brian took their packs and rifles from the corner and followed Ramiro. Nearing the front door, they heard moaning down the hallway. Ramiro whispered, "Slim is not well. His jaw pains him."

Brian looked worried. "Dad, if he lives, he will hate you."

They were led to the barracks they had seen earlier. A dozen men were already asleep. Careful not to disturb the snoring men, Nate and Brian found two bunks next to a wall. A wood stove took some of the chill out of the air, but Nate knew they would need their sleeping bags long before sunrise. They slept until Ramiro woke them

Not wanting to be the source of delay, Nate and Brian were outside and standing by the trucks in less than five minutes. They found Kendell standing in the dark by a flatbed truck, stamping his feet against the cold, his hands thrust into the pockets of his worn jacket, a wool cap stretched down over his ears.

Brian said, "Morning."

Kindell nodded to them both. "Morning. Cold and me ain't friends. I prefer heat to cold any day."

"Have any idea where Ramiro is?" Nate asked.

Kindell motioned toward the house. "Eatin' breakfast. It'll be our turn in a few minutes. People have to eat in shifts here 'cause there are too many to all eat at the table at once." He edged closer. "You have any .308 ammo you can spare? I'm down to my last six rounds."

Brian looked up at his father, keeping quiet.

Nate said, "Sure." He took his pack off and dug out a box of rifle ammunition.

Kendell opened the box and stuffed the rounds into his right jacket pocket. "We're all running low around here. I hope we find some on this trip. It ain't likely, though. People probably done took it all first thing."

"Chet has asked several times over the last few months if we could spare any ammo," Nate said, "so we brought as much as we could carry. Might as well give you guys some if you're that low."

Ramiro came out of the house and walked over to them. "Breakfast is waiting for you. Be quick. We want to be on our way soon."

"Kendell tells me you are running low on ammo," Nate said. "We have .308 and 5.56 we can spare. We also have a little twelve gauge buckshot."

"God bless you," Ramiro said. "This may save lives. Come with me to the house."

Nate, Brian, Kendell, and several other men followed Ramiro. In the living room, using the dim light from a twelve volt car taillight, Nate and Brian opened their packs and set most of the ammunition they had on the floor. Nate made sure Brian kept plenty of 5.56 ammunition for himself. Men gathered around and each received a box of rifle or shotgun ammunition. The word "gracias" was spoken many times, interspersed with a few "thank yous." Nate slipped another box of .308 ammunition to Kendell.

Mrs. MacKay and Rita wished them luck as the men readied to leave the table after a quick and meager breakfast. The men all piled onto the trucks and pickups, most had packs of some kind, but a few carried only what they had in their pockets and on their belts. Two trucks were reluctant to start, but they came to life after Ramiro opened the hoods and coaxed them patiently, while another man cussed the engines to turn a sailor's ears red. Ramiro glanced at the glowing eastern sky and smiled. "Right on time." He slid behind the wheel of a pickup and led the caravan down the drive. Those on guard saw them coming and swung the gates open for them, yelling encouragements as they drove by.

The cold slipstream chilled everyone but the few riding in truck cabs; they enjoyed the warmth of the heaters and protection from the biting wind. Brian and Nate sat on a spare tire, leaving them sitting higher and more exposed to the chill. Brian pulled his jacket collar up and his boonie hat down. He spoke into his father's ear, "Someone washed the trucks."

Nate smiled. "We must look presentable when going to town."

Brian looked at everyone riding in the pickup with them. "But we are not exactly dressed in our Sunday best." Several men laughed.

Nate wiggled his big toe through a hole in his left boot. "Keep an eye out for large boots."

"I will," Brian said. He looked at his father's boots. "Good thing you have heavy wool socks."

They passed many houses that obviously had been ransacked; some had been burned to the ground. They bumped and rattled along at fifteen to twenty-five miles per hour, depending on the condition of the dirt road. Every half mile or so, they were forced to slow to a crawl because of deep ravines cut into the road by heavy rains. They also passed a few abandoned vehicles. All along the way, Ramiro kept an eye out for tire hazards. Nate kept his eyes working the road ahead and woods line for any sign of an ambush. He grew more nervous as Ramiro increased speed.

When a windfall from a large pine tree forced them to stop, Nate jumped down and met Ramiro as he stepped out of the truck cab. "You're going too fast. I can't scan the road and tree line ahead worth a damn. Binocs are useless with the truck bouncing so much, and there's not enough time to scan the area before we're already there. All it takes is a few killers with rifles to wipe half of us out."

Ramiro tilted his head. "But we must get to town as soon as possible." Other men were cutting the windfall into manageable pieces as they talked. "This area was cleaned out by soldiers. I don't think it is dangerous now."

Nate knew he was fighting a losing battle. "The National Guard did a good job, but they damn sure didn't get every crazy in the county, and more are coming in every day. Remember, Brian and I just had to bury most of our friends."

Ramiro said. "I know your worries are well founded, but we must get to town as soon as possible. What is there to do but grit our teeth and keep moving?"

Nate sighed. He climbed back into the pickup. Some of the men were still removing the windfall, and Nate decided to take advantage of the fact. He grabbed the spare tire and threw it on top of the cab. He got down and searched the cab for rope, finding several cargo straps behind the seat. In a few minutes, he had the spare tire strapped on so tight it would not bounce loose.

Brian jumped down. "Need any help?"

"No," Nate answered. "I'm finished. Get back in the truck." He climbed up and helped Brian. "Take your pack off and put it in the corner right behind the cab." The other men had finished removing the tree and headed for the open tailgate. "Hurry." Brian put his pack in the corner. "Now lay down crossways behind the cab. Use your pack for a headrest."

Brian frowned up but did what his father told him. "Shit. This is going to be fun. The truck is going to beat me to death."

Nate took his pack off and set it down between Brian's legs to conserve room for the other men. They had plenty of room on the flatbeds, but most of the men wanted to ride in the pickups where they would have more protection from the biting wind. "Keep your carbine on top of you so it will not be beat up."

"Yeah," Brian said. "What about me?"

Nate took advantage of the spare tire on top of the cab to steady his binoculars and scanned the road ahead and surrounding area. "This is new territory; we must be careful."

"You're the one standing." Nate looked down at his son and scowled. Brian kept quiet after that remark.

Ramiro got the caravan going again. As the miles went by, they came to more crossroads, and the homes became more numerous with less empty country in between. They did not see a single living human. A cheer rose up when they pulled off of the dirt road and onto a two-lane paved road.

Nate told Brian, "We made it to the hard road. The town won't be much farther." Nate had an urge to ring Ramiro's neck when he sped up to fifty miles per hour. He scanned the road ahead as best he could. *I wish we had ridden on one of the flatbeds behind us.* Thirty minutes later, Nate pounded on the roof of the cab. "Stop."

Ramiro slowed to twenty miles per hour but did not stop. "What's wrong?"

Nate leaned closer to the open window. "The outskirts of the town is just around the corner. Take it slow."

Ramiro nodded, as he sped up to forty-five. Rounding the curve, he slammed on the brakes when he saw what was ahead. The driver in the flatbed truck following had to swerve to avoid rear-ending them. The other trucks had more time but still left rubber in the road.

A roadblock manned by ten armed men crossed the road and stretched from ditch to ditch, presenting a menacing sight. Every man had a rifle or shotgun pointed at them, resting on pickup hoods or a barricade made of old car tires piled two-deep and five feet high.

Nate's rifle hung from his shoulder. He was glad he did not have it in his hands. Though more than two hundred yards from the muzzles pointed at him, and well out of range of the shotguns, he was an easy target for anyone halfway competent with a rifle.

Brian sat up. "What's happening?"

Nate put his empty hands in the air. "Get back down. We have rifles pointed at us. There is nothing you can do. Just stay down."

Ramiro opened the door and stepped out. "We could turn around, but I would rather talk to them. They probably are just protecting the town."

One of the Hispanic men sitting in the cab said in Spanish, "The gringos will kill you." The other man nodded.

"They have not fired a shot yet," Ramiro said in English. "I am unarmed. They do not seem to be the kind of men who will shoot a man for talking."

The same man in the cab spoke in Spanish again. "You don't know. They may shoot you for being too brown."

Kendell spoke to Nate, "I will stay with Brian, if you want to go with Ramiro. We might be able to make it to the woods if shooting starts."

Nate spoke to Brian, keeping his eyes on the men down the road, "Put your pack on, but stay low. Kendell, keep low, open the tailgate. You and Brian be ready to roll out the back and run for the woods if anything happens. You will not be able to do anything for me or Ramiro, so don't bother trying, just get out of here and head home. Keep under cover in the woods."

"Bullshit," Brian said.

"Do what I say." Nate spoke in his no nonsense tone. "I think Ramiro is right about this being people protecting their town, but you never know." He jumped over the side of the pickup onto the pavement.

"Is it worth the risk?" Brian asked. "There is nothing in that town worth dying for."

"Ask me later," Nate answered. "I'll be barefoot soon, if I don't find some boots."

"We are hungry," Ramiro said, "and our children will be hungrier soon. We need food and many other things."

"Dad and I are doing okay."

Nate kept his eyes on the men at the roadblock. "Just do what I told you."

Ramiro said, "I will talk to them."

Nate spoke to Ramiro. "Don't do anything to make them nervous. If they won't let us pass, they will probably let us turn around and leave in peace. If they were trigger happy, they would have already started shooting."

"Yes, that is what I was thinking," Ramiro said.

Nate put his hands up. "Let's go." As they approached the roadblock and got close enough to see the men's faces, Nate looked them over, trying to determine which one was in charge. The last man on the left worried him. He could see hate in his eyes.

Ramiro' eyes lingered on the same man. He licked his lips and kept walking. He whispered, "I have seen hatred for my people before. I see it now on the face of the man on the left."

"Yes," Nate whispered. "But I'm not so sure it's about race. I get the same uncomfortable feeling when he looks at me."

"Trust me; I have experience in such matters."

"I understand." They were too close for him to say more.

A tall, thin man wearing a white Stetson, blue denim jeans, and jacket lifted his rifle barrel and pointed it skyward. His weathered face appeared to Nate to be fifty years old. The man's rough voice cut through the crisp air. "That's far enough."

Ramiro spoke in his best confident-sounding voice, "We are from Mrs. MacKay's horse farm. None of us have been to town since the plague hit, and we thought it was time to come in and see what the government has done to help the people."

The hard-faced man on the left laughed but said nothing.

"Mrs. MacKay still alive?" the tall man asked.

"Yes," Ramiro answered. I have been her foreman for many years now, and I can tell you with great pleasure that she is well." Ramiro smiled.

"I thought I recognized you." The tall man, who looked every bit the part of a cowboy in a Western movie, took his hat off and then put it back on with the front higher on his head and the back lower. "You men point your guns in a safe direction. I know this man." They did as he said, including the hard-faced man on the left. The tall man balanced his rifle on his hip. "Come on over."

Ramiro and Nate stopped at the wall of old tires.

The tall man nodded toward Nate. "How about the big man there, can he talk?"

Ramiro looked at Nate.

"Certainly," Nate said. "It's as Ramiro says. I'm more of a guest at her farm, though. My son and I have not decided if we are joining up with them or not. We are basically on a scavenger hunt. We have no intention of harming anyone or stealing, but thought there would be a few things left to rot after the die-off. If the owners are dead, what's the point in leaving things we need go to waste? For one thing, I need a good pair of boots. Mrs. MacKay has taken in a lot of orphaned children, and many of her employees have children who are going hungry. They are not starving and probably won't, but they are hungry."

"What's your name?" the tall man asked.

"Nate Williams. I own a farm farther south of Mrs. MacKay's place."

The tall man smiled and pushed his hat back farther. "There were some soldiers came through more than a month ago, some of them were talking about you. They said you and your boy stopped some raiders coming up from the south."

"Brian and I had help from a few friends. Some of them died in that mess."

The tall man nodded, looking Nate up and down. "Okay, you can come on in to town. Follow the signs to the warehouse and they'll give you some food, but it's not likely to be as much as you want. There's a lot of hungry people with their hands out, and that warehouse is already two-thirds empty."

"What about the other two warehouses?" Nate asked. "We were hoping to get some hardware supplies."

"Hardware?" The tall man leaned back on his heels. "There's plenty of wide open hardware stores right on Main Street. Help yourself. The owners are dead. They've been picked clean of the stuff people need, but there might be something you can use."

"Thanks," Nate said. "What's your name?"

"Chesty Johnson."

Nate stepped closer and reached his hand over the wall of tires and Chesty took it. "Come to me if you need anything or have any trouble with the town folk," Chesty said. "I was town marshal when the world went to hell. It wasn't really about law enforcement; we relied on the sheriff department for that. It didn't pay anything either. The soldiers that came through a while back told me there was a new county sheriff of a sort. But they had to kill him."

"Yeah, that idiot is dead all right," Nate said.

Chesty's eyes lit up. "It's a shame the plague took so many good people and spared so many idiots."

"That's true," Nate said. "Well, we better get moving." He did not want to waste daylight talking. They had a long list of things they needed, and he planned to gather what they could and get back to the farm as soon as possible.

Ramiro and Nate were met by worried faces back at the trucks. "It's okay," Ramiro told the others. "We will go on into town. Keep your guns pointed up and act friendly. Do not make them nervous."

Nate climbed in the back of the pickup and put his pack on. "You two stand next to me," he told Brian and Kendell. "If I tell you to bail, that means jump out and hit the ground running for the nearest cover. Hear?"

They both answered, "Yes."

"What do you think?" Brian asked. "Does it look like they mean to cause trouble?"

"No," Nate answered. "But stay alert and do what I tell you."

They passed through a gap in the wall of old tires after two pickups were pushed out of the way by several men. "They must be short on running vehicles," Brian said.

"That ain't good." Kendell bit his lower lip.

"You feel sorry for them?" Brian asked.

Kendell waited until they were down the road far enough that the men at the roadblock could not hear. "No. But if they want our trucks, they might make us feel sorry for ourselves."

Brian raised his eyebrows. "Hmm, you're right. We might have something they don't have."

Nate broke in. "That's good thinking from both of you. But I doubt they are as short on running vehicles as we are. Before the plague, there were several car lots, including one new car dealership, in town. Then there are all the cars victims of the plague left behind. I doubt they are short on cars or diesel fuel. Gas is a different matter. I haven't been in this town in years because it's farther away than the one south of our place, but I know a little about it. I bought my last truck here ten years ago."

Brian looked at Kendell and shrugged. "He's right. They should have plenty of cars and trucks."

They passed signs made from scrap plywood every few miles that were crudely painted with directions to a 'food station.' The arrows always pointed the same way they were going.

They traveled eight blocks farther and came to a sign with a painted arrow pointing to the right. Ramiro stopped, and the rest of the caravan stopped behind him. He stuck his head out of the window and asked Nate, "What do you think? Food *is* our first priority."

Nate leaned closer. "I always try not to be where potential enemies expect me to be."

Ramiro thought for a few seconds. "So we should go for the other items on our list first?"

"I think we should look for one of those big do-it-yourself stores, then a smaller hardware store if we don't find what we need at the first place."

Ramiro nodded. "Okay." He drove on, staying on the main street.

They had yet to see a single person, but there were plenty of signs of the looting that took place during the early days of the plague. Not a single store or home was untouched by vandalism and break-ins. Trash covered the streets on both sides, including the sidewalk, but someone had used a dozer to clear the streets so vehicles could get through. Many disabled cars and pickups had been pushed to the side and onto the sidewalk. They saw no skeletons, but Nate expected many of the homes contained the remains of victims of the plague. There were too many bodies to be buried by too few people.

The driver of the last truck in the caravan blew his horn three times. Ramiro checked the side mirror on his door and did a double-take. Nate looked behind them but could not see because of the other trucks following.

A four wheel drive pickup with oversized, deep-treaded tires sped past them, its horn blaring. Three teenage boys rode in the cab. The boy on the passenger side kept a shotgun barrel pointed out the window. His voice carried over the blaring horn. "Pull over asshole!" Five more teenage boys rode in the back, all screaming obscenities and threats and menacing with their guns.

Ramiro did not stop. The boys kept screaming. Nate worried that shooting could start any second, and he knew that he would have no choice but to kill as many of the teens has he could. He dare not take his eyes off the boys. He feared the men he rode with were seconds away from starting a firefight with the boys, if one of the teens did not start shooting first. His heart pounded.

The teen driving the pickup sped ahead and swerved to his right, cutting Ramiro off. Nate, Brian, and Kendell braced themselves against the back of the cab and managed not to fall when Ramiro plowed into the side of the teens' pickup, caving in the right door with the heavy bumper and brush guard. Several men riding in the back of their pickup flew forward and slammed into them, knocking the breath from Brian. Everyone in Nate's pickup piled out, rifles ready. Brian managed to jump out only seconds behind his father, despite the heavy blow he received. Those in the following trucks did the same. Three of the teens were thrown out of their pickup and onto the asphalt. By the time the other boys were able to recover from the impact, they found themselves looking down the barrel of two dozen rifles and shotguns.

The standoff lasted several seconds, Nate fearing for his son and friends and not sure if he could stomach killing a dozen teenagers. Brian stood by his father, carbine pointed at the nearest boy. Kendell stood next to Brian, his rifle aimed at a boy's chest. Another truck sped up with its horn blaring as the driver brought the pickup to a tire-screeching halt. The driver was alone. Nate recognized Chesty, the tall man at the roadblock.

One of the boys blurted, "We got looters, Mr. Johnson!"

Chesty held his hands up, palms out, "Everyone relax and point your guns skyward. The human race is small enough as it is. We don't need any killing here today." He pointed at the teens standing in the road and in a commanding voice said, "Put those guns on the asphalt right now." He pointed at the others. "You in the truck put the guns down and get out. I want all of you standing right here in front of me."

The sixteen-year-old boy who was the driver of the 4x4 pickup held onto his shotgun and gave Chesty a defiant, hard stare. "They're raiders. Hell, half of them are spics."

Chesty rushed up to the boy and snatched the shotgun out of his hands. "Not another word, Billy." He bent down and got in the boy's face, their noses only inches from each other. The boy wilted and stepped back. He looked down and said nothing.

Chesty glanced at Nate, Ramiro, and the rest of their group, relieved to see all guns pointing skyward. Several of the boys talked at once, hurling obscenities at Ramiro for ramming their pickup. "I said shut up!" Chesty's voice bounced off a nearby building and echoed down the empty street. "I told you boys before about being too quick to look for trouble."

"Look at what that orange picker did to my truck." Spittle sprayed from Billy's mouth as he threw his words at Ramiro like wild punches.

Chesty pointed threateningly. "Billy. For the last time, shut your mouth. A loose tongue and a hot head can lead to loose guns and hot lead. You boys need to think about how close you came to dying here today, and you can't think right while you're running your mouth." He put his hands on his hips and gave them a silent dressing-down with his eyes. "If you boys expect to survive much longer, you better grow up…fast." He gave them another disgusted look. They examined the cracks in the road. Chesty turned to Ramiro. "Back your truck off theirs a few feet so they can get out of here."

The engine quit when Ramiro rammed them. He got in and stepped on the clutch. Several men pushed the truck back five feet. One boy tried the caved-in passenger side door and found it jammed. He ran around to the other side and got in. Billy climbed up and slid behind the wheel while all the other boys got in the back. He cranked the engine and black smoke billowed out of the exhaust pipes. The rattle of the rough-running diesel faded as they drove down the street and turned left.

"Well, that was interesting." Nate glanced at Brian and caught him mopping his forehead.

Some of the men whispered in Spanish. Ramiro shook his head, shrugged, and answered in Spanish, "It was nothing."

Chesty stepped closer to Ramiro. "I apologize for Billy's disrespectful mouth." He looked the other men in the eye. "I apologize to all of you. Most of those boys had good parents, but they were lost in the plague, and there's no one to finish raising them. We have our problems with parentless girls too. The pregnancy rate is sky high. We're lucky enough to have a couple doctors and a dozen nurses in town, but they can only do so much without drugs and medical equipment. We've warned the girls over and over that they do not want to get pregnant right now. We lost a girl a few weeks ago. There was some kind of complication." He looked away. "We had nothing but out-of-date Aspirin. Her last hours of agony put enough fear into the girls they have suddenly learned how to say no again. Who knows how long that will last?"

"It's been about a year since I thought about those kinds of problems," Nate said. "We've been worrying about starving and getting shot."

Chesty smiled. "Yes, well you've been out in the sticks. You're in the big city now. We have a thriving population of over two hundred citizens. That's not an official number, just a wild guess on my part."

"How are they feeding themselves?" Ramiro asked.

"There's still food left in the warehouse," Chesty answered. "All the stores have been picked clean, though."

Nate spoke up. "Before the plague, there were three big corporate distribution centers on the other side of town."

Chesty took his hat off and ran his hand over his short-cropped black and pepper hair. "One of them has been taken over by a gang that moved in on us before the town had a chance to organize. Not that we're organized all that well now. One is not a food warehouse and has only merchandise. We control that one and the other food warehouse. Anyone who shows up gets a small allotment of food once a week." He looked down at Nate's toes poking through holes in his boots. "They should have boots that will fit you. I expected you to go to the food warehouse first. Word has gotten around about the food handouts, and I thought that's why you were here."

"No," Nate said. "We had no idea what to expect when we got here." He took his list of wants out of a jacket pocket and handed it to Chesty. "That's what I'm looking for. Ramiro has his own list."

Chesty scanned the note paper. "Electrical wiring; deep cycle batteries; twelve volt light bulbs; fuses and fuse receptacles…" He handed the list back to Nate. "You going into the construction business?"

"My son and I are wiring our little home for twelve volt power." He nodded to Ramiro. "So are his people. They have a waterwheel-powered twelve-volt generator."

"All the comforts of home, huh?" Chesty asked. "You people are industrious. We could use a lot more of that around here. When the food in the warehouse runs out, there's going to be a lot of hungry people." He stepped backward toward his pickup. "Follow me. I'll take you to a big do-it-yourself store. I doubt many have been as resourceful as you, so there should be plenty of wire and other electrical supplies."

Ramiro's pickup would not start. He cranked until the battery was almost dead. The driver in the flatbed truck behind gave him a push, taking several inches of paint off both bumpers. Once the engine cranked, it ran well enough, and the caravan was soon following Chesty down the street. Chesty took several backstreets, cutting across town. After pulling onto a four-lane road and traveling less than a mile, he pulled into the parking lot of a home supply center.

Chapter 12

"Dad, look." Brian pointed to two dogs on the other end of the parking lot having a tug of war with a human leg bone.

Kendell's eyes rounded for a second, then he seemed to accept what he saw and turned away to scan the area for threats.

"Keep your eyes, ears, and brain working," Nate warned Brian and Kendell.

"Any dogs you run across ain't likely to be looking for a friend," Kendell said. "They'll be looking to eat you. They're hungrier than us people."

Chesty drove right up to the front of the building, near the entrance but left enough room for a truck to be backed up to the door. He got out, a rifle in his hands. He watched the dogs fight over the bone, shaking his head, but he did not try to scare them off.

Everyone in the other trucks jumped off and walked to the building.

Chesty kept his pickup between him and the broken windows. "I doubt there's anyone in there, but it's possible. We're not far from gang territory, so watch yourself in there. Keep guards on watch out here, or your trucks might not be here when you come out. Watch for dog packs too. They've run out of dead people to eat long ago, and have eaten a few live ones lately."

"I don't like shooting dogs," Brian said.

Nate gave his son a grim look. "I'm not going to let them chew on us, so shoot if you have to."

Brian let out a lung full of air and nodded. "Yeah. I don't like shooting people either, but that went out the window a long time ago."

Nate put his hand on Brian's shoulder. "It will get better. People are starting to come together and organize a little now." They wasted no more time and made their way through the debris left by the panic of the early days of the plague, grabbing shopping carts and making a beeline for the electrical supply aisles.

Brian pushed his cart closer to Nate's. "Dad, do you think this is right? We're taking stuff, and the companies might start up again someday."

"By the time there is an economy to support any corporation, this building and everything in it will be worthless." Nate searched the shelves. "Even if this company were to come back tomorrow, not ten years from now, they would have all of this stuff hauled to the dump and the building destroyed so they could rebuild."

"There ain't enough people left alive for big companies to come back anyway," Kindell said.

Brian turned red. "Yeah, I knew all of that, but it's the first time I ever took anything I didn't pay for."

Nate turned into an aisle. "There's no shame in being honest, Brian. I feel a little strange about it too. If someone ever wants to bill me, I have money in my bank account…if the bank ever reopens and if money is ever worth anything again."

"Yeah." Brian spoke more to himself than the others.

As they made their way farther back from the front windows and doorways, the building grew darker inside. Leaks in the roof had allowed rain in, and a musty smell rose to his nostrils. Ramiro sneezed. His nose ran. "The dust," he explained, and reached for a hanky in his pocket. He found rolls of wire and soon had his cart full. Nate and Brian got what was left of the heavier wire and then grabbed thin wire suitable for wiring the inside of the bunker for twelve volt power. They took all the electrical tape they could find, as well as a dozen light switches. In less than ten minutes, everyone was pushing carts out to the trucks. On their second trip, Nate, Brian, and Kendell loaded their carts with auto headlights, taillights, dome lights, battery cables, and twelve-volt fuses. They searched for car batteries and found none. They looked for flashlight batteries, and were not surprised to discover none were left.

They found little at the garden center they could use. All of the garden hand tools were gone, and there was not a single bag of fertilizer left. An empty rack that once displayed seeds gave mute testimony to many desperate people suddenly finding vegetable gardening to be a serious subject.

"I wonder if they had any luck," Kendell mused.

"Not likely many of them were able to learn how to garden on their first try," Nate answered. "Most of those seeds were hybrid, so they only had one good shot at a harvest. If they kept some seeds to try again, they were in for a sad disappointment."

Brian spoke to Kendell, "Well, they might have gotten something edible out of the second generation but forget the third. They needed non-hybrid seeds."

Nate smiled. "You listen to him, Kendell. He's already a pretty good farmer. He should be; I taught him."

"I wouldn't mind bein' a farmer," Kendell said. At least I wouldn't go hungry."

Brian searched the shelves for hand tools, "We can teach you. But I wouldn't count on not going hungry. People can take your crops from you. It happened to us."

Nate pulled a small flashlight out of a pocket and led them to the lawnmower section where meager sunlight from the front windows made it difficult to see. All of the lawn mowers and every other small engine powered tool were gone, except for weed trimmers. "Let's go to the tool section," Nate said. "Maybe they left something we can use."

"Why did they take the mowers?" Kendell asked. "They ain't goin' in the lawn care business."

"Small gas engines to power alternators scavenged from cars," Nate answered. "Not much good now, since the gas has all been used up or gotten too old to run engines on. Keep an eye out for kits to change gas engines over to run on LP."

"I've never seen anything like that in a place like this," Brian said.

Nate saw Ramiro and several other men heading for the door with loaded carts. "No, but we might find those at a small engine repair shop. That's what I'm hoping for."

Brian pointed down an aisle way. "They left some rope and string."

Nate backed up his cart and turned into the rope section. "Let's get what we can."

At the tool section, they found a few screwdrivers, pliers, and wire cutters in the back of bins that looters had missed. Nate grabbed welding rod and other welding items, including an oxyacetylene torch, complete with pressure gauges and hoses. His welding equipment had been stolen by the raiders when they looted his farm. There were five two-hundred-twenty volt electric arc welders, and several smaller machines, but they were as useless to Nate as they were to earlier looters. All of the gas-powered welders had been taken along with all of the generators. Their carts were full again, so they headed back to the trucks.

Nate pushed his cart out the door and into the late afternoon sun, Brian and Kendell followed, their carts overflowing. Chesty stood by his truck and scanned the street in both directions and glanced at the sun. "You might have time for one more trip before we have to leave," Chesty said. "We do not want to be in this part of town after dark."

Nate threw items from his cart onto a flatbed truck. "Why?"

Chesty held his rifle in both hands. "Like I told you earlier, we're on the edge of gang territory."

Nate worked as fast as he could and nearly had his cart unloaded. "The same gang that took over the warehouse of food?"

Chesty kept his eyes on the street. "Yep. They're a violent bunch. They were killing and stealing until we resorted to security measures. Everyone must be in our part of town by dark. We have roadblocks and patrols working the perimeter every night."

Brian and Kendell loaded items from their carts onto a truck. Nate waited until Ramiro and several other men brought cartloads of items out to the trucks and helped them load onto a flatbed.

Ramiro pushed his empty cart out of the way. "I think that is all from this place."

"I agree," Nate said. "We need to find a defendable place to spend the night and start again tomorrow. Chesty says it's not safe at night in this part of town."

"Follow me and I'll set up for the night," Chesty said. "You have your choice of empty homes."

"Is there a department store on your side of town?" Nate asked.

Chesty raised an eyebrow. "Yes, of course, but it's getting late."

Nate helped Brian onto the back of the pickup. "If there's one on the way, I would like to stop there just to take a look."

"Okay." Chesty started for his pickup. "We better get going, though."

As usual, Ramiro's pickup refused to start. Nate and six other men jumped down and pushed it away from the building until a flatbed truck could get behind and push-start it.

Chesty waited, getting more nervous as the sun lowered in the sky. Movement to his left on the other end of the parking lot caught his attention. A pack of one hundred dogs, containing many different breeds, rushed toward them, with heads low and hair standing straight up on their backs. He blew his horn and yelled out his open window, "Move out now or prepare to fight for your life!"

Kendell pointed. "They ain't playin'. They're on the hunt." He shouldered his rifle.

The dogs were only seventy yards away, and Ramiro had just gotten the engine started, but it threatened to quit at any second. He revved it, afraid to let it idle.

Nate brought his rifle up and fired as soon as the butt touched his shoulder and he could look through the sights. The lead dog collapsed and slid several feet. The pack kept coming. He fired twice more, dropping a dog with each shot. The pack scattered and disappeared behind the many abandoned cars. "I had to shoot. As fast as they were moving, they would have been on us in seconds."

"I'm glad you did," Brian said. "I was just about to shoot and take your cussing for not waiting for your permission later."

Nate laughed. "When have I ever cussed you?"

"You know what I mean."

The pack turned on their dead, ripping into them with bloody teeth, snarling and snapping at each other. Nate had killed the leader of the pack, now they had to work out which among them would be the alpha male, and that would determine who would eat first. Atavism, reverting to their wolf heritage, had taken over long ago, fueled by hunger and the desire to survive.

Ramiro managed to get his pickup moving, and they left the parking lot to the dogs.

By the time they pulled into the parking lot of a department store, the lower edge of the sun had touched the horizon. Chesty kept his eyes busy as he talked. "Ten minutes and I'm out of here."

Nate, Brian, and Kendell jumped down from the pickup. Nate spoke to Ramiro. "Stay here and keep the engine running." The three of them ran inside for a quick look. One pull-down door for loading merchandise from trucks was open. Nate pulled it down and secured it with a chain and a steel pipe. No one could pull it up from the outside. They came back out and ran to Ramiro. "I have an idea," Nate said. "I think we can push a flatbed through the front entrance and park all of our trucks inside. It's just aluminum and glass. Break through that and it's plenty tall and wide enough. The gang won't even know we're here. If we are attacked it should be no problem to keep them at bay. The rear of the building is still secure."

Hesitant, Ramiro asked, "Why not go with Chesty?"

"Come daylight, we'll have more time to look through the building and then find a small engine repair shop for the other items. We might be able to find some LP and diesel tomorrow afternoon and be out of town before dark."

Ramiro looked at the two men sitting beside him, but they were no help. They just looked back, waiting for him to decide. "Okay." He got out and told the driver of the nearest flatbed truck to push through the glass and aluminum and into the building. The two men riding in the cab with him got out.

The driver put it in low and had little trouble inching his way through. The sound of safety glass shattering and aluminum posts and braces bending and tearing loose from their anchors echoed down the empty streets of the dead town. Inside, Nate, Brian, Kendell, and several other men busied themselves with clearing room for the truck and those to follow. With debris everywhere and cash register counters to be forced out of the way, it was a big job.

Nate planned to park the pickups across the entrances to help fortify the building against attack. The larger flatbed trucks had too much clearance underneath them to be of much use for that. Nate ran out to Chesty, who was still sitting in his pickup watching the sun go down and scanning the streets for trouble. "You can head home now. Thanks for helping us."

Chesty furrowed his brow. "You're staying here all night?"

"Yes. We will be as safe here as any place else."

"Well, make sure you keep a couple men on security all night." Chesty put the pickup in gear. "Good luck."

I never thought of that, Nate did not say. Chesty raced across the parking lot and turned onto the street, accelerating fast. Nate turned and ran into the building to supervise the fortifications. Ramiro had already driven his pickup inside. He grabbed Brian's backpack off the pickup and handed it to him, then did the same for Kendell. After putting his pack on, he said, "Come with me. We need to work on fortifying the back entrances." Two men followed when Ramiro motioned for them to go with Nate.

Nate led them through the dark building with his small flashlight. He saw many items they needed and took a mental note, but kept moving, dodging around obstacles left by looters.

Passing under a sign that said employees only, they worked their way past offices and many racks of merchandise until they were back at the loading dock. "Shine your light down there." Kendell pointed.

Nate saw what he had in mind. There was a massive stack of compacted and baled cardboard from boxes piled to the ceiling. "I doubt if we can find a forklift that still works. We will have to roll them into place." Nate handed his flashlight to Brian. "Stay back out of the way and keep things lit for us."

"Great, I get the easy job for a change," Brian said.

They soon had the loading door and the one three-foot-wide employee entrance blocked two rows high. Then they made the stack two rows deep and managed to add a third row of bales to the top. Nate took the flashlight from Brian and looked their work over. "That should hold. We need to check the side door that leads into the outside garden center."

They found the glass door shattered. Kendell pointed at a steel shelf. "We can turn it on its end and slide it up again the door, then pile heavy stuff against that."

The shelf weighed three hundred pounds. Brian held the light while Ramiro's men helped Nate and Kendell place it against the door. It took them only five minutes to find enough heavy objects to back up the shelf.

Nate looked their work over. "That will do."

Nate's flashlight was nearly dead by the time they made it to the front of the building. They found the others hard at work preparing to stay the night. The sun had set and there was little light coming in through the broken windows and entrances. Nate took his pack off and put fresh batteries in his light.

Brian looked out the windows. "It's going to be pitch black in this place tonight. We better eat and get our sleeping bags laid out before it's completely dark."

"Yes, we have been racing against the sun." Ramiro pointed to a row of sleeping bags in an aisle way. "We are ready to eat, but you who were in the back need to use the light you have left."

Nate unrolled his sleeping bag between two cash register counters. There was just enough room for Brian. Kendell unrolled a heavy blanket between the next two counters. He did not bring a sleeping bag. Brian put two Ziploc bags of freeze-dried lasagna on the counter between them. "Hold the bag open," he told Kendell. Brian poured a little water in. "Seal it back up and let it set a while." Brian did the same for his own lasagna. They finished their meal in complete darkness. No one talked as they gulped down their food.

"I thought I heard something." Brian threw his empty plastic bag on a shelf behind the counter next to him. He grabbed his carbine and checked the Aimpoint sight, adjusting the red dot's intensity.

Everyone listened. After twenty seconds, Ramiro said, "I hear nothing."

Two men Ramiro had put on watch looked out of the continuous line of front windows, trying to see in the dim starlight.

Nate checked the Aimpoint on his M-14. "When Brian hears something, I take notice. You on watch keep your eyes and ears working."

"But there is nothing," Ramiro said.

"Maybe." Nate reached in the dark for his canteen. He stopped short. Someone hammered on metal. The sound was faint from distance, but several of the younger men heard it. "Sounds like someone pounding on a metal door."

A man by the window spoke up. "It's down that way." He pointed to his left, but no one could see in the dark.

Ramiro was still not sure if he heard anything. "What direction?"

"South," the man answered.

The pounding grew louder and more insistent. Ramiro got up from the floor where he was sitting. "I hear it now."

"Probably scavengers like us," a man sitting on a counter said. "You men have let Chesty frighten you with his talk of a dangerous gang."

"I wish we had some of those cardboard bales in the doorways," Kindell said. "Dogs can come in right under the trucks, and we can't see nothin' inside this buildin'. How're we goin' to shoot them off us?"

Nate's voice came out of the dark. "You're right. But we didn't have time to roll a dozen of those big bales all the way from the back to here. If we have more trouble with dogs, we will have to shoot them before they get inside. Some of us have flashlights, but I really do not want a melee of wild shooting in the dark using flashlights. Someone is bound to get shot."

Ramiro gave a nervous chuckle. "No, that would not be fun. We should put two more men on watch."

"If it's okay with you," Nate said, "I would rather take the graveyard shift. That's when trouble is most likely to come, despite the commotion down the street. And I doubt that stealth is the gang's strong point."

"Okay." Ramiro looked out the windows. "I will wake you when it is time."

~~~~

Two o'clock in the morning, Nate opened his eyes in the dark and listened. He knew something had awakened him but did not know what. His rifle was already in his hands. He sat up and listened to Ramiro whispering in Spanish to some of his men. Someone was out front in the parking lot. He could here young voices and car doors slamming. Nate thought about waking Brian but decided to wait. He wanted Brian lying flat on the floor where he would be safe anyway. He sat there and listened for several minutes.

What sounded like an argument to Nate started up outside. Angry voices grew loud. Someone screamed. Brian stirred. Nate whispered in Brian's ear. "Quiet. People are in the parking lot."

Brian had his carbine in his hands in less than a second. "How many?"

"Don't know, but they just did something to somebody. Maybe killed him." Brian started to sit up but Nate pushed him down. "Stay where you are for now."

Several young voices outside laughed. "You taught that punk," a young man said. "Hey, what about this place? We can light up those torches and have a look around."

"Naw," another voice answered, "we've been in there before. There's nothing left but stuff we don't need."

"We're running low on diesel," a third voice said. "Let's head over to Fifty-Second Street and fill our tanks."

Car doors slammed in rapid succession. Engines roared, headlights came on, and tires screeched. The roaring engines raced down the street and the sound faded away.

Ramiro whispered, "They're gone." Some of the men crouched under windows released a heavy load of air.

Someone moaned.

Nate got up and moved over to the front windows next to Ramiro. "They left someone wounded out there. Must have knifed him."

Nate heard Ramiro whisper in a sad, hoarse voice, "Yes. The poor soul is suffering. God have mercy."

"There's a sliver of moon coming over the horizon." Nate raised his head above the windowsill to get a better look. "If we're going to help him, we need to do it now before the parking lot is lit up.

Ramiro looked at Nate in the dark, just making out his form in the glow of starlight coming in through the windows. "I will not ask anyone to go out there."

The moaning grew louder.

"Mother of Jesus," Ramiro whispered, his breath misting in the cold night air.

The voice in the parking lot cried out, "Somebody help me!"

Nate said, "I recognize that voice."

"Yes, the young man in the truck with big tires." Ramiro sighed, sounding as if he were in pain. "Chesty called him Billy."

"I wonder how he got himself into this mess." Nate clenched his jaw. "Maybe he was captured, but I'm thinking he may have tried to join their gang."

"I do not know, but he is out there bleeding to death." Ramiro crossed his chest in the dark. "I will go."

"I think you are too small to carry him," Nate said. "I will go. I just don't want to get killed doing it." He called to Brian. "Bring my binoculars."

Brian bumped into Nate in the dark. "Here."

"No," Nate said, "you keep them. I want you to overwatch. Scan the far reaches of the parking lot and what you can see out in the street. Someone shoots at me; you will see the muzzle flash. Shoot to the right of the flash."

"Okay, but I don't think he's worth it. I'm sorry he's dying, but he's a punk with a smart mouth. I don't like the way he talked to you."

"I'm not so sure he's worth it either," Nate said. "It's not a good idea to write off every teenager with a smart mouth, though. Society would soon be short of teenagers."

"I guess you're right. I said some things to you back when I was hurting over Mom and Beth dying that I shouldn't have. You have a lot of patience. Maybe you knew why I was like that back then, so you let it go. I guess some of it was feeling sorry for myself. Anyway, I still don't think he's worth you risking your life over."

"Probably not," Nate said, "but I'm going anyway. He's just a kid." He spoke to Ramiro. "Do you have any clean cloth I can use to staunch his bleeding?"

Ramiro asked the other men in Spanish if they had any cloth. Everyone was awake, and most were near the front window, holding their weapons. A man spoke up and dug into his backpack. He handed Ramiro a white pillowcase that had been folded into a small square. Ramiro handed it to Nate. "He had this for bandages."

Nate spoke to Brian. "Remember to keep in mind where you would hide if you wanted to shoot me. Search those places." Nate spoke a little louder. "I don't want anyone else to shoot. Brian knows what my silhouette looks like in the dark and he's not going to accidently shoot me."

"I got a good scope on my rifle." Kendell had moved up behind them. "There's enough light out there I can see what I'm shootin' at with this scope."

Nate did not hesitate. "Okay, position on the left end of the windows. Brian, you position on the right end. I have to go if I'm going. It may be too late already. He's bleeding out." Nate moved fast in the dark. He jumped up on the pickup and was over the back and jumped down just inside the entrance of the building, staying in the dark shade. He stood just long enough to make sure no one was standing against the wall, hiding, looking both to his right and left. He could see just well enough in the dim glow of the rising moon. Moving fast while trying to keep his boots from pounding the asphalt and making noise, he ran to the boy.

Nate saw the boy moving his arms, holding his hands against his side. He dropped to his knees beside him, pulled his hands away and tried to examine the wound. A large knife had been used to stab him once. They wanted him to die slow and suffer. Nate ripped a piece of the cloth off and forced it into the wound with his fingers. He wished he had cleaned his hands first, but there was no time. The boy protested weakly, "No. That hurts."

Nate pressed the rest of the cloth against the wound. "I'm trying to help you. If you can, keep pressure on the wound." He had cord in a pocket to use as a tourniquet in case the boy's arms or legs were bleeding from an artery. He searched for more wounds. Finding none, he picked him up. The boy moaned.

"Billy." Nate talked through clenched teeth. "You're heavier than you look. I'm taking you where you will be safe. Keep pressure on that wound."

Ramiro and two more men waited in the bed of the pickup. They took Billy from Nate and carried him to the other side where more men waited with outstretched arms.

In one motion, Nate climbed up and across the pickup. "Put him on my sleeping bag." He lit the way with his flashlight, holding it low to hide the light from anyone outside as much as possible. As soon as they had Billy on his sleeping bag, he turned it off and put it away. One of Ramiro's men knelt beside Billy and kept pressure on the wound. "He's out, isn't he?" Nate asked.

The man answered, "Yes."

Brian's voice echoed in the building. "Headlights coming from the south! Several vehicles."

Everyone rushed to the windows, keeping low. Two men started up an excited conversation in Spanish. Ramiro scolded them. They stopped immediately.

"It's them," Nate said. He squatted beside Brian, looking out the window. "I recognize their loud mufflers."

Someone in the lead car yelled out of a window as they raced past the parking lot, "Are you dead yet, Billy Boy?" A chorus of laughter faded away as they sped down the street.

"I think they're drunk," Brian said. "They didn't see that the boy was gone, too dark I guess."

Nate put his hand on Brian's shoulder. "I would say so. Drunk or sober, from what I've seen of them, they're not worth the bullet it would take to kill them."

Brian scanned the scene before them with Nate's binoculars. The moon rose high enough in the last minutes to light up the parking lot. "I'm sure they've done much worse. I put them in the same class as those who killed our friends."

"Chesty's people need the Guard here," Nate said, "to clean this town up. These people are not going to have any peace until that bunch is gone."

The man helping Billy spoke in heavy Mexican accent, "The boy is dead. He does not breathe."

Nate rushed over and checked for a pulse. "He's gone. You can stop keeping pressure on the wound." The familiar metallic smell of blood filled his nostrils. "Damn it. He may have grown into a decent man with a little help from someone like Chesty." Nate and the man carried Billy's body to a pickup and put him in the back.

Ramiro stood next to the pickup, looked down at the body, and crossed his chest. "He suffers no more."

"No, he's passed it." Nate went back and checked his sleeping bag, expecting it to be soaked with blood, but found little. His plugging of the wound had reduced exterior bleeding but did nothing to stop Billy from bleeding to death inside. "We can do so little for the sick and wounded now. It's one of the things that's hard to get used to. That and the needless violence."

"How much more could we have accomplished," Ramiro asked, "if not for the bad ones who would rather steal from others than work and help rebuild?"

"Yes. Brian has expressed that thought many times." Nate returned to Brian's side. "Ramiro, Brian, Kendell, and I will stand watch until daylight. You and the others might as well get some sleep. Come false dawn, we'll be scavenging again and be out of here early. There are still a lot of things on our lists we have not found yet."

"Thank you," Ramiro said. "Seeing the young die always makes me weary." He spoke in Spanish to the other men, and they went to their sleeping bags without a word.

Chapter 13

"I am freezing." Kendell blew into his hands.

Nate looked out the store window out across the empty parking lot for trouble. He could see much better with the sliver of moon higher in the sky. Stars shone above, and he knew false dawn would arrive soon. "Go get your blanket and wrap yourself up."

Kendell passed by Brian on his way to where had been sleeping.

Brian said, "Bring my boonie hat, will you? It will keep my head warm."

"Sure," Kendell said.

Brian pulled his collar up and buttoned his jacket. "Now that I'm not worried about someone getting killed, the cold is getting to me."

"Your body is not generating the heat it was when things were looking like we might be in for a fight." Nate put his hand on Brian's shoulder. "Give me the binocs and go get your sleeping bag."

Brian scanned the parking lot and what he could see of the street. "I'm okay."

Nate kept his voice low to not disturb those resting. "You're standing up to all of this well."

"Not much else to do but keep going." Brian shrugged. "I can finally see now that it probably will get better in a year or so. People are starting to come together now. But before this town can rebuild, something has to be done about that gang of morons, and I bet there are a bunch of them in the big cities like Orlando and Miami. It's gotta be hell in places like that."

"You got that right." Kendell handed Brian his hat and returned to his firing position, sitting, on a five gallon bucket someone brought from the paint section. He wrapped himself in his blanket and resumed his vigil.

Brian spoke to his father in a low voice. "Maybe Grandpa was so hard on you because he wanted you to be tough enough to take on the troubles of life."

"Well…" Nate did not speak for several seconds. "Maybe. Don't think he was abusive or anything. I don't want you to think I was complaining when I talked to you about him. He just had a different way of raising children. Society changes over time and so does society's idea of parenting. Each generation is different."

"You went easy on me, though I didn't realize it at the time. Anyway, I didn't turn out to be a wimp."

Nate chuckled. "No. I didn't have to toughen you up; life has done more than enough of that lately. I would say you are about five years older now than you were a year ago."

"That means I'm almost nineteen?"

"It means I trust you to back me in a fight the way I would trust a private or corporal in the Army. You have proven yourself."

Brian lowered the binoculars and looked at his father, just able to see him in the glow of the moon.

Nate put his hand on Brian's shoulder. "I have always been proud of you. You have never done anything to make me ashamed."

They kept silent vigil until the sky lightened from the sun's predawn glow and they could just make out the street beyond the parking lot. Kendell's eyes grew heavy, but he stayed awake. A sound from the street caught his attention and he threw his slumped shoulders back and sat up straight. "Cars comin' from the north." He let the blanket slip off his shoulders and fall to the dusty floor and rested his rifle on the windowsill.

Nate heard laughter. Several horns blared. Tires screeched. "They're turning into the parking lot."

"They seem awful happy to have just murdered someone," Brian said. He thumbed the safety on his carbine and readied himself for a firefight. "If they see the body's gone, they might come looking for it."

"Yep." Nate raised his voice. "Ramiro, get your men up and ready to fight!" A flurry of motion told Nate he had heard.

Ramiro spoke to his men in Spanish. In seconds, Ramiro and all of his men were wide-eyed and armed, muzzles pointed out the windows at the two cars and one pickup that had just stormed into the parking lot. Everyone's breath misted in the wet, cold air.

"The killers return," Ramiro said. "They come to admire their night's work."

Nate glassed the pickups. "I'm afraid Billy was not the sum total of their night's activities. They've got a girl in the back of the pickup. Her hands are tied behind her. From the looks of her, she's been attacked."

The young men in the vehicles piled out and looked down at Billy's blood. The one who seemed to be in charge said, "The bastard crawled off." Twenty heads turned right and left as their eyes searched the lot, finding no sign of Billy. The leader pointed at the building Nate and the others watched from. The young men spread out, shouldering various types of long guns.

Ramiro's face hardened and he clicked the safety off on his rifle. He spoke in Spanish, and the building echoed with the sound of safeties clicking off. The men readied for battle, taking aim. Ramiro looked at Nate. "Excuse me. But they must die. To capture and abuse women is too much to forgive."

"She's just a girl," Nate said. "About fifteen."

"Dad," Brian said, "the girl is going to get killed if we don't do this right."

Nate asked a serious question. "Can your men shoot accurately in low light?"

Ramiro nodded. "Watch. It is not far."

"Tell them I'm taking the two on the right, closest to the girl." Nate aimed. "I'll shoot their legs out from under them first, then finish them while they're on the ground. It's the only way to keep the girl out of my line of fire. Make it soon; they're getting suspicious, and it's getting light enough to see our pickups parked across the entranceways in here if they come closer."

"I understand." Ramiro spoke to the other men in Spanish and then turned back to Nate. "We will fire when you do."

Nate's first two shots were so close together; they sounded as one. Two twenty-year-olds fell to the asphalt, dropped their rifles, and grabbed their shattered thighs. Nate shot them both in the head. He had not noticed the roar of gunfire echoing in the building, but now his ears rang. Gun smoke filled his nostrils and left an aftertaste in his mouth. He saw a teen moving his arms and fired.

The girl in the pickup screamed continuously.

"I guess someone has to go out there." Brian looked past Ramiro to his father.

Kendell reloaded his bolt-action rifle. "She might be less scared of Brian. I think it's safe enough with us watchin'."

Nate stood. "Get that pickup out of the way before I come back with her. We don't know how bad she's hurt. It'd be better not to have to haul her over it. The pickup she's in is still running. I'll try to drive it up here, if she will sit still for that."

Several men pushed the pickup they had blocking the entrance out of the way. Nate stepped into the opening and checked both directions to be sure no one stood against the wall and waited for a shot at him. Gray dawn lit the parking lot. He walked straight to the pickup and screaming girl. As he passed the prone bodies, he kept alert in case one of them was not dead. He wanted to give each of them a pistol shot in the head to be sure, but he feared it would frighten her more than she already was. "Girl." He spoke loud so she could hear, but her screaming overpowered his voice. "We are trying to help you. I want to take you inside where you will be safe. Just sit where you are." He got behind the wheel and drove to the others, backing the pickup to the entrance. She stopped screaming and sat in the pickup whimpering.

Ramiro removed the ties that bound her; his gentle nature came to the surface when he saw how badly she had been beaten. "Little one, no one will harm you." He picked up Kendell's blanket off the floor and wrapped it around her.

The girl settled down and became quiet, but she shook with fear as much as cold. "Please take me home." Her eyes darted from one man to another, finding compassion and pity on every face.

"We will," Ramiro said. "Do not fear us. Where do you live? We will take you home now."

A familiar pickup pulled into the parking lot at high speed. It was Chesty, and he had six men with him. He brought his pickup to an abrupt stop and jumped out, looking around at the bodies in astonishment. Unlike the day before, he had a pistol on his side and extra ammunition on a combat vest. He also had on a badge and a faded uniform.

A forty-year-old man jumped from the back of the pickup and hit the asphalt running. Tears streamed down his face as he rushed to the girl. The girl cried, "Daddy!"

Chesty and the other men walked up and watched the father and daughter hold each other for a second, and then looked around at the others. Chesty held a full-auto M-4 at the ready. "Well, someone tell me what the hell happened here."

Ramiro nodded to Nate.

Nate gave a short version, starting with the knifing and death of Billy and ending with him driving the girl up to the building.

The father listened while he held his daughter. "Thank you. They would have taken her to the warehouse and kept her as a slave." He lost control and could not speak, just held her and cried.

Chesty's eyes darted to the bodies on the parking lot asphalt and then to the girl and father. He scratched his head and looked at the bodies again. "Well, you had no choice."

"No choice?" Nate stepped forward. "What the hell?"

Embarrassment washed over Chesty's face. "We all appreciate you saving her, but killing that filth is going to start a war. They usually go back to the warehouse around sunrise, and the others will certainly notice this bunch hasn't returned. They will come looking for them."

Brian's eyes flashed to his father but he managed to keep quiet.

"If they are murdering your boys and taking your girls for sex slaves," Nate said, "I would not call what you have peace."

Chesty gave Nate a hard stare. "You don't have to live in this town."

Nate stared back. "Neither do you. If you are that afraid of them, there are empty homes all over this county. Pack up and leave. Anything would be better than what happened last night."

"Until they all do leave, as town marshal, it's my responsibility to keep them safe. Now that gang is going to come at us with everything they have."

"They must have you massively outnumbered," Nate said. "Why are you letting a gang of punks do this to you?" Nate shook his head in disappointment. "I must have misjudged you yesterday. I thought you were a man."

One of Chesty's men protested. "Hey!"

Another said, "You don't know him."

Chesty did not flinch. "Stay tonight to witness what you started and you will see what kind of man I am."

"I apologize," Nate said. "But I don't understand your thinking at all. There are some things that can't be tolerated, no matter the cost."

Ramiro broke in. "Gentlemen, we need each other to survive. Let us not forget that. As to the killing of those over there, how could we have saved the girl without taking their life? I do not think asking politely would have worked. As to your fears of the gang's revenge, we can stay with you tonight and add our guns to the fight. If they come, more of them will die."

Chesty's eyes darted to the girl and back to Ramiro. "We need to get her to the doc. Are you coming with us?"

"We have not scavenged this building yet," Nate said. "We can meet you later. Where will you be?"

"Downtown," Chesty answered. "Just head north on this road and turn left on Main Street."

"We will be there in an hour or two." Ramiro turned and spoke to his men in Spanish. They went into the building to look for items on their list.

"The gang's not very active during the day, but they may come looking for those on the ground over there," Chesty said. "Stay alert."

"Will you take Billy's body off our hands now?" Nate glanced at the girl, still being held by her father. "You might as well use the truck she's in to take her to the clinic."

Chesty motioned with his head to one of his men. "Drive the father and girl to the clinic." The man got in and drove off. Nate and Kendell carried Billy's body out of the building. Chesty's men loaded the body in the back of his pickup and got in. Chesty then drove to the bodies in the parking lot and searched them, taking weapons and ammunition. He left the bodies where they lay. Three men got into the dead gang members' cars and drove off. Chesty followed in his pickup.

"Look." Kendell pointed at a gathering of thirty dogs at the far in of the building, their numbers growing by the minute. Several stared at him and growled, holding their heads low, stalking closer. He yelled, and they stopped coming, then seemed to lose interest and sat on their haunches.

Brian leaned out a window and watched the dogs mill around impatiently. "They're just waiting for us to leave so they can have breakfast. Gross."

Nate, Brian, and Kendell packed so they would be ready to go after scavenging the building, while two of Ramiro's men stood watch. Then they searched for the remaining items on their list. "Look for a sleeping bag or heavy blankets," Kendell said. "I'm going to freeze my ass off tonight if I don't find somethin' to replace what that girl just left with."

Brian pushed a cart in front of him. "If it comes to that, you can use mine. I won't let you freeze."

They passed a rack of throw rugs. There were only three left, but Nate stopped, went back, and grabbed what was there. "These will keep you warm, and they're the right size." He put them in his cart.

"I still want to find something better," Brian said. "Kendell needs a real sleeping bag. We have plenty at our place, but they aren't doing him any good there."

Ramiro and several men rushed by them with half-full carts. "Do not waste time in the food section, every can is gone."

Nate kept moving as he yelled after them. "I guess you checked for dried goods also."

"Yes," Ramiro yelled back. "No beans, rice, nothing."

"Not surprising," Nate said more to himself than anyone there.

Kendell rushed to the sporting goods section, stepping on broken glass from an empty gun cabinet. "We need to check the employee area in the back." He quickly scanned a smashed ammunition cabinet when he went by. As he expected, it was empty. "They probably had a safe they kept guns in that were not on display."

They entered the employee area. Nate stopped at an office. "Wait here." He searched every likely hiding spot, but the place had been gone over many times, and there was nothing left. Even a safe had been broken into. Nate looked up at the air-conditioning vent. He noticed scratch marks on the screw heads. An overturned table nearby became his stepping ladder. He reached up and yanked the grill until he ripped it loose and threw it aside. It was dark in the office, but he could see well enough. Now, he needed his flashlight. Shining it in the air duct illuminated a hidden cache. He lowered his head and smiled. "Bring a cart in here."

Brian and Kendell helped him load more than two hundred rounds of ammunition, three shotguns, two rifles, and four handguns into the cart. Most of the ammunition was twelve gauge buckshot; .308; .38 Special; 9mm; and .45ACP. The ceiling was sagging from the weight, despite a brace holding up that part of the air duct.

Kindell examined a stainless steel .38 revolver with a two-inch barrel. "Must have been an inside job, as they used to say on the police shows."

Nate jumped off the table. "That's all there is."

"How did you know?" Brian asked.

"If you worked at a place like this and the world was going to hell, people were dying by the millions, and the power went out for good, killing the security cameras, wouldn't you put a few things somewhere looters could not find them?" Nate dug a box of .38s out of the cart and handed it to Kendell. "You don't have a handgun. Load that little revolver and keep it in your pocket until we can find a holster for you."

"Whoever hid this stuff was probably planning on coming back but never made it." Brian pushed his cart into the hallway. "I bet a lot of stuff was taken by employees when things started looking bad." He looked across the hall at an open door. "There are a lot of offices; maybe there's some food hidden in one of them."

"Maybe," Nate said. "We will certainly check them all."

Forty minutes later, Kendell held Nate's flashlight and looked into an air duct. They had searched every office and found nothing. This office was their last chance. "There's something in this one." He handed half a dozen boxes down to Nate, who placed them on a nearby desk. "That's everything." Kendell jumped down.

Nate opened a box. "Pharmaceuticals." He opened the rest of the boxes. "It's mostly antibiotics and painkillers."

Brian paid little attention. He looked down the hall and checked his watch. "Probably too old."

"There are some syringes here." Nate held a bottle up and read the label. "Out-of-date of course. The main trouble is the stuff has been up there for more than a year in the heat of summer." He put the bottle back in the box. "We'll take it anyway. Chesty says they have doctors and nurses in their town. They should know if this stuff is safe to use."

Kendell put a handful of loose .38 Special cartridges in his left jacket pocket. "Anyone check the pharmacy department yet. Probably picked clean, but it's worth lookin' at."

"We'll ask Ramiro when we get back." Nate led them down the hallway and into the rear warehouse. They spent nearly an hour searching the shelves for anything useful. Their carts were overflowing when Nate said, "Time to get back to the trucks and see what the others are up too."

They found Ramiro trying to start his pickup. His men were all packed, and most were sitting in the backs of pickups or flatbeds waiting for Nate and his group to show.

When Ramiro saw Nate, he stopped trying to crank the engine and got out, slamming the door. "Every time, this devil refuses to start!" He looked up and muttered, asking forgiveness for losing his temper.

Nate saw how the others had simply loaded their carts onto the flatbeds and tied them all together so they would not turn over, and then tied the mass of carts to the truck with cargo straps. He and Kendell lifted a cart up, and two men on the flatbed took it. Their eyes rounded when they saw the guns and ammunition.

Ramiro looked on in astonishment. "Where did you find such things?"

"Hidden in an air-conditioning duct." Out of the corner of his eye, Nate saw a man come from somewhere deeper in the building and join them. "Have you checked the pharmacy?" he asked Ramiro.

"Yes. There is nothing left." Ramiro told the man who just came up on them to do a body count and make sure they were not leaving anyone behind. He turned back to Nate. "We will leave soon. But first we must push this devil of a truck out of the building so I can have a push."

Nate smiled as he shed his backpack and put it in the back of the pickup. He slung his rifle across his back, out of the way. "Get in and drive." Five men helped Nate, Brian, and Kendell push the pickup out the door and into the parking lot, leaving room for one of the big flatbed trucks to maneuver behind it.

The man reported to Ramiro that all were accounted for. Ramiro nodded. After pushing Ramiro's pickup halfway across the parking lot with one of the larger trucks, the engine finally coughed to life and they were on their way.

They drove down Main Street and entered the downtown area. Ramiro saw a roadblock ahead and slowed to ten miles per hour. Men at the roadblock pushed a car out of the way and waved them on. At the roadblock, a man stepped closer and pointed. "Two blocks down. Chesty's expecting you."

Ramiro sped up, waving as he drove by. A tall, rawboned woman armed with a pump shotgun yelled at them, "God bless you for saving Christina!"

People ran down sidewalks, grim determination on their faces, looking as if they were preparing for battle. Everyone carried a long gun; some also had a handgun strapped to their side.

Kendell rubbernecked as they drove down the street. "They're more excited than a hive of bees."

"And they're all armed with stingers," Brian added.

A church parking lot seemed to overflow with people and vehicles. Nate recognized Chesty's pickup. He slapped the roof of the cab. Ramiro yelled, "I see it." He turned into the parking lot.

Brian stood in the back of the pickup and looked around. "I haven't seen this many people in one place in a year."

"It does seem crowded, don't it? As long as they ain't wearin' white sheets and burnin' crosses." Kendell jumped down after Ramiro found a place to park.

Brian jumped down beside him. "That's not funny."

Kendell smiled. "You think it ain't funny? Try bein'black."

"There's more than a few black people here," Brian said. "Don't worry about it."

"Oh, I ain't worried." Kendell waved him off. "It does seem strange, though, after all this time, seein' so many people."

"You two stay with me," Nate said.

Ramiro told is men to stay with the trucks. The four of them walked across the parking lot and approached the entrance to the church. One of Chesty's men saw them coming and went inside. By the time they got to the steps, Chesty appeared at the door. The sound of a heated debate between several men came from inside. "We have a problem." Chesty closed the door behind him. "The people are too spread out to protect, and no one wants to abandon their home and move closer to the food warehouse where we can protect them."

Nate asked, "Why would you want to wait for them to come to you? Why not go to them, and hit them where *they* live?"

Chesty gave Nate a strange look. "Do you know how many there are?"

"I'm guessing there must be at least a thousand. You have been acting as if you are terrified of them since we got here."

"No, not a thousand," Chesty said. "But more than us. And they are all young and ruthless."

"You mean young and stupid," Nate said. "As to ruthless, I do not believe that anyone can be as ruthless as a parent protecting his or her child. There must be some ex-military and law enforcement people in your town. Let them lead you."

Chesty gave Nate a hard look. "This isn't your town. We appreciate your help, but we have plenty of leaders already."

"I see," Nate said. "I was not volunteering myself as your new leader, just trying to help. Do you have a map of your town? I need to take a look at that warehouse where the gang is."

"Come on." Chesty led them into the church and past the pews where fifty people were gathered.

A tall, heavyset black man in his early thirties and wearing a faded deputy uniform threw his hands up. "We're wasting our time here. If we cannot get people to move to safer areas, we cannot protect them. Then they will lose their homes *and* their lives."

The clamor of many dissenting voices echoed in the church.

"I think this whole little party of yours is nuts," an elderly man in tattered overalls said. He held a double-barreled shotgun with the business end pointing at the high ceiling. An image of Mary holding Jesus looked down from a stained glass window. "We should go down there and clean those little snot nose bastards out." His thin body made his small beer belly all the more conspicuous. He scratched his bald head for a few seconds while the deputy and several other men argued.

The deputy pointed. "Have a seat, Pops."

"I've got a better idea." The old man walked away and started down the aisle. He nearly collided with Nate's bulk, stopping just in time.

"Don't run off," Nate said. "You're making more sense than the others."

The deputy raised an eyebrow and gave Nate a good stare-down.

Chesty moved in between them. "These are the men I was telling you about." He spoke to the deputy. "Tyrone," he motioned to Ramiro, "Ramiro," the deputy nodded, "and Nate."

"Nate and Ramiro, this is Deputy Tyrone Samson."

"Glad to meet you," Nate said. He got straight to the point. "How many of these hoodlums are there?"

"We don't know." Tyrone shrugged. "Several hundred would be my guess."

"Well, there are twenty fewer of them now. The ones who took the girl and killed the boy called Billy are dead." Nate saw a map taped to the wall with a red line drawn around the downtown area. He moved closer. "Is this supposed to be your safe zone?"

Tyrone grunted.

Not losing patience, Nate asked, "Is that a yes or no?"

"It wasn't my idea. It's BS." Tyrone's broad chest deflated and his shoulders drooped. "It's completely dependent on the supposition that roadblocks will keep them out, but there is absolutely no reason they can't drive off the streets and go around the roadblocks. So the security line has too many holes in it."

Nate looked the map over. "It's doable. But, as you say, there are several places they can drive off-road. This park is one place, the golf course another. You have a lot of side streets to deal with also. Your best bet is to take the fight to them before they have time to come to you. If you can kill enough of them, the rest will leave town."

"You take killing easy, don't you?" Chesty put his finger on the map. "This is the warehouse the gang occupies. They have it fortified. There it is an eight foot chain-link fence around the place, and the only entrance from the road is always blocked by a semi."

Nate looked over the area surrounding the warehouse. "Have any idea how much diesel fuel they have?"

"They have a tanker they took from somewhere," Tyrone answered. "I doubt they have used much of it. They were smart enough to steal a dozen or so brand new diesel pickups from a car dealership after the first big die off. It was about that time that they also took over the warehouse. Killed three of our town's people doing it. They had been placed there to guard it. Should have put more men on the job. We made a lot of mistakes early on. We were not thinking straight. With all the grief and misery, I think many of us were not sure we wanted to live at the time. It looked like the end of the human race there for a while. Then the disease started to lose strength as more and more of us got sick but did not die. Then there were those who seemed to be immune."

"The doctors explained it to me once," Chesty said, "but most of it went over my head. It seems there are always or at least most of the time, a certain percentage of people who have a natural resistance to the disease causing a plague. Over time, the people who get sick but do not die develop stronger antibodies." He glanced at the people gathered around. "This one was a real bitch."

"Where are the doctors?" Nate asked.

A woman spoke up and stepped forward. "Doctor Stein is working his shift at the clinic. I will fill them in on the meeting when I get back."

"This is Doctor Brant." Chesty stepped aside so she could meet the others.

Brian broke in. "How is the girl?"

The doctor's eyes lit up at the question. "She should recover physically, emotionally is another matter. It was kind of you to ask."

"You would be doing more good by getting ready for the wounded that's likely to show up at your clinic tonight." Chesty's voice held a tone of concern. "Also, you both need to get some rest while you can. Same goes for the nurses. You will be busy once the trouble starts."

"Brian, go get the pharmaceuticals from the truck," Nate said.

Doctor Sheila Brant kept her eyes on Nate as Brian and Kendell passed by her on the way to the truck. "Pharmaceuticals?"

Nate saw a glimmer of hope surface on her face. "We found some medical supplies hidden in an air-conditioning duct. I'm afraid most of it may be of no use. It's been setting in that air duct for over a year, and the heat probably ruined the medicine. There are some syringes and a few other items that I am sure you can use, though."

Defeat washed over her face. "We are in desperate need of antibiotics."

"I understand that," Nate said.

She looked up at the ceiling. "Excuse me for expressing the obvious."

"Not at all." Nate wanted to say something more; something to make what she and most everyone else in the church knew was coming less frightening, but he had no such words. "Have you tried primitive methods?"

She tilted her head inquisitively. "Such as?"

"In ancient times, ground copper mixed with water to make a paste was used as an antibiotic. It was applied to the wound."

"Oh." She reacted in a way that told Nate she had already dismissed his suggestion. "I remember reading about that early in my training. I don't think anyone has used that method in hundreds of years. It certainly was not taken seriously in class. There are many old remedies that even under these conditions I would consider malpractice."

Nate shrugged. "If I had an infected wound, I would try it in a heartbeat."

"Yes. Well, desperate people do desperate things." Though a tall woman, she had to look up as she talked to him.

"Honey is another natural antibiotic. We were taught that stuff in the army."

"To use in a survival situation," she added.

"And what would you call this?"

"Hell on earth," she answered, "if my clinic is filled with wounded tonight. Wounded we can do little for. Have you watched people die, people you cannot help?"

"Like everyone here, I've lost loved ones in the plague. I have also lost many friends to violence in the last year."

Brian and Kendell came back with a shopping cart loaded with pharmaceuticals. Doctor Brant eagerly dug into the boxes. Her eyes devoured the labels. Her forehead wrinkled. "Well, desperate times…"

"If someone is dying, it is certainly worth the risk of using this old stuff," Nate said.

Doctor Brant put a box back in the cart. "I certainly do thank you for your effort. Many items here have no expiration date and will be a great help. The syringes for example. I will get this to the clinic right away."

Nate turned the cart around for her. "Have you used a week solution of carbolic acid on open wounds? I'm sure you have read about doctors of the past using a weak acid solution to clean the wounds and their hands. One pioneering doctor even kept a mist of weak acid sprayed continuously in the air of the operating room to help prevent infections."

She appraised him with a renewed respect. "Yes of course we doctors have studied the pioneers of medicine and know of such primitive methods. They did work well enough to reduce deaths from infection by a great degree. Did they teach you all that in the military?"

"No. I read it somewhere."

Chesty nodded to a man standing nearby. "Help Doctor Brant get this cart to the clinic. Then give them any help you can. Stay there all night and protect the clinic. Find someone to go with you."

The man grabbed the cart. "I will take my son with me."

"Fine," Chesty said.

Nate spoke to Brian and Kendell. "Go get the shopping cart with the guns and ammo in it." The two jogged up the aisle and disappeared out the door. Nate spoke to Ramiro. "I would like some of the .308 ammo I gave your men back. I will exchange it for the ammo we found in the back office."

"What is the purpose?" Ramiro asked.

Nate moved to a table against the wall and took his pack off. "I know where my rounds shoot. I have no idea where the rounds in that shopping cart shoot in relation to my sight settings. At long range, that can make a fatal difference. I would rather be shooting my own ammo and hitting what I shoot at."

Ramiro's face broadened with a smile. "I see." He called his men forward and told them to give back Nate's ammunition. They were confused at first until Ramiro explained.

When Brian and Kendell brought the shopping cart in, the men dug into the ammunition.

"Do any of your people need the guns and ammunition in this cart?" Nate asked Chesty.

"Many are unarmed and many who are armed are low on ammunition." Chesty squeezed himself between two of Ramiro's men and dug into the shopping cart.

Ramiro raised a brow and gave Nate a questioning look.

"Wait until Ramiro's men have taken what they need," Nate said.

Chesty stepped back. "Sure. My wife could sure use a box of .38s."

"Take a box," Nate said. "I doubt many of his men have a need for .38 ammo. I have not seen too many revolvers among them. There probably will be plenty left after everyone gets a box."

Chesty dove in and grabbed a box of +P hollow points.

Nate stepped close enough to speak low and have a somewhat private conversation with Chesty. "I would guess you have your wife in a safe place tonight."

Chesty listened and nodded. "As safe as any."

Nate whispered in Chesty's ear. "We can stop them before they reach the downtown area. We can kill them before they ever leave their little gang headquarters or at least bloody them so badly that they damn sure will not want to tangle with us again tonight or any other night."

The crevices on Chesty's face deepened. "I'm willing to listen to anything you have to say, but you might as well say it to everyone else at the same time. Deputy Samson may be your first ally."

The deputy had been examining the map for many minutes, while everyone was talking. He looked over his right shoulder. "Chesty, I think your friend there may have the best idea so far. I don't like looking for trouble, but in this case trouble will be coming to us tonight. I think the best place to ambush them is on the road just far enough away from their hangout they can't hear the gunfire. We wipe out there assault team, then we move in on the warehouse. I'm not thinking we can take it. The price would be too high. What we *can* do is more damage and maybe put the fear of God in their asses."

"Now you're talking." Atticus grinned and scratched his bald head. "Punks like them can dish it out but they can't take it. Last night's crimes against our children prove to me there's no living in this town as long as those punks are on this side of the county border. Christina deserves justice, and she's not likely to get it from anyone other than us. How many more girls and women, how many more teenage boys have to suffer and die before we put a permanent stop to it?" His face changed from anger to melancholy. "Billy needed a trip to the woodshed, but he damn sure didn't need murdering. He was bad, but not in their lowlife class in any way. They had no business killing him. Now it's time for them to pay their debts on this side of hell, afterwards, it will be the devil's turn to extract payment."

Nate looked at the map. "Anyone here know what is across from the entrance to the warehouse parking lot? It looks like woods on the map, but this map is not exactly high quality, and the scale ratio does not allow for any detail." Nate turned from the map and looked at the faces looking back at him. "We need a topographical chart of that area. Barring that, I need to question anyone who has firsthand knowledge of the warehouse and the surrounding area."

Tyrone raised his broad shoulders and bent backward to stretch his aching back. "I've been there many times before it all went to hell. Used to patrol the area. There's a little shack that was abandoned years ago just a couple hundred yards west of there. There's an open farmer's field behind it and more fields beyond that. So there's little cover around the shack." He put his finger on the map, showing Nate, who stepped closer to see. Tyrone stepped out of the light coming in from the stained glass windows. "There's plenty of cover over there." He moved his finger a fraction of an inch. "Lots of trees and woods."

"All along here?" Nate ran his finger along the side of the road on the map a half an inch.

Tyrone nodded. "Yes. Plenty of cover for hundreds of yards."

"How many acres of woods? I don't want to find myself in five acres and surrounded by open field. I need ingress and egress."

"Oh no, man, there are thousands of acres of woods there to hide in, except around the shack."

Nate gave up on the poor quality map and turned his back to it. "Has there ever been a case of these people setting up booby traps that you know of?"

Tyrone shook his head and frowned. Nate searched the faces around him. No one spoke. Chesty said, "Oh God, I hope not." He rubbed the stubble on his face then added, "They have not done anything like that yet."

Nate looked at his son, as if he were talking to him alone. "We better expect *anything*, including booby traps." He directed his attention back to Tyrone. "What about the other side of the road and the perimeter of the warehouse property? I want to set up a sniper hide. Maybe not tonight, but later, if they do not pack up and leave."

Tyrone's brow furrowed "You're putting yourself deep into our troubles. How come? Justice for a girl and boy? To help people you barely know?" He stood with his feet apart and stared at Nate. "How much of what's in that warehouse do you want?"

"Christ, Tyrone." Chesty's voice echoed in the church.

"It's living in this world that makes me so distrustful." Tyrone continued to stare at Nate.

"Ramiro's people do have hungry children at home," Nate said. "I'm sure they would be grateful for any food you give them."

Ramiro started to speak, but he caught himself and remained quiet.

Tyrone's face did not soften. "As long as you ask."

Nate heaved his massive shoulders and sighed. "We didn't come here to take. Scavenge yes, but not steal."

"I can't see where these people deserve that, Tyrone." Chesty looked embarrassed.

"The situation is like this," Tyrone said. "We will run out of food in about six or seven months, unless we take that other warehouse. We've been living on short rations, trying to stretch out our food, hoping help from the government would get here before we starve. As a last resort, some of us thought we might try to take the other warehouse from the gang, but we all knew that would be our last, desperate act. So we don't need outsiders coming in with their own self-serving plans."

"So you're thinking what?" Nate did not wait for an answer. "I'm trying to talk you into taking the warehouse so we can get some of the food? Even if that were true, so what? If some of us die taking the warehouse, I think a bag of beans is poor payment."

"Yes." Chesty crossed his arms. "I would like for you to spell it out in plain terms so we can get back to planning for tonight. We don't have much time, so make it short and straight to the point."

The crowd had been silent, hanging on every word, now several people spoke up. A rising murmur echoed in the church. Atticus broke in. "If you know something we don't Tyrone, spit it out. We have work to do. There's killers a coming at us in a few hours."

Tyrone hooked his thumbs in his belt. "I'm just saying we don't know these people, yet Nate here has become our chief war counsel all of a sudden."

Something washed over Nate's face that chilled those who saw it. Brian whispered in Kendell's ear. "Look out. My dad's mad now."

"What I was offering you is something I don't appreciate seeing spit on. I was offering to put my life and the life of my son at risk to help you. I really would like to know what the hell you think is more valuable than that. These people, who came to town with me, are nearly every friend I have left. They too, were offering to risk their lives to help you. And you stand there and spit on it as if I'm a used car fraud trying to sell something." Nate looked around the room and settled his gaze on Ramiro. "I don't know how you feel or what you're going to do, but Brian and I will stay in town tonight. They can forget about me helping them take the warehouse or run the gang out of town. We promised Chesty we would be here to lend our rifles. Well, we're here. But the warehouse is their problem."

Ramiro nodded. "I agree. We will help to protect the town, but that is all."

Atticus spit on the church floor. "Well, confound it! We need these people, Tyrone. It ain't like you to be such an asshole."

If Tyrone were not too dark already, his face would have turned red. "It just seems too damn pat, them showing up like this. Hell, the National Guard promised us six months ago they would be back in a few months with food and medical supplies." He looked disgusted. "The Guard never shows up but they do." He pointed at Ramiro and Nate. "They're here for the food. They won't admit it, but that's what they're here for. We need the food in that other warehouse to buy us more time. Maybe the Guard will show up tomorrow. Maybe the Guard is never coming back. Then again, they just might come back a week or two after we're all dead from starvation." He looked at Nate, nodding slightly, his eyes two ice-cubes. "Sure, we could use their help. But not at the expense of ten percent of the food."

"And where did you come up with that figure?" Nate asked.

Tyrone swept his eyes around the room. "I see quite a few of your men here. I don't know how many more people you have back at your farm, but I would bet what you brought with you is only a small fraction of the number of people you left behind. If you help us take the warehouse, it would be no surprise to me if you demand a large part of the food."

Ramiro kept his eyes on Tyrone as he spoke in Spanish. His men moved toward the door. "We demand nothing from you." Ramiro spoke to Nate. "We will be with the trucks."

Kendell looked at Chesty. "You guys just stepped in shit. Because of him," he pointed at Tyrone, "more of your people will die, and you might not ever get that food now. Ramiro and the others are good people. They and Mr. Williams could have helped you take that warehouse." He turned and walked out of the church.

Chesty spoke to Nate. "If you're still going to help us protect our people, we could use you at the park and the golf course. We'll have all the main roads blocked, and the side roads will be guarded. They're not likely to get through the park in trucks because of the trees, but they can go in on foot. The golf course is a different matter; they can just drive right across it."

Nate clenched his jaw and looked at his son. He turned to Chesty and nodded. "Do you have any radios with good batteries? We need to be able to communicate and coordinate our efforts."

"They're probably afraid we will steal them," Brian quipped.

Atticus coughed and looked up at the ceiling.

"We have three working police radios," Tyrone said. "They're sheriff department issue."

"It would be nice if we were able to have one of them to call for help if we need it." Nate took one last look at the map. Before, he had paid little attention to the area of the golf course and park, since he was not planning on being stationed there. *The golf course is wide open. We will need long-range rifles there. Rifles heavy enough to disable pickups.* He gripped his M-14.

Chesty rubbed his forehead. "There is no way we can protect everyone, they're too spread out. The perimeter is too damn big. The line too damn long. There are too few people to keep the perimeter tight. Hell, some families live outside the perimeter, and they won't abandon their homes."

"Tell us something we don't know," Atticus said. "We've already been through all that. Tyrone put the kibosh to it. We have to deal with what we have and not what we could've had. We don't have the time to wish in one hand and shit in the other and wind up with nothing but a handful of shit."

Brian smiled but kept quiet.

"Well," Chesty said. "We need to send people out one more time and try to get everyone behind the perimeter lines."

"I will need you at the ambush," Tyrone said.

Chesty checked his wristwatch. "Yeah well, someone needs to stay here and supervise. If they get by your ambush, there will be nothing between those animals and our people. I want to be here."

"Okay," Tyrone said. "But I need to pick the men who come with me. I figure fifty will do it."

Chesty flinched as if he had just been shot at. "No way we can spare fifty."

Tyrone threw his head back and closed his eyes. He stayed that way for three seconds. When he opened his eyes he looked at Chesty. "It will be suicide with fewer than twenty."

"Fine." Chesty motioned toward the door with his head. "But get going now. You have to go over whatever plan you come up with, with your men and then you've got to get the hell out there and get set up."

Tyrone looked straight ahead when he passed by Nate. "Don't forget to give Nate one of your radios," Chesty said.

Tyrone stopped and pulled a radio out of its carrier on his belt. He looked Nate in the eye. "I've got a man at the roadblock you passed through when you came into town. If he calls for help on the radio, let Chesty or someone know about it. Send one of your people to sound the alarm if something happens before I get to the other radios I have at home."

Nate took the radio and turned the volume up just enough he could hear. "I will."

Tyrone took three steps and stopped again. "Atticus, you coming with me?"

The old man smiled and rubbed the gray stubble on his craggy face. "Why are you asking? You know I'm coming. Might it have something to do with the fact you've had your ass on your shoulders today and made the rest of us look bad?"

Tyrone blew a lung full of air out of his broad chest and rolled his eyes. "Are you coming?"

Atticus patted his jacket pockets. "Thanks to our visitors, I have fresh buckshot to pepper the asses of a bunch of lowlifes that need a damn good killing bad. Of course I'm coming. Wouldn't miss it for the world." He took off in a rush, passed Tyrone, and talked over his shoulder. "Stop wasting time let's get the hell out of here."

Tyrone stepped up his speed. "You should have taken one of those pumps. That damn double-barrel is obsolete."

"So am I, Tyrone. So am I." Atticus disappeared through the door with Tyrone close behind, but his voice could still be heard. "Just call me the obsolete man." He tried to adapt his impromptu lyrics to an impromptu tune. "Just caaall meee the obsoleeete maaan."

Several people in the church laughed.

Brian said, "That old guy reminds me of Mr. Shebang."

"Yep," Nate said. "People made fun of his last name, but nowhere near as much as he did."

"Every time we met him, he had a new Shebang joke to tell us." Brian looked up at his father. "I didn't realize how much I missed people like that."

Chesty spoke loud enough everyone in the church could here. "Men, it's time for you to go to your positions and man the perimeter."

"It's nowhere near dark yet," a man in his thirties said. "I wanted to spend some time with my family first." He held a small girl in his lap as he sat in a pew. His wife sat next to him, tears running down her face.

Chesty checked his wristwatch. "Best to be in position early and get yourself well hidden, Bill. It might save your life. There's no rule that says they can't hit us before dark. They've always hit us late at night before, but that could change."

"Keep behind something that will stop rifle bullets," Nate added. "Don't just hide, stay behind protection."

People slowly flowed into the aisle and out the door. Few said a word; those that spoke did so in a low whisper to a nearby loved one.

"Well." Chesty rubbed the back of his neck. "You've seen the map; I guess you can find the golf course and park yourself."

"Yes. No problem." Nate looked up at a large painting of Jesus holding his open hands out while standing under at a glowing sky. "Where's the preacher?"

"Dead. Died in the plague, his wife too," Chesty said.

"This church could be a good gathering place in the morning, if the killing is over by then. Someone could stay and organize things. Those with minor wounds could come here for treatment instead of overloading the clinic. Move some of the pews out of the way; they could sleep on the floor. Some of the townspeople could cut up clean sheets for bandages."

"Yeah." Chesty's eyes focused inward, his thoughts elsewhere as he spoke. "We will gather here tomorrow after the fight. I'll tell everyone." Chesty grew silent for a moment. "I expect Tyrone's ambush will stop them. If they make it to town, it won't take much to turn them around. Kill a few of them, they usually run like hell."

Nate's eyebrows knitted. "That's not what you said this morning. You said they would be madder than hell and would come looking for blood. I think your first instincts were correct."

Chesty jerked his head and looked at Nate. "We will know in the morning," he said in a low, even, tone. Nate and Brian left him standing alone in front of the map.

Chapter 14

Ramiro stopped the pickup in front of the golf course. The caravan of pickups and trucks halted behind him. Nate stood in the back behind the cab, Brian and Kendell beside him. "Just sit still for a few," Nate said, yelling to Ramiro.

Ramiro got out and looked the area over. "Okay, but we will have to park in the trees in the park somewhere. We must hide the trucks."

Brian pointed to a stand of trees on the east side. "Set up some long rang rifles over there, maybe."

Nate lowered the binoculars. "Yes. It's the best place for two or three men to snipe from." He jumped down. Brian landed next to him. Nate looked up at Kendell. "I take it you can hit a man at two hundred and fifty yards with that bolt-action."

Kendell smiled. "Of course." He jumped down.

Nate handed Brian one of his canteens. "Fill this up and all of yours."

Brian and Kendell sprinted to the third truck in the caravan that had two thirty-five gallon barrels of drinking water strapped to the back of the cab.

"Any advice?" Ramiro asked.

"Place your men where they can do the most good. Keep them behind cover that will stop bullets. Use all the concealment available. Consider the range, accuracy, and power of the weapon your man is using as well as his own shooting ability. Keep in mind you may have to stop those trucks with rifle fire, utilize the most powerful rifles for that and position them with that in mind. Hide your trucks well and put them where they will be out of the line of fire if possible."

Ramiro looked at his men waiting patiently in the other trucks. "I am not a soldier. At this moment, I wish I were. I pray I do not let my men down. They are simple men who know horses and farming, not guns and fighting. Their profession is hard labor and simple tasks. They love their families and fear god. They do not want to die and they do not want to kill."

The scene seemed surreal in its peaceful beauty. Birds sang and a gentle breeze created waves in a green sea of grass that had not been manicured in more than a year. Someone had tied a cow to a tree to take advantage of all the lush grazing. It stood there on the edge of the golf course, munching on grass looking at the men.

Nate nodded. There was really nothing he could say. "I can use one of your men. Someone armed with a high powered rifle and can shoot."

Ramiro looked past Nate at the last truck in the caravan. "Carlos!" A man jumped down from a flatbed truck and ran to Ramiro. "I need you to go with him." Ramiro said, nodding toward Nate. Ramiro pointed toward the cow. "Cut it loose so it will not get shot. It will run when the shooting starts." Carlos nodded and ran through the tall grass.

Brian and Kendell returned. Nate put his full canteen in a side pocket on his pack.

"We will be off now," Ramiro said. "Carlos speaks English well and is a good shot."

"Good," Nate said. "Keep your head working and you'll be okay."

Ramiro climbed behind the wheel and drove off, the other trucks following.

"Let's get out there and behind cover," Nate said. They walked along the edge of the golf course, staying just inside the tree line until they were two hundred and fifty yards from the road. Nate stopped there because it was the right range for the others, otherwise, he would have decided on a longer range, using distance to provide more safety and time. Distance is a sniper's best friend. "You two wait here and stay alert. Keep hid and behind bullet stopping cover. Decide on the best position for you to shoot from with a steady rest for your weapon. While you're sitting here waiting for me to come back, think about what they are likely to do when the shooting starts and how you will handle it. We must keep them from rushing us and getting too close. They will have us outnumbered, and that means letting them get too close will be fatal. They will overrun us. We will need accurate firepower.

Not just slow-fire accuracy and not just a lot of noise, but *accurate* firepower. Hits are what counts."

Brian took his pack off. "Where are you going?"

"To find a good fallback position. I think it will be that rise over there where the trees jut out into the golf course. I'll be back in a few minutes."

Kendell licked his lips. "I have a bolt-action; I can't shoot but so fast with it. I'm thinking he should have asked for more help."

Brian set his pack in front of him so he could shoot from behind a thick pine tree and use the pack for a rest. "When he gets back, you can ask him why he did not ask for more help. I expect those bastards will run as soon as the shooting starts anyway."

"Maybe. Maybe not."

"I guess we'll see."

Kendell coughed. "Yeah, I guess so."

Nate met Carlos coming back from letting the cow loose. "Come with me," Nate said.

Carlos turned and followed.

When they reached the spot Nate was thinking of, he told Carlos, "This will be our fallback position. It all depends on how brave they're feeling tonight. Maybe they have their blood up, maybe they don't." Carlos nodded. "The thing is we cannot count on anything and therefore must be ready for anything."

Carlos looked toward the road. "Whatever happens, we must keep them off us."

"Yes," Nate said, relieved that Carlos understood. "We must shoot them off of us. Our bullets will be our shield. If they overrun us, we're all dead."

Carlos sighed. "Ramiro will come if our battle lasts long." He looked up at Nate. "I trust him and the others with my life."

"Good, because it may come to that. If the gangbangers are insistent on going through the golf course, then I'd expect Ramiro will join the fight, because they will be useless hiding in the woods if the fight is here."

"The gang may never come. They may drive past and not stop."

Nate took one last look around, finding several places to shoot from behind cover. "Let's get back to the others." As they walked, Nate went over the battle plan with Carlos. "One of the worst things that can happen is for one of us to be wounded at the first position. That will make it very difficult to fall back under fire." He shook his head. "I am not leaving anyone, not Brian, not Kendell, and not you. That means one of us will have to carry the wounded one. And it means those left will have to keep them off of us while we retreat. If more than one of us is wounded, we will have to stand at the first position and fight to the end, or until Ramiro arrives."

"I think you worry more than is needed. These are cowards and murderers, not soldiers. They do not have so much fight in them as you think."

"True," Nate said, "but we must not bet our lives on such variables. You never really know what people will do."

Brian and Kendell had found a log back in the trees. Nate and Carlos found them in the process of placing it in position to provide better cover. Brian wiped his dirty hands on his pants. "Kendell has some questions for you."

"Good. That means he's thinking," Nate said. "The log is a good idea, but one of you should've kept your eyes on the road." He took his pack off and sat down. "We haven't eaten all day. All of you eat while I keep watch."

Kendell drank from a canteen and chewed on jerky. "Why didn't you ask Ramiro for more help?"

Nate kept his eyes on the road. "I've been told there are hundreds in the gang. If true, there is no way we can stop them, no matter how many of Ramiro's men we had. If they want through here bad enough, we're going to have to back off and let them pass. Also, Ramiro's position dictates close quarters fighting and that means he will need all the fighters he has. We have some open ground here that makes it possible to keep them off us, but they will flank our position by coming in through the trees on our left. That means we will have to fall back before they have a chance to do that, and fall back again, if they keep coming."

While they ate, Nate went over as many scenarios as he could think of and how to react to them. He explained that

Ramiro was their reinforcements and would outflank their attackers if the firefight lasted very long. He also explained how they would retreat on his command, if it came to that.

"Brian finished eating. "You might as well eat now, Dad. The sun is down and it will be dark soon."

Kendell took a last drink and put his canteen away. He grabbed his rifle and got comfortable behind the log.

"You two put your packs back on." Nate said. "If we have to change positions, we will have to move fast."

Brian protested, "I was going to use the pack for a shooting rest."

Nate gulped his food down. "No, use your normal prone shooting position. Stay behind that pine tree as much as you can."

~~~~

Minutes ticked away into hours. In the dark, they could see little of the road. The temperature dropped fast and cold seeped through their jackets. Brian turned his jacket collar up and pulled his hat down.

The radio in Nate's pocket came to life. He took it out and turned the volume up. Chesty's voice blared. Nate turned the volume down a little. "They got around Tyrone's ambush. Came in through some back roads. Tyrone's men are heading back into town."

"Any idea where they are now?" Nate asked.

Chesty's voice came back. "They could be anywhere. We only have three radios and no other way to communicate. Just be ready for anything."

Nate signed off and turned the radio volume down.

Brian commented, "Not exactly full of useful information, is he? The fog of war has settled in already."

"Be ready—sounds like good advice to me," Kendell said.

"Have you checked the intensity of the reticle on your Aimpoint?" Nate asked.

"I have it set low," Brian answered. "It's as dark as the inside of an Eskimo's winter coat out here."

"And twice as cold," Kendell added. "Wouldn't you turn it up in the dark?"

"No," Brian said. "You turn it up in the bright daylight and down in the dark. At night, if it's too bright it will drown out the image of your target and you can't see what you're shooting at." He held his carbine out. "Here, have a look."

Kendell shouldered the carbine and looked through the Aimpoint sight. "Wow! You just put the red dot on the target and pull the trigger?"

"Yep, it has to be sighted in of course," Brian said. "At long range you have to aim a little high. But at this range you just put it on target. The main thing is it's fast."

"Batteries must last a long time."

"You can leave it on for years," Brian said. "And we have extra batteries."

Nate broke in, "Okay guys, you need to work your mouths less and eyes more."

Brian held his left hand up. "Cars coming."

Everyone held their breath and listened. The whining and drumming of deep treaded tires grew louder.

Nate checked the eastern sky where the moon remained low and hidden. "I was hoping we would have moonlight to shoot by before they got here. Don't shoot unless I tell you to. At first you will have to use their headlights and taillights as reference points and aim according to where you believe the men are. Once they start shooting back at us you aim just to the right of their muzzle flash."

The road lit up from distant headlights. Nate could hear the breathing of the others. Brian was the first to thumb his safety off. Three trucks raced by. Down the road, the trucks slowed down and came to a stop. The lead driver hit the gas and drove another one hundred yards and then stopped again. Nate and the others could not see, but they heard well enough to know that Ramiro's men were about to be in a gunfight.

A sudden roar of gunfire reverberated across the golf course and faded into the trees. Another short, hot flurry, and then engines roared and tires spun in mud. Young men screamed, horns blared. Headlights flashed in the road.

Nate yelled, "Get ready!"

Two pickups came racing forward then slowed. Nate shot, emptying his twenty-round magazine. The others fired. The sound of bullets hitting metal bounced back to their ears. The back of the pickups lit up from muzzle flashes. Bullets slammed into the trees and ground around them. Brian was blinded when fragments of tree bark flew in his face. He laid down on the ground and tried to brush the debris out of his eyes with his fingers. The second truck swerved around the truck in front and took off, tires smoking. The others' weapons were empty, but Nate had already reloaded. He stood and pumped bullets into the back of the pickup where he saw muzzle flashes as it sped off. Instead of the sound of bullets slamming into metal, the hollow thud of bullets hitting flesh came back to their ears.

Nate saw Brian lying flat on the ground. "Is anyone hit?"

Everyone answered no.

Brian sat up. "I'm okay."

"Stay behind cover," Nate said. "Everyone load your guns. It might not be over."

"They left one of their trucks back there." Kendell's voice revealed his excitement.

Nate used his binoculars' light-gathering ability to see better in the dark and glassed the road. "That's Ramiro's problem. I expect they left a lot of dead men back there too." He held the binoculars steady. "There are people in the road. It appears they are dead or dying."

Kendell exhaled with enough force his breath whistled through his front teeth. Nate knew the realization that he may have just killed someone had suddenly come over him. "Everyone breathe and force yourselves to calm down." He waited a few minutes. "It's time to fall back to our second position." No one asked why or argued with him. They just got up and silently followed. He kept in the dark shade of trees. When they reached the place he and Carlos had decided on, they settled in behind bullet stopping cover.

Carlos took a long drink from a plastic bottle he carried in his pack. "You think they may come back and look for us where we were before?"

"If they come back," Nate said, "we do not want to be where they expect us to be."

"There were only three trucks," Brian said. "And one of them and those in it, are back there with Ramiro and his men. It doesn't seem like they would want to come back."

"If that gang is as big as Chesty says it is, we have not met their main force yet." The radio in Nate's pocket came to life. He turned the volume up and Chesty's voice came in. "We have been hit in three places. They broke through our perimeter and made it to the downtown area. We've lost some people and some are wounded. Have you seen anything at your location?"

Nate put the radio close to his mouth. "We just had a skirmish with three truckloads of the bastards thirty minutes ago. We have no wounded here. Ramiro and his men clashed with them also. I do not know if Ramiro has casualties."

Chesty's voice came from the radio. "We need help in the downtown area. Can you relocate and reinforce us?"

Nate did not hesitate. "No. We cannot do that."

"Why the hell not?"

"It's too dangerous. We will get the same treatment we just gave them. Traveling by vehicle is too dangerous now. If we had been able to catch them all in one place, like at the warehouse, it would be a different story. Your people should hunker down and prepare to fight where they stand."

"Thanks a lot."

"This is your town and you wanted to fight this fight your way. We're doing our part and more. If they come back this way, we will give them hell."

Chesty's voice came back. "Out."

Carlos commented, "He sounded angry."

Nate turned the volume on the radio down. "You just saw what happens when you drive into an ambush."

"Si," Carlos said. "I saw it."

Kendell cupped his right ear with his hand. "I think I hear something out there on the road."

"Yeah," Brian said, "I hear it too. At least one of those bastards is lying in the road hurting."

"We're a long ways from the road," Kendell said. "He must be moaning and crying real loud."

"Sound carries far at night across an open space like this golf course." Nate resumed glassing the road. "Don't talk anymore unless you have something important to say. We need to be using our ears and eyes, and not our mouth."

~~~~

Nate caught movement, low to the ground, out in the open. A thin crescent of moon had been above the horizon for more than an hour, and he could see the open golf course well with binoculars. A fox dug in what was a sandpit, now partially grown over with weeds and grass. *How did you sneak out there without me seeing you?*

Kendell pulled his throw rug tightly around him and shivered. Brian had wrapped his upper body in his sleeping bag, using it as a blanket and leaving his legs free so he could move fast by casting off the sleeping bag in a second. His breath was lit by the moon's glow and Nate watched the rhythm of his breathing for ten seconds, and then went back to glassing the area, spending more time on the tree line than the open golf course. He swept the road once a minute, methodically covering every inch he could see from his position. *If they come back, it will be in force and looking for revenge, and they will try stealth this time.*

Fog had just started to thicken three feet above the ground. It had formed hours before, but until recently, was thin, now it worried Nate. He could no longer see their first position, and that was important to his plan. He originally planned for their first position to be the new kill zone. He expected the gang to believe them to still be at the old position and move in. There were two possibilities that might save them from the fog: The wind might pick up and blow the fog away, though that did not look probable at the moment, and the gang might come late enough that the heat of the rising sun would lift the fog so Nate and the others could see under it. False dawn began to brighten the eastern sky moments earlier. If the gang did not return in the next two hours, they would not be coming.

Carlos proved tougher than the teens. He endured the cold without complaint, not even stuffing his hands in his thin jacket pockets. He did pull a black wool cap down past his ears. He had no sleeping bag or blanket with him. Nate gave him his. He wrapped himself in it but kept his arms free and his rifle in his hands, cold be damned. Nate lowered his binoculars and looked at Carlos. *He's a fighter. Ramiro was good enough to give me one of his best men. I will have to remember to thank him for that.*

A faint, distant drumming of tires on asphalt came to Nate's ears. He knew the others had heard. Their ears were younger and had not been damaged so much from the sound of gunfire and explosions.

Carlos removed Nate's sleeping back and carefully rolled it up and put it aside.

Brian whispered, "Dad."

"I know." The drumming of tires grew louder until it was obvious there were many trucks coming.

Kendell aimed his rifle at their first position and scanned the area through his scope, looking under the fog. "I don't see nothin' yet."

"They're going to try to come in quietly." Nate lowered his binoculars again. "I expect it will take them thirty minutes to work their way to where they think we are. It all depends on how careful and quiet they try to be as they move in. Concentrate on keeping yourself calm so you can shoot straight. Breathe deep. Focus on our old position so you will recognize something different about that area when they arrive. These are not professionals. There's a good chance they will get lost, so watch the surrounding area also."

"They are bound to go after Ramiro too," Brian said. "Some of them will probably sneak along the other side of the road back in the trees and try to get to the others."

"I guarantee you they brought a lot more friends with them this time," Kendell said. "They're pissed off now."

"We kill a few of them, the rest will run again just like before." Brian clicked the safety off on his carbine.

Carlos remained quiet. He settled into a steady prone position with his rifle shouldered.

"You guys be quiet now and don't shoot until I do." Nate glassed the area constantly. "Stay alert. It may be a while before the fun starts. Remember, breathe deep."

Brian shed his sleeping bag. Then Kendell shed his throw rug of a blanket. Nate smiled in the dark. *You two starting to sweat, are you? It doesn't seem so cold now, does it?*

Thirty minutes came and went. Another thirty minutes came and went. The eastern sky glowed red and orange and the fog lightened to grey. Birds began to chirp. The more minutes that ticked by, the more Nate worried. Why would it take them so long to get into position? Either they had a more complex plan than Nate expected they were capable of, or there were so many of them it was taking them a long time to maneuver. Either possibility made Nate nervous. He contemplated calling Chesty on the radio, but doubted Chesty would send help. Their relationship was not exactly cemented with strong mortar. Another thought came to him, and he hoped it would prove true. Just maybe the gang was waiting for daylight, thinking that somehow their attackers had had the advantage in the dark before. *Maybe they think we have night vision devices.* Nate gripped his rifle, his stomach churning from a nagging feeling that there was more to this gang than he realized.

Movement in the trees caught Nate's attention. He glassed the tree line and could make out indistinct forms moving toward their former position. The woods were swarming with people. He needed more information to decide on his next course of action, so he pulled the radio out of this pocket and turned up the volume a little. "Chesty, they're moving in on us as I speak. Can you give me a situation report?"

Chesty's voice came over the radio. "It's been quiet in town for over two hours. I think they have headed home."

Oh shit! "They're not heading home, they're moving in on us. We are facing all of them."

"I don't believe it. They're heading home."

Nate put the radio up close to his mouth so he could speak in a low, determined voice. "It's been quiet in town because they've been moving in on us for two hours now and waiting for daylight. I realize you don't give a damn about us, but this is your chance to wipe them out. "If you move in on them now, you can catch them unawares from behind. I expect most of them who came to attack your town are here. There's a lot of movement in the woods and a lot of trucks parked down the road."

"I only have ten men with me. It will take a while to gather up more. I don't want to attack them with less than thirty men."

Nate's mind raced. "How long is a while? The fight is about to begin at any moment."

"Well, it will take at least half an hour to get out there even if we drive as fast as possible. I expect it'll be close to an hour."

"Make it faster than that even if you have to come with only ten men."

"I'll be there as soon as possible. Out."

Brian kept his eyes working the tree line. "We in trouble, dad?"

"Get ready to move out fast." Nate tied his sleeping back to his pack. Kendell and Brian scrambled to get ready to leave. "Stay down," Nate said. "Hurry, get your packs on."

Carlos kept watch. "You have little confidence in Chesty and his people, don't you?"

"We will see," Nate said.

"And what of Ramiro and my people? Will you leave them to fight alone?"

"We are not leaving, just moving to a place we cannot be so easily overrun by massive numbers. I am hoping to make this a long-range fight and keep them off of us."

"Long range? Is this not already long range?" Carlos asked.

"More like medium range." Nate bent over and prepared to run. "Follow me and stay low."

They ran through the pine trees at top speed, not caring for the noise they made. Speed was of the essence. Nate depended on what little dark remained and the fog, and there was not much left of either. They ran for two hundred yards. He turned left and exploded out of the tree line and led them around the contour of a rise, keeping low, depending on a swell that ran across part of the golf course, keeping it between them and the enemy for cover and concealment. He caught Brian trying to see over the swell as he ran. "Keep your head down." It wasn't enough to hide them completely but it hid the lower two feet of their bodies.

The last fifty yards they crawled, relying on the tall grass for concealment. They could see movement back in the trees. The gang moved in on their first position. Several shots rang out.

"What are they shooting at?" Brian asked.

"They think they're shooting at us," Nate said.

But we ain't there," Kendell said. He snickered nervously. I guess they know we ain't there now."

Relief washed over Nate as they entered the trees on the far side of the golf course. Staying back in the trees, Nate led them to the left and headed back towards the road one hundred yards. They found a place where large rocks had been pushed up when the golf course was built. He let Carlos decide where he wanted to shoot from; for the others, he found good positions where rocks offered bullet-stopping cover, yet they could see well enough to shoot.

Nate scanned with his binoculars. "We have Ramiro and his men behind us and wide open space across our front. Now we have to hold them off until the townspeople arrive. You see a target, kill him."

Chapter 15

Carlos fired the first shot, shooting a man through the chest. The man collapsed where he stood.

The gang replied with a roar of gunfire. Though dawn had arrived and the golf course was well lit, Nate saw the muzzle flashes back in the shade of the trees. A covey of quail rose up from the tall grass near the middle of the golf course; the image of their wings blurred by speed, gained altitude and was swallowed by the rising fog.

Nate yelled, "Make your shots count." He was gratified to see the others taking deliberate aim and firing only when they had a target. Between shots, they could hear a gunfight taking place at the road and knew Ramiro's group was under attack also.

Several of the gang members jumped up and charged. They were cut down in less than ten steps. Bullets chewed at trees all around them and sent sparks flying off the rocks. As more of the gang members discovered their position, their fire became more accurate. "Keep your heads down behind the rocks and let them waste ammo," Nate yelled.

"Did you see that?" Brian yelled. "They tried to charge across that wide open space. They must really want us bad."

"If they keep that up they're going to run out of people," Kendell yelled.

Carlos remained quiet. He looked for targets. He fired and a man fell.

Nate pulled the radio out of his pocket. The rock he used for cover spit sparks from the impact of bullets. With the radio held close to his mouth, he yelled above the roar of combat. "Chesty, what is your ETA?" He could just make out Chesty's voice. It sounded like Chesty said fifteen minutes. "If you drive up now, you can cut them off from their vehicles and prevent their escape." Nate put the radio down to help repel ten men in full charge—cut down the same as the others.

"Geez," Brian yelled, "I can't believe they're that stupid. Why are they doing that?"

The battle raged on for twelve more minutes. Carlos raised his head a few inches to get a better shot. He aimed. His head snapped back and he collapsed to the ground. Nate took one look at the wound and knew he was dead. Kendell and Brian turned their heads and saw Carlos. Their faces turned cold, all emotion washed away. They fired with renewed anger, deadly seriousness on their face.

Nate yelled, "Stay down! Stay as low as possible." He snatched up the radio. "What is your ETA?" He heard Chesty say one minute. Nate turned the radio off and put it in his pocket. He rolled back into the prone firing position and started killing.

The roar of gunfire increased to a new intensity. After several more minutes, the battle started to wane, but in the distance the sounds of Ramiro's battle continued strong. Nate wondered if Chesty's group had reached the gang's trucks. Several more minutes went by. Firing from the other side of the golf course slowed. He suspected that the gang was in the process of exercising a flanking move of some kind. Glassing the tree line revealed nothing. He scanned the area toward the road. A dozen men ran across to their side. Nate fired, but managed to hit only one of them before they disappeared into the tree line. During the lull in gunfire, Nate heard shooting coming from down the road. *Cut them off from their trucks, Chesty.* He tapped Brian and then Kendell on the shoulder. "Time to go." They gave him a puzzled expression but did not argue. "Stay low. Crawl on your belly, head down." Nate stopped long enough to grab some .308 rounds from Carlos' pockets. *Sorry, Carlos. I'll tell the others how bravely you fought.*

Fifteen yards into the trees, they began to crawl on all fours; ten yards farther, they rose to their feet and ran hunched over for half a mile before they stopped. Nate looked around, finding a sinkhole-like depression fifteen feet across and four feet deep. They slid into the hole on a thick layer of leaves and lay on their bellies. "Okay, catch your breath," Nate said. He glanced at the two teens who were on his left. Their chests heaved, faces rigid with tension, eyes scanning the woods.

Kendell's right arm dripped blood. Nate ripped his pack off and dug out his meager medical supplies. "You're hit, Kendell."

The Brian saw the blood for the first time. "No!"

Nate cut Kendell's jacket sleeve away. "Keep watch, Brian. I doubt they'll come this far, but stay alert." He examined the shallow graze and saw that it was not life threatening, but deep enough to cause bleeding. He tied a strip of clean cloth over it.

"That's good enough," Kendell said. "Don't waste any more time on it. Killers are coming."

"Probably not," Nate said. "But we will retreat farther into the trees."

Brian jerked his head around and looked at his father. "Abandoned the others?"

"We've done our part. My job now is to keep you two alive."

"I don't know as we have done our part," Kendell said.

Nate put his pack on. "We have. We cut their numbers down substantially, just the four of us. Chesty's men have arrived. If he has any sense, he has already cut them off from their trucks and they have no escape except on foot. This will soon be a mop-up operation. Now let's go."

They walked until they came to the park's border on the far side. Someone's home stood only fifty yards away. They could still hear gunfire in the distance.

"What do we do now?" Brian asked.

"It looks empty." Kendell held his rifle at the ready. "I don't see anyone around. Doesn't look like anyone has lived there in a long time."

"It doesn't matter," Nate said. "We will retreat back in the trees and stay there until the shooting stops."

Once they settled in at their new hide Brian spoke his mind. "Is it right to leave them like this?" He looked at his father. "We're hiding while they're fighting."

Nate sat on the ground and watched mist rise from his wet pant legs in the cold morning air. Brian and Kendell blew mist with each breath. Little clouds rose and drifted away in the gentle breeze. All three shivered. "You guys wrap yourself up again before you suffer hypothermia," Nate said.

They listened to the battle in the distance. The shooting was less frequent but continued on. Nate answered Brian's question. "When it comes to who lives, I will always put you first. At the moment, Kendell is number two."

Kendell blinked. "Wow," he muttered under his breath.

Nate continued. "I like Ramiro and his people, but you're my son and you will always be my first concern."

"But is it right?" Brian asked.

"It's my right as a father. It's not like we did not do our part. We left a lot of them dead back there. And the day is not over. We could be in another firefight at any moment. Keep your eyes and ears working and stay alert. Some of them will scatter in the woods and try to run. A few of them are bound to run this way. You will probably get a chance to kill again before the day is over. So don't feel bad about being here instead of where the gunfire is now."

Brian pulled the sleeping bag tightly around him and looked down at his feet for a few seconds. He looked up and scanned the woods. "The woods are thick here, and there are lots of dry leaves on the ground. We should be able to hear them coming."

Nate loaded a fresh magazine into his rifle. *I hope he understands. It looks like he has accepted it. It was just too hot back there, too many rifles firing at us. They knew exactly where we were, the rocks and the open land of the golf course saved us. Sure we were killing a lot of them, but it was only a matter of time before more of us got shot.*

Kendell jumped and raised his rifle when two squirrels emerged from their nests and scurried from limb to limb, shaking dew drops from leaves that bombarded palmetto fronds below. To their fear-heightened senses, it sounded loud in the quiet forest. The squirrels chased each other for several moments and then scurried away, leaving the forest quiet again.

More minutes ticked by, and the distant battle waned. Quiet spells between renewed flurries of gunfire became more frequent and lasted longer. The three of them sat in concealment and cover, watching and listening, waiting for danger to come to them. All three shivered in the cold.

Brian jerked his head to his right. He lifted his carbine. Wild crashing in the brush warned them. By the time the three men emerged from the wall of green and exploded into a small opening in the woods, rifle sights were aimed at them. Despite the cold, they were drenched in sweat. Their eyes were wild with fear. They gulped air into heaving chests. Nate, Brian, and Kendell fired. It was only after they were lying in their own blood on the leafy forest floor that Nate noticed none of them were over twenty.

Kendell worked the bolt of his rifle, pushing a fresh round into the chamber. "They were running for their lives, scared shitless," he whispered. "Might be more coming. Be ready."

Brian looked at his father. "We're still helping, even here."

Nate's eyes locked with Brian's. "That's because we're still alive. Dead people are useless."

Brian searched the woods. "How long are we going to stay here?"

"Until long after the shooting stops and all of the gang members are dead or have had time to flee the area."

They sat in silence for two more hours, prepared to kill again if need be. The sun rose in the sky and melted away the sharp bite of the morning chill. More than an hour had passed since they heard the last shots fired. Brian's eyelids grew heavy. His shoulders slumped. Something collided with a palmetto frond. Instantly alert, Brian straightened up and shouldered his carbine.

Nate and Kendell heard also. The sounds of movement in the brush grew louder, and it was obvious there was more than one person coming. Nate pushed the safety of his rifle off with the back of his trigger finger. Looking through the brush as if it were a picket fence, Nate saw the face of a teenage boy not much older than Brian. He wanted to locate at least one more target before revealing his position, so he did not fire. As they approached, Nate realized there were more than two or three of them. He wanted to warn Kendell and Brian not to shoot until the last moment but did not think there was time. He and the two boys were well hidden in concealment and cover. *If those two don't shoot too soon, we can wait until they are right up on us and kill them all before they can escape.* His fear was they would not wait that long before shooting. It was only at times like this that he wished he had a full-auto M-4 carbine in his hands instead of a semi-auto rifle. He reached over and put his left hand on Brian's shoulder and mouthed the word *wait*. Brian nodded.

Nate didn't see the man who shot him. He was watching two young men inch closer, along with the teen Brian's age, when a blade of fire cut across his back at a forty-five degree angle. Nate swung his rifle and fired twice into the man's face. He swung back to the left looking for targets and found more than he wanted to. The forest roared with gunfire for nearly a minute, then the firing stopped so fast its echo could be heard fading into the distance.

A man dashed between trees. Nate tried a snapshot and connected, as much by luck as skill. The man doubled over, dropped his shotgun, and fell. He coiled into the fetal position and held his stomach. He and several other men moaned as they lay hidden in the woods. Between moans, Nate could hear Brian and Kendell breathing fast. He slipped his backpack off and pushed it aside.

Brian glanced Nate's way and saw the blood. His eyes rounded. A bullet cracked within inches of his right ear and went on to ricochet off a rock fifteen feet behind him. He ducked and lay flat on the ground as more rounds flew over only inches above his back.

Kendell fired several rounds, working the rifle's bolt as fast as possible. Nate fired at anything that looked suspicious. Then he emptied his rifle into the wounded. Brian followed his example and sprayed the woods until his firing pin clicked on an empty chamber. Nate had reloaded and was looking to his left when three men rushed them from the right. Despite the ringing in his ears from all the gunfire, he heard them pushing through brush and turned to fire. A bullet struck his rifle and ricocheted away, screaming through the air. His head jerked to the side for some reason. There was no time to aim, he looked over the Aimpoint sight and fired rapidly. The men fired back and kept firing as they fell. Someone was shooting over his head. He glanced over his shoulder and saw Brian on his knees, firing. Brian stood and stepped over him. Then he charged the men, firing as he ran. Nate yelled, "No!" When he stood to run after Brian, he became lightheaded, stumbled and fell. He pushed himself up from the ground and crawled on his hands and knees. He heard Brian running through the woods, firing. He yelled, "Kendell, bring him back here!" He turned and saw that Kendell was gone. He could hear them both screaming and firing, running through the woods shooting, at what, he did not know. The only gunshots he heard were Brian and Kendell's. He prayed it would stay that way and forced himself up from the ground. His vision blurred immediately after standing, and he knew he had lost a lot more blood than he originally thought. He stumbled forward, keeping his rifle at the low ready. A man lying on the ground moaned. Nate shot him in the head and kept stumbling forward. Brian and Kendell had worked their way around in a semicircle, and were coming back to Nate. A man, he must've been running from the boys, ran across Nate's vision from right to left. He swung on the man and fired. The man ran faster and disappeared into the woods. He heard the boys coming just as his legs collapsed under him. He fell to his knees and the woods spun around, with him in the center. His head throbbed. He touched it. He pulled his hand away and saw it painted red. He looked past his hand and saw Brian coming, his face white, eyes locked on his. The last thing he saw was Brian running to him.

Chapter 16

Nate opened his eyes. He had no idea where he was, but there was a ceiling and four walls. Ten seconds later, he realized he was in a room, lying on his stomach in a bed. There was a blanket over him and he was warm. He coughed, and a bolt of fire burned across his back. His head hurt. He reached and touched it and felt cloth wrapped around his head. He did not remember being shot there, only his back.

He heard someone cough, but he could not see anyone. He slid closer to the edge of the bed, reawakening the pain that throbbed through his head. He looked down and saw Brian sleeping on the floor, his sleeping bag under him. Voices came from another room. He recognized Ramiro and Chesty. Chesty seemed to be excited and happy. He thanked Ramiro several times.

The bedroom door slowly opened, and Kendell stuck his head in. His eyes lit up when he saw Nate. He spoke to those in the other room. "He's awake."

The door swung open further and Ramiro and Chesty walked in. "My friend," Ramiro said, "you will be well soon."

"That's what Doctor Brant tells us," Chesty said.

Awakened by the voices, Brian jumped to his feet. Hours of worry had left him looking much older. "The fight is over, and Kendell and I are okay. So relax. The bullet that hit your rifle also grazed your head. That's why you passed out. You bled a lot from your back, but it was the head wound that made you pass out."

Nate touched the bandage on his head. "I did not feel a thing when it happened, only my back." He began to relive the events that occurred just before he blacked out. "You should not have charged them like that. Never leave cover and expose yourself for no reason. You saw what happened to them when they tried to charge us."

"You're right," Brian said, "but at least wait until you're better before jumping on me about it. I saw your back covered with blood and you get hit in the head. I expected you to be dead or at least out soon. It looked like we were about to be overrun on your side, so I reacted."

"You should be proud of your son," Ramiro said. "He and his friend did well. They bandaged your wounds and dragged you out of the woods on Kendell's rug. Then they took you to a nearby house. The house we are now in. The owners died in the plague."

Nate looked up at Brian. "The house we saw earlier?"

"Yes."

Nate rolled onto his side. The pain forced him to roll back onto his stomach. "I can't understand why so many of those bastards happened to run our way when they fled. I chose that spot to get away from them."

Brian laughed. "It was bad luck. We killed a lot of them because of it, though."

Nate doubled the pillow over to make it thicker, in an effort to get more comfortable. "I get the feeling there is more to it than bad luck."

Chesty explained. "This afternoon, we learned the gang was using a house a mile down the road. We learned of this while we were sweeping the area to hunt down the rest of them." He looked away. "Mostly, it was used as a place to take rape victims. The ones you tangled with must have planned to retreat to the house. They had ammunition stored there; maybe that's what they were after. It was just your bad luck to choose that spot."

Atticus walked in. He had been listening through the open door. He held up a pump shotgun. "Got this off of the bastard that shot my boy."

"I hope he didn't kill him," Nate said.

Atticus shook his head. "Nah, Tyrone's fine. You're hurt worse than he is. It still made me mad. I gave the asshole both barrels."

Nate looked confused. "You call Tyrone your boy?"

Everyone in the room laughed.

Chesty spoke up. "Atticus raised Tyrone."

Atticus corrected Chesty. "My late wife Irene and I raised him. He's our son, legally adopted. We couldn't have any kids of our own, and his parents died in a house fire, so we took him in when he was six."

"I see," Nate said. "Now I know it wasn't just respect for the elderly that stopped him from kicking your ass when you dressed him down in the church that time."

"He knew he was in the wrong," Atticus said. "He wouldn't hit an old man anyway; I raised him better than that."

Chesty cleared his throat. "I have to say I'm proud of our townspeople. Everyone has done their part. The whole town's had enough and was on the warpath today. We pretty much cleaned that gang out. There is one more job: take that warehouse."

Atticus waved Chesty off. "Can't be many left of those gangbangers. That warehouse will be easy."

"I'm not ready for that until we have a real plan." Chesty gave Nate a serious look. "As soon as you're up to it, I wish you would advise us on how to best go about it. None of us but Atticus have any military combat experience."

Brian broke in. "Right now Dad needs to rest."

"He's right," Ramiro said. "We should leave him now. Perhaps tomorrow he will be stronger."

Nate's mind went back to the fight. "Did you see to it Carlos received a decent burial? He was a good man."

"Yes," Chesty said. "We buried him on the same day we buried several others who died in the fight. They're all in the cemetery."

Ramiro nodded. "Carlos was a good man. We were all at the funeral."

"Good." Nate's eyes locked on Ramiro. "Thank you for giving me one of your best men. It made a difference out there."

Ramiro lowered his head. "I only wish it did not cost him his life."

"I know." Nate's eyes flashed to Brian for a second. "It could have been any of us."

Everyone but Brian left the room. "Do you feel like eating? We have freeze-dried stuff or freeze-dried stuff. For drink, we have water."

Nate shook his head. "How secure is this house? Do they have guards posted?"

"There are probably fifty people staying in other houses in the neighborhood. They have two guards outside also." He sat in a chair. "Don't worry. There might be a few of those gangbangers still alive, but not many."

"Where's my pack? I should have some water left in my canteen."

Brian opened a closet door and brought Nate a canteen of water.

After he drank, Nate said, "Anything happens, wake me. Don't leave this house while I'm asleep."

"Don't worry. I'm worn out myself. As soon as I eat, I'm hitting the sack again. You might wake before I do."

~~~~

Doctor Brant checked Nate's pulse while he held a thermometer in his mouth. "Too early to tell if your wounds will become inflamed. I cleaned them with a weak solution of carbolic acid when I first treated you several days ago." She stopped talking for a second and gave Nate a thin-lipped smile that stretched across her face. "I took your advice and had someone hunt up a few bottles of carbolic acid. We have those antibiotics you found, but I will not allow them to be used except as a last resort. They spent too much time stored in less than favorable conditions."

"You didn't stitch my back up yet, did you?" Nate asked.

She glanced up from reading the thermometer. "No. If there is no sign of inflammation tomorrow, I will close it. It's actually two wounds, since the bullet skipped over the small of your back, missing your spine by a fraction of an inch."

Chesty walked into the room.

Brian got up from his chair. "He's not ready to be bothered with planning the raid on the warehouse yet."

"Oh, don't worry about that." Chesty put his right hand out so he could lean against a wall. He casually lifted his hat off his head and hung it on the back of a chair. "We sent a recon mission out to the warehouse. I just got a radio report from them." He smiled at everyone in the room. "Whatever was left of that gang has packed up and left. Atticus said it looks like they loaded a few trucks up with food and left town. We have setup schedules to keep twenty-four/seven security going out there."

"So it's over?" Brian asked.

"The gang is kaput," Chesty said, "but we're not on Easy Street by a long shot. We still have a lot of work to do around here. Some of us have been thinking we should abandon the downtown area and set up shop closer to farmland. We've wasted a whole year waiting around for the government to come in and provide for us. I think now the people have finally got it through their heads that isn't going to happen anytime soon, if ever. And the warehouse food's not going to last many more months. We have people scouting for a good place. It looks like it might be the south end of town. There are plenty of empty homes, and it's not far from good farmland."

"Don't forget water," Nate said."

"Yeah, that's at the top of the list of things we're looking for. There are plenty of deep wells on the south end, and we got a few men working on steam engines to power the pumps."

Nate cleared his throat. "You need surface water, like a big lake, in case your steam engines don't pan out. You can dig irrigation ditches with gates to control the water level."

Chesty nodded. "There's a chain of lakes, with rivers and canals connecting them. We thought that could come in handy for transportation. Who knows? We might be hearing the whistle of steamboats again for the first time in way over a hundred years."

Doctor Brant smiled. "I hope to rejoin the twenty-first century, not the nineteenth."

Chesty tilted his head and shrugged. "Well Doctor, we just might have to go backwards a little more before we can go forward." He looked at Nate. "Now, when you get better, I would like to hear more about those waterwheel generators you were speaking of a while back."

Nate smiled. "Sure. But first I want someone to tell me Ramiro found a pickup that starts every time. I'm tired of hearing him cuss in Spanish."

Brian laughed. "His men found one days ago."

Characters in books 1 & 2 that are either in book 3 or may be mentioned in book 3 by other characters.

Nate Williams: Main character, a farmer and ex-Army Ranger struggling to give his son a chance to survive the chaos and lawlessness long enough for society to rebuild.

Brian; Nate's thirteen-year-old son. He turns fourteen in book 3.

Susan: Nate's wife, died in the plague in book 1.

Beth: Nate's daughter, died in the plague in book 1.

Deni Heath: A twenty-four-year-old woman who befriends Nate and Brian. A soldier on leave who was trying to get to her fiancé when the plague and the resulting chaos hit. In book 2, she is wounded and taken to a military hospital by the National Guard.

Mel: Neighbor, avid survivalist, called to duty by Army National Guard. He has a survivalist retreat that Nate and Brian use when forced to abandon their farm because of roving gangs of looters.

Chuck Shingle: A prison escapee and old nemesis of Nate's who dies in the first book.

Caroline: A woman who was captured by sadists and rescued by Nate. She is wounded and taken to a military hospital in book 2 at the same time Deni is.

Carrie: A teen who was captured by the same sadists as Caroline and rescued by Nate at the same time.

Ben Neely: A construction worker before the plague. Killed in a shootout in book 2.

Martha Neely: Ben's wife.

Cindy: Ben and Martha's teen daughter.

Tommy: Ben and Martha's little boy.

Sam Boonbeck: An auto mechanic who is killed in a shootout in book 2.

Synthia: A little girl rescued by Nate and taken into the survival group. Her parents were murdered.

Colonel Joe Greene: Comes into the story late in book 2. A colonel in the National Guard that Mel serves under.

Also by John Grit

Feathers on the Wings of Love and Hate:

Let the Gun Speak

(Volume 1 in the series)

Feathers on the Wings of Love and Hate 2:

Call Me Timucua

(Volume 2 in the series)

Apocalypse Law

(Volume 1 in the series)

Apocalypse Law 2

(Volume 2 in the series)

19197682R10130

Made in the USA
Lexington, KY
10 December 2012